P

W9-BWU-949

so by Katherine Stone
Large Print:

nagine Love
usions
vins
oommates

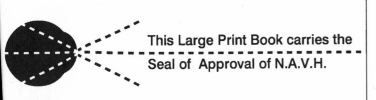

This Large Print Book carries the
Seal of Approval of N.A.V.H.

HOME at LAST

HOME at LAST

KATHERINE STONE

Thorndike Press • Thorndike, Maine

Published in 1999 by arrangement with Warner Books, Inc.

Thorndike Large Print ® Basic Series.

The tree indicium is a trademark of Thorndike Press.

The text of this Large Print edition is unabridged.
Other aspects of the book may vary from the original edition.

Set in 16 pt. Plantin by Juanita Macdonald.

Printed in the United States on permanent paper.

Library of Congress Cataloging-in-Publication Data

Stone, Katherine, 1949–
    Home at last / Katherine Stone.
        p. (large print) cm.
    ISBN 0-7862-2165-8 (lg. print : hc : alk. paper)
    1. Large type books.   I. Title.
    [PS3569.T64134H66   1999]
    813´.54—dc21   99-36546

HOME at LAST

ONE

"Galen Chandler would like to see you. Sir."

"Do I know Galen Chandler?"

"No," the rookie cop conceded. "I suppose not."

Even though the rest of Manhattan did.

But Lieutenant Lucas Hunter had been out of town — indeed out of the country — for the past month, since just before Christmas, a full week before Galen Chandler's first appearance on-air. He'd been in Australia, at a compound in Queensland where cult leaders had been promising extinction not only for their brainwashed devotees but for a nearby village as well.

The promised annihilation had not come to pass. Thanks to hostage negotiator Lucas Hunter. And this evening, just as the lieutenant's flight from Sydney was touching the tarmac at JFK, a hostage situation had begun to unfold in Manhattan. Lucas had been rushed, sirens blaring, to the hospital where the terrified hostages were being held.

Of course Lieutenant Hunter didn't know of Galen Chandler. And the man who was consumed with far weightier concerns — crime, murder, death — might well have ignored her inconsequential, albeit riveting, difficulties even if he had been in town.

"She's KCOR's new anchor. For the past three weeks she and Adam Vaughn have been co-anchoring the evening news. She says it's essential — actually, she said *imperative* — that she speak with whoever is in charge of the negotiations here tonight."

"She's a reporter?" Lucas's sharp query suggested in no uncertain terms that this particular rookie needed to familiarize himself with the practices and policies of his superiors on the force. "I have no intention of seeing her. Now. Or ever."

"She's really insistent, sir."

"Sure she is. Reporters tend to be."

"She asked me to give you this." The novice cop offered a meticulously folded note.

Lucas swore softly as he read its single word: Becca. How the hell did KCOR's new anchorwoman know about Becca? True, Memorial Hospital's administrators knew, as did the girl's frantic parents. But they all understood the danger of such a revelation. The man who held hostage the eight young patients was watching with interest the television broadcasts about his escapade.

So far, to him, his captives were simply girls, beloved daughters, yes, but without other claims to fame. Until this moment, four and a half hours into the standoff, neither the criminal nor the media knew that one of the hostages was the eleven-year-old daughter of Chicago billionaire Nicholas Paxton-Wright. Very few people in fact, and none of them members of the fourth estate, were even aware that the software mogul's family was in town, much less that Becca had undergone an emergency appendectomy two days before.

Until this moment.

And what was Galen Chandler planning to do with her knowledge? Lucas knew, of course. The ambitious Ms. Chandler would use this stunning scoop for her personal gain. She had not, however, capitalized yet. For some reason — confirmation, perhaps — she was coming to him first.

"Where is she?"

"Right outside."

Lucas sighed. "Show her in."

"Outside" was a remote corner of the doctors' parking lot, and "in" was NYPD's state-of-the-art mobile command unit, a converted yet still plush RV, a gift from a grateful citizen.

The trailer was lavishly equipped and supremely silent. All six television monitors were close-captioned, faxes arrived in a soundless *whoosh,* and e-mails came and went in utter stealth. Even the telephones, all save the line to the captor, did not ring. They merely blinked. The computer screens were programmed to go blank in a keystroke, which they did at this moment as a reporter entered the sacrosanct space.

Lucas watched as she entered, studied her with his famous — and notorious — glacial gray gaze. The lieutenant's cool yet intense appraisal could remain absolutely calm, relentlessly unrevealing, no matter how horrific, or how dazzling, the image he beheld.

Lucas's ice gray appraisal revealed nothing now, despite the fact that what he beheld was a complete surprise. KCOR's new anchorwoman should have been impeccably coiffed, flawlessly clothed, a transcendent portrait of sophisticated grace. Her makeup would be subtle, virtually unnecessary and artfully applied, the tiniest strokes of a feathery brush on an exquisite countenance framed in gold.

Impeccable. Flawless. Artful. Golden.

Galen Chandler was none of those things.

Her hair was red, every blazing hue of fire.

And her coiffure was pure chaos, an inferno gone wild. Her face was thin, stark, makeup-free, and with skin so pale Lucas wondered if it had ever been touched by the sun.

The winter wind had caressed her snow-pale flesh, raking its icy fingers across her cheeks, painting splotches of crimson before fanning further the frenzied flames.

She wore tennis shoes and jeans and mohair. *Faux* mohair surely, for what designer would craft from the real thing a coat such as this? This shapeless, this billowy, this turquoise blue?

It was a remarkable — impossible — blue, destined to clash with any other color nearby . . . unless that color happened to be an identical match . . . as was the case with the mittens she wore.

Mittens.

Had this been April first, and had Lucas Hunter been the kind of man anyone would dare to tease, this flame-haired creature in turquoise might have been an April Fool's joke — a stripper who could disrobe provocatively before his eyes. Off would come the tangled fire, a wig concealing raven tresses, and her pallor would be less haunting once the garish blue coat was gone, and —

But this was January twenty-third, not

April first, and this was neither a night for jokes nor for a welcome-back-to-Manhattan surprise. Eight little girls, sick little girls, were being held hostage to terror.

This was no joke.

Although, one could reasonably argue, *she* was. This was the woman who had won the prize, the KCOR trophy that was every reporter's dream? This woman who looked as if all her dreams had been long ago shattered and who seemed so fragile, so lovely, so lost?

Lucas felt a kaleidoscope of impulses, none of them good — although some quite wonderful — and all defying reason. She was a reporter, he reminded himself, in possession of information that could kill. And she was holding him hostage with that knowledge as surely as Anthony Royce held hostage eight innocent little girls.

"Ms . . ." Lucas shrugged. "I'm sorry. The officer mentioned your name, but it seems I've forgotten."

His voice was dark, dangerous — and accented, Galen realized. Faintly British, undeniably elegant, impeccably well bred. In another setting, with another woman, this gray-eyed gentleman would have stood.

But he did not stand now. Not for her. Although even seated he presented an im-

12

posing presence that commanded respect.

And inspired fear. He, whoever *he* was, was clearly the person to whom she had asked to speak. The man in charge.

Had he truly forgotten her name? Galen seriously doubted he was capable of such a lapse. It was merely a cruel reminder of who she was, an embarrassment the good people of Manhattan would happily forget.

And would forget. Swiftly. Gratefully. *Soon.*

"I'm Galen Chandler," she replied as evenly as she could. "I happened to visit 6-North about seven this evening —"

"Happened to?"

"Yes."

"For what reason?"

"Does it matter?"

Yes, Lucas thought, it matters very much to you. He had assumed she was on 6-North because of Becca, because she had not only discovered the Paxton-Wrights were in Manhattan but had learned of Becca's emergency surgery as well.

Now he wasn't so certain.

"No," he admitted. "I suppose not." *Except that I want to know.* It was a self-indulgent impulse, which Lucas condemned to sudden death. "What matters is that you're asking me about Becca. Why?"

13

"Because she was in the playroom where the hostages are being held."

"So you happened to see someone who you believed to be Rebecca Paxton-Wright in the playroom on 6-North."

"I *know* it was Becca."

"Oh? How?"

"When I worked for Gavel-to-Gavel television I covered the copyright infringement trial involving her father's company. Becca was never in court, but a photograph of her circulated among the reporters covering the case."

"And you concluded, based on a photograph you once had seen, that the girl you saw tonight was Becca?"

"The girl I saw *was* Becca. We wouldn't be talking if she weren't."

We wouldn't be talking, Galen thought. But you *would* be smoking.

His glacial focus was on her. Intense, unyielding, fearsome. Yet he was mindful, too, of the cigarette in his hand.

Even as he gazed at her, as he interrogated her, he was drawing periodic — almost measured — breaths of nicotine and smoke. Deep breaths, punishing ones, holding the fire within until there was only pure air to exhale.

The gentleman-inquisitor exhaled now,

away from her lest the slightest wisp of smoke remained, and responded to her proposition that they wouldn't be talking if Becca Paxton-Wright were not in peril.

"True," he conceded easily, effortlessly, as if not a concession at all. "You say you happened by 6-North around seven, just minutes before the standoff began, and it's almost midnight now. I have to wonder why it has taken you so long to come forward."

"I only heard about the situation when I turned on the eleven o'clock news."

"You weren't called to cover it?"

Was this another cruelty? A reminder of yesterday's scathing critique?

The blistering commentary had appeared in Manhattan's most widely read newspaper, in its most avidly anticipated column: *Start Spreading the News* by gossip aficionado Rosalyn St. John.

The columnist had been on Galen's case from the start, had seen her for the disaster she was. Until yesterday, however, Rosalyn had taken only small yet excruciating shots.

But yesterday Rosalyn's entire column had been an analysis of Galen's first three weeks on the job. Her three-week report card. It was an accurate analysis, to be sure. Every clever malicious word.

According to Rosalyn, Galen Chandler's

grade was F, as in *f*ailure, *f*iasco, and so much more. Such as *f*lat, which perfectly described the new anchorwoman's affect, both as she read the news from a prepared script and as she engaged in impromptu exchanges with KCOR anchor Adam Vaughn.

How difficult, Rosalyn wondered, could it be to read the news with *f*eeling? Not difficult at all, she suggested. Unless you were Galen. And as for light banter with the handsome Adam Vaughn? Well, that was every woman's *f*antasy. Although, Rosalyn admonished, *f*lirtation per se belonged only to Adam's lovely wife, *F*ran.

F was also for *f*rown, which is what Galen did with *f*labbergasting regularity, as if the news she was reporting was entirely *f*oreign to her and each story went by *f*ar too *f*ast.

The *f*ormer Gavel-to-Gavel reporter was NOT dyslexic, Rosalyn asserted. It was an assertion she had personally investigated and confirmed. Speaking of Gavel-to-Gavel — and investigative reporting — the chronicling of trials was perhaps the *f*ailed anchorwoman's true *f*orte, her only *f*orte, a specialized sort of journalism conducted at a *ph*enomenonly leisurely pace, one story, one trial, at a time.

*F*ace it, Rosalyn had concluded. The Galen Chandler experiment, the *f*olly of catapulting a *f*arm-girl *f*ashion disaster to *F*ifth Avenue *f*ame, had miserably if spectacularly *f*ailed.

Face it. Face it. Face it. Which Galen had. But KCOR's management, the three people who had recruited her with such inexplicable passion and unyielding persuasion, professed belief in her abilities still.

"Having one's name in print is always good," KCOR owner John McLain had reassured. "Always," anchor Adam Vaughn had seconded. And "Rosalyn is an absolute *twit*," news director Viveca Blair had proclaimed. "She has *no* talent combined with an *even more meager* brain. Go home, Galen. Take a bubble bath. Drink champagne. And don't think about the news, or KCOR, or Rosalyn St. John for the entire weekend. We need you rested and refreshed for Monday. Thanks to *Start Spreading the News*, Monday's audience will be huge."

Of course it would be. Curiosity seekers would flock to their television sets like gawkers to a car crash, craning to see if the catastrophe was as immense as Rosalyn had portrayed.

Galen had and had not followed Viveca's advice. She thought about KCOR, and little else, even as she forsook the news and silenced her phone.

For all she knew she *had* been called to cover tonight's hostage crisis. And why not? The Memorial Hospital standoff was precisely the sort of story Galen Chandler *could* handle. Serious. Life-and-death. With no requirement whatsoever for emotional repertoire or vivacious repartée.

"I wasn't available earlier."

"But you're here now."

"Yes."

"And you would like to know if Becca is one of the hostages."

I wanted *you* to know that she *might* be. For her. For you. Not for me. I'm leaving New York, you see. Galen was tempted to tell him the good news, to let him be the first to know.

Him. Her inquisitor. Whoever he was.

He wore no police uniform, nor the Brooks Brothers ensemble of those more senior in rank. He could be FBI — assuming the Bureau's standard issue included T-shirt and jeans the color of midnight, with collar-length hair in a similar shade.

His hair was black. His eyes were gray. His mouth was at once sensuous and cruel.

And everything else was hard: the patrician features carved from granite, the powerful column of his throat, the sleek sculpture of his arms, the muscles lean and taut beneath his clothes.

He gazed at her with the deceptive nonchalance of a predator, a great male beast about to kill.

Or seduce.

He needed no weapon. His bare hands and naked gray gaze afforded ample artillery with which to destroy . . . or to claim.

"Sir?" The query came from one of the three uniformed policemen who stood nearby. "We've just received the phone number for that, er, person you've been hoping to reach."

He, whoever *he* was, resented the insanity that had invaded this winter night with a fierceness that bordered on madness.

But he wanted to be here, Galen decided. *Chose* to be.

And as his smoke gray gaze raked over her, Galen realized something else. This elegant warrior wanted to be rid of her. Needed to be. As if she were as loathsome as the madman overheard.

As if she were the enemy.

"What do you want, Ms. Chandler?" It was a harsh question, softly posed; a coup de grâce which yielded at the final instant to a reprieve of sheer grace, as if in that instant the warrior saw the truth: this enemy was no threat. Her wounds were already mortal ones.

He needed only to grant her final request.

What do I want? Galen's thoughts swirled. So many things. Impossible things. And yet, for an astonishing moment, it felt as if he were a gray-eyed sorcerer who would give her, *wanted to,* whatever she wished. Or dreamed. "Want?"

Lucas gazed at her, this lovely, fragile creature of turquoise and flames. She was bewitching him, bewitching *him* . . . who could not be bewitched.

All softness vanished. "In exchange, Ms. Chandler, for restraining from on-air speculation regarding the identity of any of the hostages."

Galen wanted nothing in trade for her silence. Nothing? Well, if she, *they,* could revisit however briefly the magnificent illusion that he had wishes to grant. Dreams to bestow.

There are no wishes. No dreams.

Galen gave him the reply he expected, the go-for-the-jugular demand of the journalist she would never be.

"An exclusive. With you. After."

"Done."

"Immediately after."

Her inquisitor, so solemn and so dark, was able to smile. It was a warrior's smile, of course, intense and grim.

"Don't you trust me, Galen?"

"No more than you trust me." *Sir.* Whoever you are.

His smile became a fleeting memory, but its menace lingered. "Okay. An exclusive with me immediately after. Now if you don't mind . . ."

Galen felt his impatience. His coldness. His disdain. She might have run screaming into the bitter cold night. Don't worry! I'm leaving! *Forever.*

But Galen neither ran nor screamed. At least her scream was not out loud. "I think I saw him," she said. "The man who's holding Becca and the other girls. He was getting off the elevator just as I was getting on."

It *had* to be him. His attire had been appropriate, casually correct, but — she realized now — there'd been something unsettling about him.

"We know who he is."

"Oh," she murmured. *Of course.* How else would he have known to locate the unidentified person awaiting his call? What an idiot she was. Rosalyn St. John was *so right.* "Yes."

Galen started to turn away, to scurry away, to give him precisely what he wanted: the end of her.

"Do you remember what he was wearing?"

His query was gentle, as if they were co-conspirators after all, not merely opposing players in a bribe — future confidences from him in a quid pro quo for her silence now.

"A stethoscope. Draped over his neck."

A spark of amusement glittered in his dark gray eyes, a silvery glint from the sensual fires that blazed within. "Was he wearing anything else?"

"What? Oh yes. An oxford shirt, and khaki dockers, and polished loafers. Without pennies. Very Ivy League, very Yuppie." *Very mad.*

"No white coat?"

"No. No coat at all. As if his office were nearby."

"Anything in his hands?"

"No."

"In his pockets?"

Galen's own mittened hands had been buried within the pendulous pockets of her billowy coat. Fisted there. But now, as she closed her eyes and the remembered image came into view, a mitten appeared, unclenched, and drifted toward her heart. "A pack of cigarettes . . . here."

As the mittened hand emerged from hiding, Lucas saw the remarkable design knitted in the turquoise: a fuchsia Christ-

22

mas tree adorned with silver garlands and topped with a bright purple star. "And in his slacks?"

Galen's eyes remained closed as her hand moved down.

"There was something here," she said as the fuchsia tree and its star pointed to the left front pocket of her faux mohair coat. "Something the size of a fist. Egg-shaped. No, pinecone-shaped."

So Anthony Royce wasn't lying about the grenade. Lucas's thought was punctuated by bright blue eyes suddenly open, a dazzling exclamation point of comprehension and alarm.

"Anything in the right-hand pocket?" he asked calmly.

"Two more packs of cigarettes," Galen murmured as she looked from his placid gray gaze to the cigarettes beside a nearby phone. There were three packs, one partially consumed, *being* consumed even as he interrogated her.

"Anything else? An AK-47 perhaps?"

"No. *No.*"

Lucas smiled. "Well, good. In summary we have a Yuppie armed with three packs of cigarettes and a pinecone." And in summary, he thought, we have lovely, intelligent, worried blue eyes — which Lucas felt an improbable yet overpowering urge to reassure. "Piece of cake. It would seem, Ms. Chandler, that we shall be seeing each other again very soon."

TWO

"I am truly impressed."

The words greeted Galen as she stepped from the brightness of the trailer into the darkness of the night. Warm words in the midnight chill. And spoken by a familiar voice.

Adam Vaughn. KCOR's premier anchor. The man with the silver-screen looks and Ivy League intellect with whom evening after evening Galen had failed to ignite even the slightest spark. It was her failure, not his. Adam had been enormously kind and so popular in his own right that despite her ineptness KCOR's viewership had remained loyal.

"Hello, Adam," Galen replied. "Impressed?"

"Truly impressed. Every journalist here, myself included, would kill to have been permitted into the inner sanctum. I must confess when Paul" — Adam gestured to a second figure a few feet away — "said he saw you heading this way, I had my doubts. But it was not an optical illusion after all. Just the zoom-lens vision of our star cameraman. For here you are, emerging from the very center of this stunning story. How on earth did you manage it?"

"Oh, well, I just had a thought I felt I should share with whoever was in charge."

"And was the good lieutenant interested in your thought?"

"The good lieutenant?"

"I assume it was Lucas Hunter to whom you spoke."

"Lucas Hunter? He's returned from Australia?"

"Yes. Just. He came directly from JFK to the crisis here."

"The Queensland siege is over?"

"It is. It ended quite badly for the cult's lunatic leaders, but very well for everyone else. Even before the smoke cleared, and the Waco debacle notwithstanding there *was* smoke, Lucas was en route to New York. It sounds as if you took Viveca's advice about how best to spend this weekend: a moratorium on the news . . . at least until now. Now you're back with a vengeance."

Back with a vengeance. That described Lucas Hunter, not her. Lucas Hunter. The same Rosalyn St. John who had spent the past three weeks ravaging KCOR's hopelessly inept new anchor had raved, during those same twenty-one days, about the "devastatingly gorgeous" homicide lieutenant.

Rosalyn sang Lucas's praises and celebrated his gifts. There were his private gifts, the intimate talents enjoyed by his lovers, and there were gifts, also generous, bestowed for the greater good.

Lieutenant Lucas Hunter possessed an "uncanny understanding of the criminal mind." It was an aptitude, Rosalyn St. John explained, that translated into not only the successful pursuit of murderers but dialogues with lesser criminals as well, the kind who held hostage compounds of innocent devotees and hospital playrooms of little girls.

The lieutenant was rich since birth, a staggering wealth that replenished itself no matter how much he gave away. And Lucas gave lavishly to his cause, his "personal crusade" for victims' rights.

Lucas drew no salary, no compensation at all, either from NYPD or the myriad other law-enforcement agencies, domestic and abroad, where the elegant hunter pursued his prey.

This time the murderous quarry was

haunting the hunter's very home. Manhattan. And it was even more personal than that, for the knife-wielding killer chose as his victims, three so far, the city's most dazzling women. *Lucas's* women.

The intimate link between the beautiful victims and the sexy lieutenant was made by the killer himself in a letter sent to Rosalyn St. John after the second brutalized body was found. The letter read:

"Lucas's ladies — Lucas's *lovers* — are dying. And they will continue to die until he comes home to play."

The letter itself yielded no clues. Modern-day criminals, the ones who'd been paying any attention at all, knew about fingerprints and trace evidence and DNA. In this instance the message was a collage of letters cut from the Christmastime issue of *Playboy.*

Rosalyn dubbed the murderer the Lady Killer, and *spread the news* to Lucas in Australia, and became a conduit for the police when they urged vigilance for all Manhattan women, whether they "knew" Lieutenant Lucas Hunter or not.

It was an urging which wasn't heeded, for a third woman was slaughtered in her home. And the killer's subsequent letter queried:

"What lucky lady will be next, Lieutenant? If you want to find out, just stay where you are."

But, Rosalyn implored murderer and anxious Manhattanites alike, Lucas had no choice. He had to remain in Queensland. Eighty lives were at stake. Children's lives. And although Rosalyn had no doubt that the sexy — if infuriatingly private — homicide lieutenant might have a comparable number of lovers in Manhattan, the Lady Killer could not ravage Lucas's women at once as the cult leaders in Australia were threatening to do with their hopelessly captive flock.

But now, thanks to Lucas, the captives were safe. Free.

And now the hunter was back. With a vengeance.

"Do you know him, Adam?" Galen asked.

"Socially, yes. Our paths cross from time to time. But professionally, no. Lucas makes a habit of not speaking with the media. It must have been quite a thought you wanted to share."

Galen shrugged. "It was just a thought. He did agree to an interview after the crisis is resolved."

"I repeat, Galen, I am truly impressed. And also quite superfluous." Adam smiled. "So superfluous, in fact, that I'm going home."

"What? No. I mean, I'm sure Viveca knows you're here." *And wants you here, like the rest of Manhattan.*

"Yes. She does. Marty's officially on call this weekend, and he and his crew are stationed out front. But given the potential size of the story, a second team seemed a good idea. Viveca didn't call you because we'd all agreed you'd have the weekend off. But this is your story now, Galen. And well deserved. We should tell Viv the terrific news. Your cell phone or mine?"

Galen's phone, issued by the station, was in the right front pocket of her billowy coat. But her mittened hands did not plumb the turquoise depths.

"Yours," she said. "You call her."

"With pleasure." Adam flipped open his phone and keyed in the code that automatically connected him to the Park Avenue apartment of KCOR's news director Viveca Blair. "Hey, Viv. It's Adam. Galen's here and guess what? She's got an exclusive with Lucas as soon as the crisis is resolved. The journalistic coup of the century, wouldn't you say? Yes. Absolutely. So I'm heading home. Yeah, well, maybe. Okay. *Yes.* In the meantime Marty and crew are out front, and Galen and Paul will hold down the command-post fort, and I for one am getting out of the cold . . ."

"She wants you to do the interview," Galen observed when Adam flipped shut the phone.

"What makes you say that?"

"There was a 'yeah, well, maybe' that made me wonder."

"Actually, she was just suggesting that I come back after the denouement in the event there are ancillary stories worth covering — the families, the press conference — while you're interviewing Lucas."

"He won't be at the press conference?"

"Not a chance. No matter the outcome. If the girls survive, we'll hear from the police commissioner, with the mayor at his side, and if they don't, it'll be handled by a heretofore unknown spokesperson from the force. Under no circumstances will anyone hear from Lucas Hunter. Except through you. And since you can't be two, much less three, places at once, I'll return with Wally just in case. Your mission, yours and Paul's, is to make sure the good lieutenant doesn't get away. Okay?"

"Yes. Okay," Galen agreed, despite her wish that it would be Wally not Paul with whom she'd be holding vigil throughout the night.

Paul undoubtedly shared the wish. The

KCOR cameraman had known from the start that Galen would fail, and like Rosalyn St. John, Paul had not bothered to conceal his contempt.

"This isn't a miniseries," he had scoffed during their first joint foray to cover breaking news. "We're talking sound bites here, Galen. Little tiny nibbles. Got it?"

Yes. But how did one reduce an entire life into a few pithy remarks? Galen couldn't do it. But Paul could and sometimes did, to show her just how easily it was done.

It was with such clarity and economy that Paul shared with Galen the KCOR saga, the story of Adam and Viveca and Fran and Marianne and John.

Of the five, only John had been born with nothing, less than nothing. But by the time John McLain decided to expand his vast media empire to the Manhattan television station that was on the verge of collapse, he also enjoyed extravagant wealth.

The floundering station was precisely the kind of challenge John liked, and with the instincts of a gifted director, John McLain assembled a blockbuster cast. His first choice for anchor was Adam Vaughn, the celebrated war correspondent who could have commanded a high-profile position at any network he wished. But Adam liked challenges too, and risks, and Manhattan. And so he said yes.

John's first choice for news director was Viveca Blair. She was already in his employ, at a station in Dallas, but when he asked her to make the move to New York she agreed. It was Viveca who came up with "KCOR." Officially, John McLain's station was and would remain WKCR. But for those in the know, and eventually *everyone,* the W became silent, and KCR became KCOR, and it was the perfect name for the station that was to be the center, the *core,* of the Big Apple . . . and the heart, the *cor,* of Manhattan.

Adam solo-anchored KCOR from obscurity to number one, and Viveca and Adam together chose the ladylike Marianne, their own Grace Kelly, from the myriad audition tapes that arrived once the word was out that the top-rated station was searching for a female anchor.

Marianne had already captured her viewers' hearts when she and John fell in love. It was at their rose-garden wedding in nearby Chatsworth that Adam met Marianne's sister Frances. And six months later Fran and Adam, too, were wed.

Paul told Galen how KCOR had started and how it had thrived, with strangers and sisters and talent and love. But Paul did not share, nor did he need to, the most recent chapter in the tale, the one dated December 14, the death from cancer of Marianne McLain.

Marianne. The beloved, courageous, gracious — and irreplaceable — woman whom Galen Chandler had been brought in to replace.

Galen wondered, as Paul spoke with such clarity and such ease, if *he* wanted her job, Marianne's job. Paul had the ability and the looks.

But not the interest, Galen discovered. Paul preferred still photography, the artistry of shadow and light. Paul's KCOR cameraman job, like the crime-scene photowork he'd previously done for the NYPD, was simply a way to pay the rent.

"He probably feels sorry for you." Paul's words created a shimmering mist in the midnight air.

"Yes," Galen conceded as she watched through that frosted veil Adam's vanishing silhouette. "I'm sure he does."

"I meant Lucas Hunter. Why else would he meet with you?"

But, Galen thought, Lucas Hunter doesn't know anything about me.

For the three weeks she'd been at KCOR,

he'd been away. Rosalyn St. John might, however, have kept Lucas apprised of other Manhattan goings-on as well. It's not *all* grim in the Big Apple, she might have e-mailed to Australia. Amidst the murder and mayhem there's a little comic relief. KCOR's new anchor is an absolute stitch, so relentlessly awful it's almost funny. Too bad our killer doesn't visit *her*.

"You're definitely not his type," Paul elaborated. "The good lieutenant, the *stud* lieutenant, is a connoisseur of beauty, of success, of style. Witness the women who have died."

It was true. Absolutely. Which meant, what? That Lucas Hunter's willingness to speak with her was sympathy? Charity? A generous donation from the aristocratic advocate for victims' rights — even though she was a trivial victim: a fashion fiasco, a career catastrophe. And, Galen knew, she was an impostor victim as well, for she had no one to blame but herself.

"This is going to be *such* a pleasant night."

"Actually," Paul countered, "it will be. While you're guarding the stud I'll be making some other woman very happy."

"But . . ."

"Don't worry, Galen, I'll be nearby. Just page me if anything interesting happens."

35

"Interesting?"

"You know, like little girls being tossed out the sixth-floor window? On second thought, don't page me for that. We'd use the network footage anyway. This is a hostage situation, Galen. Nothing dramatic, at least nothing *cine*matic, is going happen."

Unless the lunatic decides to explode his grenade. Which he won't, Galen told herself. Lucas won't allow it.

"Page me, Galen. And I'll come running. I promise. I wouldn't miss your exclusive with Lucas Hunter for the world."

THREE

"No." It was a syllable of sheer terror spoken by Elizabeth Royce, wife of the Wall Street guru who had gone berserk. "I can't speak to him. Cannot. Don't you understand?"

Lucas did understand. Of course he did. But . . . "Just over the telephone, Mrs. Royce. That's all I'm asking."

"How did you even *find* me?"

How? It hadn't been easy. Elizabeth Royce was sheltered in the dedicated embrace of women determined to protect their sisters, their mothers, their daughters . . . a haven far safer and far more hidden than any bureaucratic offerings might provide. But Lucas had made some calls to women he knew — women who trusted the man who cared with such passion about victims' rights. "It was necessary to find you. It *is* necessary. We won't tell him where you are. We would never tell him. I just need to have you assure him, over the phone, that you'll let him see your daughter."

"Let him see Sarah? Never, Lieutenant. *Never.* He almost killed her once. He *did* kill her spirit, her hope. She's so confused now. So *frightened.*"

"Just like the eight little girls he's holding hostage."

"That's not fair!"

"None of this is fair, Mrs. Royce." Including what he, Lucas, was doing to her. Elizabeth Royce was not about to speak her husband's given name, to humanize, personalize, him. *It.* Nor would Lucas refer to him as Anthony. But Lucas addressed her as Mrs. Royce, a relentless refrain, an unfair and yet so necessary reminder of her unique and essential bond. "You said he almost killed your daughter?"

"Yes. My precious Sarah. She's only *five*, Lieutenant. Just a little girl."

"Tell me what he did to Sarah."

"It was right before Christmas." Elizabeth Royce's reply came in a rush of relief. Once the lieutenant knew the truth, he'd realize how impossible his request really was. "I had some last-minute shopping to do. He'd be happy to baby-sit, he said. *No problem.* But there was a terrible problem. Sarah fell down the stairs, he said, tripped over a tennis shoe that had fallen out of the laundry basket I'd taken upstairs before I left. Sarah was rushed to Memorial Hospital. She spent two days in intensive care, *intensive care,* before being transferred to 6-North. Her bones were broken, as was her spirit. I didn't understand why. Then I discovered the spreadsheets decorated with gold stars and giant Christmas trees in his study at home."

"Sarah's decorations."

"Yes. Sarah's joy. And the trigger for his rage. He's a stockbroker, you know. It had been a bad week, a terrible week. The volatility in the Asian markets had wreaked havoc over here. I should have *known* not to leave Sarah alone with him. When the markets are volatile, he is volatile."

"And violent?"

"Yes. Sometimes. With me. Only with me, until that day."

"Did the doctors suspect child abuse?"

"I don't know. Maybe they wondered. But his story of the accident was plausible, and he was so distraught."

"There's no doubt in your mind, however."

"He *confessed,* Lieutenant. To me. But even as he was admitting what he'd done he was blaming her, and me. I *might* have dropped the tennis shoe, such things had happened before, and I was the one who'd taught her to draw pictures *everywhere.*"

"What a stand-up guy. So you threw him out."

"I tried to. I even got a restraining order."

"Which he ignored."

"Of course! And he sobbed, and he raged. But most of all he terrified my wounded Sarah. So we left, Lieutenant. *We* disappeared. Until tonight I believed we could not be found."

"You can't be found. Not by him. I promise you, Mrs. Royce, he'll never see you or Sarah again. But he needs to believe that he will."

"You want me to lie to him."

"Yes." *Please.*

"He'd kill me for helping you."

"He's going to spend the rest of his life in prison."

"But money speaks, Lieutenant Hunter. Surely you know that. And he has lots of money. He'll meet men behind bars, convicted murderers who'd be delighted to kill again for the right amount of cash. I wouldn't *care* if it was just me. There were times before Sarah when I wanted to die. But who would love my precious little girl? The courts? The system? You?"

No. Not me. I don't love.

"Don't make me do this, Lieutenant. Please."

Lucas grimaced at the plea, as if he could — and would — manipulate her as her husband so obviously had.

Lucas Hunter didn't negotiate nearly as well with normal human beings as he did with psychopaths. It was scruples, perhaps, conscience about negotiating with the innocents of the world, the principled creatures who did not lie.

Lucas was asking Mrs. Anthony Royce to lie. But he could not lie to her.

"Your husband will never be released from prison. That's a promise. And I can and I will make certain there's always a safe place for you and Sarah to live."

"The only way we'll be safe, our only hope, is if *you* lie to him, if *you* tell him you tried to find us and failed. I'm sorry, Lieutenant. I can't help you. I just *can't.*"

Her voice shimmered with apology, as if she were responsible for the monster she had married, as if his actions, his evil, had tainted her as well.

Guilt by association.

How well Lucas knew that anguish.

The phone line went dead, the end of hope for the young hostages' easy release, just as the only telephone that wasn't muted began to sound. The phone was right beside him. But Lucas answered only after the fifth ring.

"How're you doing, Tony?"

"*Anthony.* How you *think* I'm doing, Lucas, waiting for you to call? But you *haven't* called, have you? So I'm calling you. Have you found her yet? Have you found the bitch?"

"I thought we agreed you'd watch your language."

"*You* agreed I'd watch my language. But hey, I'm an easygoing guy. So, Lieutenant Hunter, have you found my precious wife?"

"No, and it doesn't look like we're going to."

"You'd *better.* You know what happens if you don't. Or would you like me to spell it out again for the girls?"

An entire dictionary of four-letter vulgarities would be trivial compared to a repeat of Anthony Royce's already verbalized threat to "blow them all to kingdom come."

"No. I remember. But you need to tell me how to find her, Anthony. I've tried every police venue I know. And nothing. *Nada.* She's vanished. The logical next step would be a public plea for her to come forward. Every station would be delighted to carry it. But you've said you don't want your name released to the press."

"You've got that right. I don't. My clients are some of the world's most famous financiers, and this is a *private* matter between my *precious wife* and me. Besides, Elizabeth isn't all that public-spirited. She wouldn't come forward. *You* need to find her, Lucas. And soon. I'm going *crazy* in here."

"You could come out."

"Right."

"Maybe if you let some of the girls go . . ."

"Just open the door, you mean? To the SWAT team hovering on the other side? I don't *think* so. And if anybody out there tries anything cute, well, I simply pull the pin and everybody goes poof. Everybody. Including, and this is the good part, these damned dolls."

"What dolls?"

"These effing — pardon my French — Barbies. Picture this, Lucas. I'm surrounded by a circle of whimpering little girls, each of whom is clutching a doll, as if the little plastic tart could protect them." Anthony Royce spoke, shouted, at his frightened hostages. "They *can't* protect you, get it? *Nothing* can."

"Easy, Anthony," Lucas urged calmly as he scribbled a note — Find out about the Barbie dolls — to an officer nearby. "You're sounding a little tense."

"A little tense? What is that, cop humor? Of course I'm tense."

"Too many cigarettes."

"One pack and counting. And I *am* counting, Lucas. I trust you are, too."

"Every puff."

"I gave them up, you know? Cigarettes. That's probably why I'm feeling the effects so strongly now. I gave them up. For her. For *them*. My so-called family."

"You did a lot for them, didn't you?"

"*Everything*. And what do I get in return? Betrayal. She's got someone else. I *know* she does. That's what this is really all about. Another man. Do you know, Lucas, what I'd like to do with this grenade?"

"I can imagine."

"I doubt you can."

Lucas inhaled deeply, inhaled smoke, his seventh puff on his twenty-second cigarette since 11:45. "Sure I can. Let's see, it has something to do with your wife's anatomy."

Lucas Hunter's utterly calm suggestion was greeted with stunned silence at both ends of the telephone — sudden silence from the hostage-holder six flights above and a deepening of the hush within the trailer, as if its other three occupants, police officers all, had ceased to breathe.

The three officers knew Lucas's reputation for conversing with psychopaths as if he were one of them, as if he knew *and shared*

44

their murderous lust. It was a technique that could not be taught, not ethically, not morally, not practically, for what sane person would imagine such barbarism, much less dare suggest acts that might fuel further the madness?

No sane person. Only Lucas Hunter. Rogue. Rebel. Seducer of the most beautiful of women . . . and the most evil of men.

Lucas's track record for seducing — and subduing — criminals was quite astonishing. And even though the other officers were discomfited by his approach, each would have chosen Lucas over an entire army of touchy-feely psychologists had a loved one been at risk.

In the breath-held silence, as they awaited Anthony Royce's reply, the officers steeled themselves for a dialogue of madness.

But the Wall Street broker seemed shocked, too, by the image of a grenade so explicitly placed. "I actually had something a little more . . . civilized in mind."

"Like in her car? Or beneath her lover's bed?"

"Yeah," Anthony whispered with relief. "Something like that."

The relief and even the whisper exposed Mr. Royce for what he was. A bully not a psychopath. A man whose bluff had been well and truly called, and who could not possibly go one-on-one with Lucas Hunter when it came to the fantasies of madmen.

Anthony Royce was a run-of-the-mill abuser, with neither the staying power nor the perversion of true psychosis. Which was not to say the Wall Street maven wasn't dangerous. He had a weapon and his thoughts were scattered, cast asunder by anger, frustration, and nicotine.

"Do you have a position on Gemstone?"

"What?"

"I'm asking your professional opinion about Monday's initial public offering for Gemstone Pictures. I understand it's being offered at eighteen. You think that's high?"

With his reply Anthony's voice transformed to the smooth persuasive tone of the successful stockbroker he was. "No. In fact, in my estimation, the share price could double within the first few hours."

Lucas thought so, too. He was banking on it.

It began then, not a dialogue of madness but a discussion of the market. They talked stocks and price-earnings ratios and whether Anthony remained bullish despite the frothiness of the Dow.

The atmosphere within the trailer became lighter, frothier too, and decidedly bullish.

It was going to be all right, each of the officers silently decided. Lucas would prevail.

It might take a while, these things often did, and despite the hopefulness they all felt, the officer to whom Lucas had scribbled the note about the Barbie dolls had dutifully e-mailed the message to the computer on 6-North, where even now the head nurse was preparing her reply.

But they were all breathing. Ever more calmly.

Even as Lucas's veins filled with ice. With evil. With an evil that had nothing to do with the voice that was chattering with near euphoria into the speaker phone, the minor-league bully who had taken a gigantic and irrevocable step into major crime.

This glacial chill was true evil. Without conscience. Without care. *And on the prowl.*

Lucas glanced at his watch, a deceptively casual glance that was interpreted by the others as idle curiosity, the lieutenant checking to see if the time from onset of crisis to its peaceful resolution would represent for the master negotiator a personal best.

3:13. Manhattan's Lady Killer was on the move, on the verge of murder, and there wasn't a damned thing Lucas could do about it. Nothing. Except sense it, *feel* it, the

47

restless hunger, the insatiable lust.

The evil filled him, flooded him, froze him, as Lucas permitted it to, as he needed it to. He needed to sense, to know, to feel whatever he could for as long as he could, no matter that the glacial claws stilled his heart and shredded his soul.

The evil did not linger long on this winter night, just an eternity for Lucas of fury and pain, and as the icy malevolence began to recede, Lucas himself began to move. It was a motion, to those who watched, that mimicked the leisurely yet menacing grace of a jungle cat.

But it was restlessness not leisure that compelled Lucas to the nearby window, a sudden and powerful impulse that had no name but would not be denied. A need perhaps to stare into the empty shadows of this winter night? A *desire* to do so?

But the nighttime shadows were not empty. For there she was, in her turquoise coat and matching mittens, motionless save for her flames of hair, which were fanned without mercy by the bitter wind.

Had she been there all this time? Alone in the cold? Trusting him even as she froze?

Trusting him. Believing him. Waiting in the frigid blackness for him to keep the promise *that was a lie.*

Lucas swore silently as the unnamed impulse *and desire* that had compelled him to the window wanted even more, to compel him into the bitter-cold darkness to the lightness, the brightness, of her.

But something darker, colder, more bitter — the truth — intervened.

Go away, mittened shepherd. Go *away*.

FOUR

Anthony Royce puffed literally and figuratively for almost two hours, a soliloquy fueled by nicotine during which he chronicled his investment achievements to date and forecast even more stunning successes to come.

The officers within the trailer grew weary of the boastful tirade. And impatient. But Lucas listened alertly, and patiently, to every self-aggrandizing word. He knew the crash would come, Anthony's descent back to reality, and he had to be ready to deal with it when it did.

The crash came precipitously shortly before dawn.

"Lucas?"

There was sheer panic in the once-arrogant voice. Panic, claustrophobia, and disbelief. Lucas knew precisely, felt precisely, Anthony's desperate thoughts. What was he doing in this playroom of whimpering girls and Barbie dolls? He was a financial wizard. He was supposed to be on

50

Wall Street making multimillion-dollar —
no, billion-dollar — deals.

"I'm here, Anthony. What can I do for
you?"

"Get me the hell out of here."

"That's easy. Just open the door."

"And get arrested? No way."

"It's the only way."

The officers within the trailer groaned in-
wardly at the master negotiator's intransi-
gent reply. For a man who happily broke all
the usual rules, why wasn't Lucas Hunter
following the perfectly acceptable ones
now? It was permissible to lie to criminals,
especially when hostages were involved.
False promises were made all the time.

But for reasons known only to him, the
lieutenant had chosen the candid approach.

"Have you forgotten the *grenade?*" The
demand, made by Anthony Royce and with
a renewed burst of arrogance, was the precise query the officers might have made . . .
had they dared.

"No. I haven't forgotten. But you know
what, Anthony? My shift is almost over. In
fact," the rogue negotiator lied at last, "my
replacement's already here. I'm tired. I want
to go home. I think I'll turn this conversation over to him right now."

"No, Lucas." The financier's panic re-

turned. "You *have* to see this through."

"Not really, Anthony. I really don't."

"Are you saying you don't *care* what happens, Lucas?" He was whining now, the man who had complained about the whining, frightened little girls. "It doesn't *matter* to you if I pull the pin on this grenade?"

"I'm saying it's your choice, one which I guess I'll learn about on the evening news. I'm going home, Anthony. To bed. It's been a long night."

"*Wait*. You *have* to get me out of here. *Now*."

"Just open the door."

The officers, weary no more but impatient still, were on high alert. Anthony Royce, captor of little girls, had become a captive himself — of Lucas, dependent on Lucas for survival itself. Or so, apparently, Lucas had decided. But was he right? Or would the next sound be the explosive destruction of girls and dolls and the broker himself?

There was no explosion. Merely the sound of abject defeat.

"Will you tell them not to shoot me?"

"Sure, Anthony. I'll tell them."

Within ten minutes of Lucas Hunter's assurance to the hostage-taker, the assembled media were informed of the news. The crisis had ended. Peacefully. All eight girls were safe. And the perpetrator, unnamed by the police until formally charged, was already en route to the nearest precinct, an evacuation accomplished through a subterranean tunnel to an awaiting van.

The press conference, to be hosted by both the police commissioner and the mayor, would commence soon, as the first rays of daylight limned in gold the skyscrapers overhead.

Paul appeared precisely eight minutes after Galen placed the page.

"See?" he queried. "What did I tell you? No sudden drama. No precipitous ending. You could have gotten a perfectly good night's sleep. Which," he added, "would not have been such a bad idea. I hope you've also paged —"

"Adam and Wally. Yes. I have."

"Actually, I was going to say Jose-Felipe."

"Very funny."

"Believe me, Galen. It was not a joke. For reasons known only to themselves, Viveca and Adam and John have been unwavering in their support of you. But I can assure you that Viveca will not be happy if you appear on camera looking this way."

This way. The way she truly looked. Without the expert intervention of super-stylist Jose-Felipe or the *Vogue*-style wardrobe provided by Saks.

As a reporter for Gavel-to-Gavel TV and for her entire life before, Galen's hair had been long, and so heavy it could not possibly curl. She had worn it unbound. Always. A cascade of fire.

And if errant flames whipped her face? So what? Gavel-to-Gavel viewers, like those of ratings-rival Court TV, expected such wind-ravaged authenticity, an unrehearsed reality that paralleled the unplanned drama within the nation's courts.

But the wild, impromptu look wouldn't fly in Manhattan, Viveca explained, especially since Galen would be broadcasting from a climate-controlled studio, not the meteorologic potpourri of courthouse steps. Moreover, given the timing of KCOR's evening news, Galen would be in essence a dinner guest in the viewers' homes.

She needed to look her best. Which meant a makeover at JF, Jose-Felipe's chic Fifth Avenue salon, five days before her KCOR debut. The renowned stylist himself supervised the entire extravaganza and personally revamped her hair, *cut* it to a length that caressed her shoulders only when she shrugged and which would have curled exuberantly had it not been for Jose-Felipe's artistry with a hair dryer and mousse.

The result was smooth, sleek, glossy — and round — which, Jose-Felipe observed, gave necessary fullness to the face that was uncommonly thin, was it not, *sharp?* JF's makeup specialist imparted additional fullness, softness, and artfully enhanced her one authentically appealing feature: her eyes.

Jose-Felipe was pleased with the result, as was Viveca, a JF regular, who appeared at day's end. It was a "look," Jose-Felipe assured, that would be easy for Galen to maintain. His minions showed her how and provided written instructions as well, with relevant phone numbers just in case.

It was important, Jose-Felipe admonished Galen, that she wear her JF look, her KCOR look, always.

"This includes," he clarified, "anytime you leave your apartment. Even if it's just to check the mail." His expression indicated that he'd had clients who had failed, in that precise manner, to comply, and who were absolutely mortified when their unguarded images were captured by the ever-vigilant tabloid press.

"There's no excuse for any celebrity to be caught off guard *ever*," Jose-Felipe told Galen. Then smiling ingratiatingly at

Viveca, he added, "And as the new anchor-woman for Manhattan's *best* station, you'll be a celebrity right away."

She had at least become *known* right away. And even though, almost right away, it would have been nice to hide, out of respect for Viveca, Adam, and John, Galen had conscientiously obeyed Jose-Felipe's fashion-conscious advice.

Until tonight.

Not that tonight represented flagrant defiance. It didn't. Not defiance, merely happenstance. Galen had been toweling her just-washed hair, a preamble to meticulous moussing and drying, when she heard the news. Even before the report was through, she had tossed the towel aside and dressed in tennis shoes, T-shirt, jeans.

Not the KCOR wardrobe, she realized vaguely. Not the stylish assortment of slacks, blouses, and boots to be worn beneath the tailored charcoal coat as she walked to and from the station; and most assuredly not the on-air attire into which she changed once there.

But neither the KCOR look nor the KCOR wardrobe were suitable for the mad dash she was about to make.

So she grabbed her beloved — and forsaken — turquoise coat, and her even more beloved turquoise mittens, and ran to share with whoever was in charge her worries about Rebecca Paxton-Wright.

And now Paul was telling her that stylish, beautiful, supportive Viveca would not be happy if she appeared on camera *this* way, when the night's floating mists had tangled even further her unruly curls and the winter chill had contracted even more the translucent thinness of her face.

"Photogenic is one thing," Paul was saying, a reminder of the astute, albeit contrary, compliment he once had made. Galen looked good on camera, the photographer-artist said. She had one of those unusual faces that actually looked *better* on film than in the flesh. "But we're talking trick photography here."

"Thank you *so* much, Paul. But this is about eight little girls" — *and the man who saved them* — "not about me."

Besides, Galen didn't believe that Viveca *would* care. Yes, Viveca Blair was herself a fashion plate. And yes, Viveca had felt strongly about the way Galen looked during scheduled broadcasts from the station.

But Viveca was a newswoman, committed first and foremost to the story. And when the story, the *news*, unfolded on a wind-ravaged night and anxious Manhattanites themselves spent the entire night riveted to their television sets — well, it was acceptable for a concerned reporter to appear less than fully rested and impeccably coiffed, wasn't it?

Viveca wouldn't care . . . as long as Galen got the story.

Which Paul's next comment cast into sudden doubt.

"Of course," Paul said, "the likelihood that the interview's even going to happen is about zero."

"What?"

"You heard me. Lucas Hunter would have promised you the moon to get rid of you."

"But . . ."

"But what? The interview *has* to happen just because KCOR's been hyping your exclusive all night? You heard what Adam said. Lucas Hunter doesn't make a habit of giving interviews. Which means, Galen, in case you missed it, he *never* does."

KCOR had been hyping her interview all night? *Of course.* It was a promise that no other station, networks included, could make. "Viveca wouldn't have run the hypes if she didn't believe it."

"Is that right? She *had* to run them on the off chance the interview came to pass."

"Adam would have told me. Warned me."

"He *did*."

"Warned Viveca, then."

"Viveca's been at this game as long as Adam has. No warnings needed there. Besides, who knows? Maybe it *will* happen. Maybe I'm dead wrong."

"Dead wrong about what?" Adam asked as he and Wally drew near.

Wally was the cameraman with whom Galen worked whenever Paul managed to be assigned somewhere else; and who had so proudly showed her his wallet photograph of his wife and kids; and who had confessed without apology his devotion to the courageous Marianne; but whose unassuming manner told Galen that despite such devotion he would give *her* a chance.

The contrast between Adam and Wally was striking. Always. But it was especially pronounced on this winter dawn. Adam appeared rested, confident, and, as always, in complete control. And Wally? His demeanor was meek, uncertain. As always. But there was more. He looked exhausted, nervous, and on edge, the *very* edge.

"Wally? Are you all right?"

"Oh, sure, Galen. Thanks for asking. It's just that I was up all night watching the coverage, worrying about those little girls, knowing how frantic I would have been if one of them had been my Annie."

"Dead wrong about what?" Adam asked again.

"Paul thinks my promised exclusive with Lucas Hunter was merely a ruse." *A lie from the master negotiator contrived to send the pathetically inept and trusting reporter on her merry way.*

Adam frowned slightly, briefly, then reassured. "If that's the case, it will be Lucas who looks bad, not you. So go get him, Galen. Go on in and ask all the tough questions."

FIVE

All the tough questions. Those were not,
Galen supposed, the questions that had
danced in her mind throughout the night. Or
perhaps they were.

What does this do to you, Lucas Hunter?
These negotiations with madmen? What
does their madness do to your heart and to
your soul?

And what of Monica, Marcia, and Kay?
Those dazzling women you have loved —
have *loved* — and who are dead, murdered,
because the killer wanted *you?*

Have you grieved the monumental loss of
love? Or has there been only torment, only
fury, at the truth: the invitation from a murderer engraved in your lovers' flesh?

Galen knew that Lucas was still in the
trailer.

And alone.

Throughout the night she had watched a
procession of uniformed officers come and
go. And she had seen, within minutes of the

end of the crisis, the command post empty of everyone save him.

Like a Broadway superstar, Lucas remained closeted within, reluctant to leave until the last of his admiring audience was gone. And like that thespian, perhaps, Lucas needed time to recover from his remarkable yet grueling performance, to make the transition from fantasy to what was real. Or, in the case of the homicide lieutenant, from madness to life.

To life? No, Galen realized. To *death*. To the murders Lieutenant Lucas Hunter had returned to Manhattan to avenge.

"It seems our bird has flown the coop," Paul remarked as Galen's tentative knock yielded no reply.

"No. He hasn't. He probably just didn't hear."

But the door opened before Galen knocked a second time.

And Galen's questions were instantly answered. The journeys to madness were excruciating for him. Devastating. Ravaging.

His skin was drawn, his muscles taut, his eyes the darkest gray. But from the darkness came a glint of silver, a glitter of welcome, for her.

"Hi," Lucas greeted softly. "Time for our interview?"

No, Galen thought. Not ever, if it will require you to return to such pain. And not now, especially not now, when you are looking at me like —

But the glittering moment had vanished, an enchanting, disturbing, thrilling mirage. And now the gray eyes, empty and cold, turned to Paul.

"I know you."

"I used to take crime-scene photographs for NYPD."

Lucas Hunter's expression revealed nothing except appraising granite. "That's right. Galen and I need to speak privately before we commit the interview to tape. So if you'll excuse us?"

"Sure." Paul was being dismissed. His parting shot was a dismissive reminder to Galen. "I'll be right outside if you need me."

Then Lucas and Galen were alone in the trailer, in its hushed silence and lightless gloom. Outside, somewhere, the winter dawn blossomed. Somewhere else. What golden rays might have caressed the trailer were blocked entirely by the hospital's massive bulk.

But Lucas saw her clearly. Because he was a master at peering into shadows? Perhaps. Yet she seemed to glow, luminous and pure.

Her hair sparkled, fire and mist, flames and diamonds, a glittering crown atop a face as white as snow and a shimmering halo for her eyes.

They were blue, those eyes, the light, bright sapphire of the firstborn sky following the harshest of winters, a newborn heaven filled with the hope and the promise of spring.

That was the blue of Galen's eyes. But where, Lucas wondered, was the promise? The hope? Missing, as if wedded still to winter. As if once long ago she had hoped for spring, only to be rewarded with a killing frost.

She was tall.

He was taller.

Lucas found himself wondering if it had been difficult for her as a girl, being the tallest in the class, and worrying that it had been. Certain of it.

But she had survived, this luminous creature of flames and snow. Fragile and tough. Determined. And resigned.

"There isn't going to be an interview," she said. "Is there?"

What would she do, Lucas wondered, if he told her no? Would she pout? Would she rage? No, he decided. She would merely nod, a regal tilt of her fiery crown, as she accepted with dignity *and as if her due* this latest killing frost.

"Yes," he countered. "There is."

Surprise glimmered. "But there wasn't going to be."

"No. There wasn't."

So what had changed since midnight? Galen knew, of course. One of the other officers had undoubtedly told him about her, and might have even downloaded for the lieutenant a copy of Friday's blistering *Start Spreading the News*. "You feel sorry for me. You're just being nice."

Now he was surprised, this man for whom even the most horrific of carnage was no shock at all. "Sorry for you? No. Nice?" A faint smile curved the harsh lines of his haggard face. "Never."

"Then why?"

Why? Because there was something about this flame-and-turquoise creature, this woman of shattered dreams. "Because I promised."

"Promises get broken all the time."

Yes they do, Lucas thought. All the time. What broken promises, he wondered, littered her life? "But not this time. Although, if you don't mind, in the interest of helping the interview flow smoothly, we should probably discuss a few ground rules first."

Galen was accustomed to such discussions. During her days with Gavel-to-Gavel, she had conducted numerous interviews, on-camera and off. Defense attorneys and prosecutors alike, not to mention officers of the police, almost always had ground rules to set.

And now, if Galen answered "sure," Lieutenant Lucas Hunter would enumerate his requirements, and maybe they'd negotiate — or clarify — for a moment or two, and then it would be time to call for Paul, and . . . Galen didn't want Paul, that intrusion, not yet.

"No ground rules?" Lucas asked softly.

"I was just thinking maybe we could do a practice interview instead? If you don't mind."

"I don't mind. I'm Lucas Hunter, by the way."

"I know. I didn't know earlier. But I do now."

"May I take your coat?" *Your mittens?*

His voice was soft, as if he wouldn't mind touching her coat, as if the gentleman was not the least repulsed by the "bag-lady atrocity" — Rosalyn St. John's description — worn by Galen during her Gavel-to-Gavel days.

Lucas Hunter was offering to touch her

coat, to be careful with it, protective of it, and there seemed even more promise in the gentle offer, to take care of her, protect *her*, if only she would let him touch.

Oh, Lieutenant. You would be so repulsed.

"No. Thank you. I'm fine."

"Have a seat then and ask away."

She did, and did. She sat across from him, an amorphous bundle of faux mohair, her mittened hands folded tightly in her lap.

But the journalist began with a statement not a question, a forthright assertion embellished by an earnest and unflickering gaze.

"You don't usually give interviews."

"No. I don't. I'm afraid I have a somewhat narrow definition of what I consider newsworthy, and I find myself drawing a fairly clear distinction between the public's right and its need to know."

"A distinction based on?"

"Risk-benefit analysis. I'm hard-pressed, for example, to assign much benefit, despite an abundance of risk, to disclose just how easily one can disguise oneself as a physician these days."

"The public doesn't benefit from knowing he had no difficulty gaining access to a ward of little girls armed only with a casually draped stethoscope and a hand grenade?"

67

Lucas smiled. "In my estimation, no. The people who need to know, hospital administrators here and elsewhere, are acutely aware. Security is being tightened even as we speak."

"Why did he do it? Do you know?"

Lucas smiled no more. "He was desperate."

"And crazy?"

"Not in any psychiatric sense. He was angry, frustrated, and in way over his head. As long as we could prevent him from doing something stupid it was just a matter of time until he gave up. The Barbie dolls really helped."

Galen had been looking at him, interested, intelligent, open, *safe*. But now she frowned and looked away, down, as she murmured to the mittens clasped — and now clenched — on her turquoise lap, "The Barbie dolls."

Lucas spoke very softly to the fallen crown of diamonds and flames. "It may well have been his wish to escape from the Barbies that compelled him to surrender as easily as he did. The Barbie doll story is pretty interesting. In fact to me it's far and away the most interesting aspect of this case. Would you care to know what I know about the dolls?"

Was he mocking her? *No.* Galen Chandler knew how it felt to be mocked. This was something different, something she had never known, something that felt like gentleness, like wonder, a most tender caress.

She looked up from fisted fuchsia Christmas trees to him.

"Yes." *Please.*

"All right," he said, and smiled. "This is according to an e-mail I received from Casey, 6-North's head nurse. On Christmas Eve, Casey writes, a woman she neither recognized nor knew showed up on the ward with a Barbie doll. Not just any Barbie, but one clothed in a striped bathrobe and a blue-cotton gown exactly like the ones worn by hospital patients everywhere. The woman had just moved to Manhattan to begin a new job. Sewing was her hobby, she explained, and she particularly enjoyed making doll clothes. Barbie doll clothes. Assuming Casey approved, she would like to donate batches of dolls, one for each girl hospitalized at any given time. She'd done this before, she said, in other towns where she'd lived. The dolls would arrive in their inpatient attire, but there would be other clothes as well, outfits for when doll and girl went home.

"Not surprisingly, Casey loved the idea,

and they agreed the first delivery would be on New Year's Day. Our benefactress left the prototype Barbie with Casey, who in turn gave it to her most needy patient, a frightened, battered five-year-old girl. The girl's name was Sarah, and it was her father who'd caused both her injuries and her fright."

"Oh," Galen whispered. "Poor thing."

"She'll be okay," Lucas reassured her. "Her mother loves her very much. She would move heaven and earth to keep Sarah safe."

"Oh," Galen whispered again. *"Good."*

This whisper came with relief. And something else. Longing, Lucas decided. And loss.

"And of course," he added gently, "Sarah has her Barbie." *The gift — from you — that meant so much.* "Here's where the story gets really interesting. It was Sarah's father who appeared last night with a stethoscope and a hand grenade."

"Oh, *no.*"

"This is a good story, Galen. A very good one. Anthony Royce had been to 6-North before, when his daughter was hospitalized there. And do you know how Sarah would greet him when he visited her? With fear, and with her Barbie. She'd hold the doll between herself and her father, as if he was a vampire and the Barbie was a crucifix. Which is why, I suppose, the dolls came to symbolize to Anthony the end of his life as he knew it. As it happens, shortly before he arrived last night, the mystery woman made another delivery."

"The mystery woman," Galen echoed quietly, searching for contempt, for mockery. And seeing none.

None.

"Casey never reveals her name. Our heroine wanted it that way. It seemed a simple if astonishing request, and easy to honor . . . until the generous seamstress became familiar throughout Manhattan. It became a little cloak-and-dagger then. She and Casey would meet in the hospital lobby, or even here in the doctors' parking lot. But last night Casey was too busy to get away, so the mystery woman made the delivery of joy herself. 'Delivery of joy' is a direct quote, by the way. Casey also writes that the doll clothes are works of art, both in craftsmanship and design. And, she says, they're sewn entirely by hand. I wonder why that would be."

He was interviewing her and his technique was quite stunning, a gentle inquisition that made her want to confess all

71

manner of foolish things.

"Well," she replied cautiously. "Given the smallness of the dolls, and of their clothes, I suppose it's just as easy to sew the old-fashioned way, with needles and thread."

With needles and thread and, Lucas mused, with her hands. He wondered about her hands, hidden now, clasped within turquoise. How would they look, he wondered, as they danced with soaring needles and shimmering thread?

"It occurred to me," he said, "that if she travels a lot — and remember she told Casey she'd donated Barbies in a number of towns — it would prevent her from having to lug a sewing machine from place to place."

That was the *real* answer, of course, the incautious confession, the pathetic truth. She could spend her days inside courtrooms, covering trials, and in the evening she could retreat to her motel room and sew.

"Yes," Galen admitted. "It would." She seemed lost for a moment, and so lonely. But only for a moment. As if she would not permit a heartbeat more. "You said there was a delivery of dolls last night?"

"Of joy," Lucas corrected softly. "Yes. And just in time. When Anthony bolted himself and his eight young captives in the playroom, he held hostage the Barbies as well. The girls clutched their dolls, just as Sarah had clutched hers, and it felt to Anthony as if he were surrounded by a coven of tiny witches, each one casting a potent spell. And he wanted out. Desperately. It's a good story, isn't it? A nice one. Too bad it's not newsworthy."

"It's not?"

"Not unless the mystery woman wants it to be. It would be good, nice, for the people of Manhattan to know that such generosity exists. But as extraordinary as the story is, her privacy, her wishes, should come first."

He was protecting her, this man of privacy and wishes, protecting her as he would have protected her coat. And he was caressing her still, with his voice and with his eyes, and now it felt as if she — not merely the Barbie doll story — were extraordinary.

And it was too much. Too great a lie.

Galen looked away, had to, from the smoky gray gaze . . . to ashes . . . and back.

"It's the cigarette aspect of the hostage crisis that's most interesting to me."

An elegant black eyebrow arched and a glint of silver sparked in the smoldering smoke. "The cigarette aspect, Galen? Tell me about that."

"Well. Anthony had three packs, and you had three packs, and when I was here at midnight, you were smoking, slowly, rhythmically, methodically."

"Not the way I usually smoke?"

"I don't believe you smoke at all."

Lucas inclined his midnight black head. "Okay," he conceded. "So why was I smoking last night?"

"Because *he* was. Anthony was. And you wanted to know how the nicotine was affecting him, the kind of power he was feeling, the edginess and the rush."

"But you said I was smoking methodically. Rhythmically."

"Yes." A mittened hand abandoned its ferocious clasp, and its nest of turquoise fluff, and began to move rhythmically, methodically, up and down, up and down, a knitted metronome of grace. "Maybe the cigarettes were how he chose to measure time to his ultimatum. If his demands weren't met by his final puff . . . well. He was probably smoking erratically, in nervous bursts. But there was no way you could mimic that. So you smoked slowly and surely, hoping it would even out."

"The hare and the tortoise."

The tortoise? No. Lucas Hunter was a panther . . . who had slowly but surely — and deeply and punishingly — smoked all but two cigarettes from the three packs. The

74

remaining duo lay on the table nearby, slender ghosts of the fifty-eight comrades that had seared his lungs.

"Do you know how many cigarettes he had left when he surrendered?" Galen asked.

A wry smile curved his lips as he looked from the twin ghosts to her. "Two."

"So you convinced him to give up with time to spare."

His expression became solemn. Intense. "I told you, Galen, it was the Barbie dolls that got to him."

"But the cigarettes are interesting. Too bad they're no more newsworthy than the dolls."

"They're not?"

"I don't think so, at least not using the benefit-risk formula. Negligible benefit. Substantial risk."

"How so?"

"Well, aren't criminals sometimes copy-cats?"

"Often," Lucas said.

"So, let's say some would-be hostage-taker hears the cigarette story and likes it, thinks it has a certain flare. But he wants to give it his own spin, just to prove he's an original after all, so instead of keeping time with nicotine he decides to go with crack cocaine. What's the hostage negotiator to do then?"

Galen had her answer, at least from *this* arbiter of madness. Lucas would do whatever was necessary. *Whatever.* No matter the personal risk.

"This takes so much out of you," she said.

Now she was caressing him. With gentleness. With caring.

For several magnificent moments, selfish bastard that he was, Lucas indulged in pure fantasy.

He and Galen would leave the trailer. Now. Before it was too late. And they would simply disappear. For a while. Perhaps forever. They would talk of Barbie dolls and turquoise mittens and fuchsia Christmas trees with bright purple stars.

They would discover spring, even on this wintry day. Spring, with its myriad promises and glorious hopes.

Before it was too late.

But it was already too late, *had been,* long before the icy foreboding that had come at 3:13. Lucas could not, would not, wish his dissolute soul on anyone.

Least of all this mittened waif.

"I'm afraid, Galen, that there's really not much to take." *And nothing — good — to give.*

His voice was ice, his eyes were glacial, and even as the air within the trailer was growing bitter cold, the door opened, permitting more chill. And startling her.

But not him.

Lucas had been expecting this intrusion, Galen realized. Waiting for it.

Dreading it.

And biding his time chatting with her.

The officer in the doorway was someone new, someone fresh, a day-shift face to replace one of the several that had kept vigil throughout the night.

"I'm sorry, sir. But this was just called in. There's been . . ." The officer stopped abruptly. If he wasn't mistaken, this was Galen Chandler, a disheveled version and a stricken one, pleading for a chance, perhaps, to prove herself undeserving of Rosalyn St. John's scathing critique?

If so, if the disgraced anchorwoman was hoping for a career-saving scoop, the information he was about to reveal to Lucas Hunter would definitely fit the bill. Which meant he had no intention of revealing it until she was gone.

"Another murder," Lucas said quietly. "The Lady Killer has killed again."

"Yes."

"Do you have her name?"

"Yes, sir. I do." The officer cast a meaningful glance at Galen, as if he knew that once armed with the information she would rush from the trailer and announce the tragedy to the world.

"Her name." Lieutenant Hunter's command was taut. Raw.

What was he thinking? Galen wondered as the officer consulted his notes. Was the master negotiator brokering some deal with fate . . . or with his God? Was he pleading that the killer's latest victim *not* be the woman he had been missing, wanting, during his month-long exile in Australia, the beautiful woman with whom he would have spent this night had it not been for the hostage crisis on 6-North?

And if Lucas *was* sending such a silent pleading, was he tormented by guilt, even more guilt, that by pleading for the life of his current lover he was tacitly dooming another, discarded lover to death?

"Brynne Talbot."

"Brynne," Lucas echoed.

His eyes closed briefly, ebony lashes over anguished gray, as he permitted a moment of grief, of mourning, of rage. Then they opened anew, stark and glittering and clear, and he was a hunter again, drawing from the fearsome passion deep within, the fierce,

78

dark place from which he had told her there was so little to take.

"Is the scene secure?" Lieutenant Lucas Hunter asked.

The scene. The *crime* scene. Assuming the Lady Killer had not deviated from his established M.O., the place of carnage would be the victim's home, to which he'd gained access without forced entry and from which he'd vanished without leaving so much as a chromosome of DNA.

"Yes, sir. It is. The officers at the location say that nothing has been touched."

"Good." Lucas stood. Strong. Powerful. And weighted by immense invisible chains. "Let's go."

No! Don't go! It was a silent cry from a foolish heart. But there were things she wanted to say.

Thank you, Lucas, for looking at me, for that rare and wondrous moment, as if I were special. Extraordinary. I'll never forget it. Never. And take care of yourself, will you? Please? Be gentle with yourself. As you were so very gentle with me.

Galen said those things in silence. But even had she shouted such foolishness aloud, Lucas Hunter would not have heard. His mind was already far away — from the plush trailer that caged him still.

But then he turned. To her. And the ferocious gray eyes devoured her with longing, with apology, with regret. As if he knew she was leaving Manhattan, *wanted her to leave,* yet wanted something — quite different — as well.

"Lucas?"

The hunger vanished. And there was only ice. Only death. "Good-bye, Galen."

Good-bye.

"Galen?"

"Oh! Paul." Galen stood as moments earlier, an eternity earlier, Lucas had arisen with his chains. "Let's go."

"No exclusive after all?"

"I'm sorry. I guess I wasn't clear. I should have said 'Let's roll tape.' "

"Here and now? With you looking like death? Turquoise is *not* your color, Galen. It's too vivid for your skin. The camera's going to see turquoise, and red, and in between, where your face should be, nothing at all."

"Fine." I may look like death, she thought. But Lucas is seeing it, touching it, touching the brutalized body of a woman he has known, has caressed, has loved.

"Fine." Paul tossed her the wireless microphone. "You might at least want to re-

80

think the mittens."

Galen answered his suggestion by curling her mittened hands around the microphone.

"Whatever," Paul said. "Whenever you're ready."

Galen was ready, without rehearsal. The words simply flowed.

"This is Galen Chandler, reporting live — and apologizing live — from inside the mobile command unit where I've just finished interviewing Lieutenant Lucas Hunter of the NYPD. It was a comprehensive interview, as the lieutenant had promised it would be. But I'm afraid I have nothing to report. The specifics of this negotiation cannot be revealed. To do so would be to subject the public to unnecessary risks of similar crimes."

SIX

"There's really no excuse for such brutality," the electronic voice asserted without prelude when Galen answered her telephone at 10 o'clock on Thursday night.

"I'm afraid you have the wrong number."

"No, Galen Chandler, I assure you I don't. Speaking of which, a *listed* phone number? I'm not complaining, mind you. It made my task of reaching you at home far easier than it might have been. But listing one's phone number? In *this* city? In *this* day and age? Your naïveté is delightful, Galen. So charmingly Midwest."

"Who is this?"

"All in good time, my dear. All in good time. Besides, since we've already detoured to a discussion of your listed home phone, and your Kansan charm, I should also chastise you — again gently, because it helped me no end — about your carelessness. To wit, carrying your cell phone in the pendulous and eminently accessible front pocket

of that awful turquoise coat. Such temptation is candy for even the most novice pick-
pocket, an invitation that becomes irresistible when you toss the coat aside whenever the camera begins to roll."

"You have my cell phone?"

"I do. Have you really not missed it yet?
No, I suppose not. Since the hospital hostage fiasco you probably haven't gotten
many — any? — requests to abandon your
weather-girl duties to cover breaking news."

Her weather-girl duties. The electronic
description itself was an exaggeration, a
promotion from the actual facts. Galen had
been reporting the weather, not forecasting
it. Admittedly this week's weather had been
news. Last evening in fact the newscast had
led with it, ahead of the twin stories that had
dominated since Sunday: the rescue of eight
little girls held hostage at Memorial Hospital and the slaughter during that crisis of
Brynne Talbot . . . *Dr.* Brynne Talbot, the
brilliant and beautiful oncologist who had
cared for Galen's predecessor, Marianne
McLain, from the beloved anchorwoman's
diagnosis to her death.

Galen's role as KCOR's on-the-scene
chronicler of Manhattan's meteorologic
whimsy had been entirely voluntary. And
logical. As of her Sunday morning telecast

there could be no more pretense about *any-thing,* beginning with the way she looked.

So what if raindrops splattered from soggy curls to naked face? At least KCOR's viewers knew they were getting the unedited truth; could *see* that truth even when Galen's chapped lips were numb. And mum.

The electronic voice was right. She hadn't used her cell phone for days. Hadn't even reached for it since paging Adam, Paul, and Wally on Sunday at dawn.

And now the voice was saying it — he? — had plucked the phone from the cavernous pockets of her turquoise coat. That was the *how.* And the *when* and the *where?*

At either end of the day as she walked along Fifth Avenue to and from work. Or *as* she worked on location as a weather girl.

On Monday, perhaps, in Battery Park. With artist and critic Paul. The bright yellow KCOR rain slicker did nothing, he noted, for the pallor of her face. However, the yellow contrasted dramatically and aesthetically with the sea-green silver-crested waves. Besides, by the time her turquoise coat was tossed into the unlocked van, the faux mohair was thoroughly drenched.

Or on Tuesday with Wally, when the winter sun shone so brightly that grateful Manhattanites flocked to Central Park for lattes and lunch, and jogging and Rollerblades, and even to fly their kites. Galen's coat spent most of that balmy day on a nearby park bench, its bountiful pockets accessible to legions of sun-worshiping passersby.

Or on Wednesday, when Wally's down-filled parka provided a last-minute substitute for snow-matted fluff.

Or today. No, *not* today. Today's weather had been seasonable, reasonable, temperate and calm. Galen had spent the entire day at the station, puttering in her office, cleaning up, cleaning *out*, as she awaited her 4:15 appointment with John McLain . . . the appointment during which she would tell him that she was leaving KCOR.

Galen would have told him first thing Monday morning, tried to. But John was away until Thursday afternoon, his secretary told her, a long-scheduled business trip which would detour on Wednesday to the funeral in Toledo for Brynne Talbot, the slain doctor who had fought so hard to save his wife.

Galen needed to announce her decision to John, first. He had been the most impassioned about her coming to KCOR, and his support for her had been unwavering, generous and heartfelt, even as he himself remained so obviously broken, shattered, by the death of Marianne.

"Why?" she asked the electronic voice that had been silent during her own silent reflections on the hows, the whens, the wheres.

"Why what?"

"Why do you have my phone?"

"I'll get to that. Never fear. But back to my original point: the brutality of your colleagues in the fourth estate. Rosalyn St. John is the worst. 'A Galen-force disaster.' How catty can one get? But she's been hissing at you from the start and now everyone's jumped on the let's-trash-Galen bandwagon. In fairness, this week's criticism *is* deserved. Lying to one's viewers is not perfect, Galen. Not perfect at all."

"I didn't lie."

"Let's establish the ground rules right now. There's no need to lie to me. Ever. In fact lying to me would be a big mistake. Lucas Hunter tricked you. *Lied to you.* I, for one, thought it was classy, if incredibly naive, to let him off the hook. Very Joan of Arc. Of course, like Joan, you — at least your career — have gone up in flames. Courtesy of yours truly, however, you will rise triumphant from the ashes. You're about to be rescued, Galen Chandler. By me."

But I don't need to be rescued. I did that myself, at four-fifteen this afternoon, when I met with John.

86

"I'm him, Galen."

"Him?"

"Manhattan's Lady Killer, at your service. Unlike Lieutenant Hunter, when *I* promise a lady an exclusive *I* deliver. And that's my promise to you. Exclusive after exclusive."

"I don't believe you."

"What part do you doubt? The promise of exclusives? Or that it's really me? Never mind. The answer is obvious. If it's *not* really me, an exclusive would be valueless on its face. Ergo, you doubt it's me."

"Yes," she managed, even as her stomach churned and her mind raced. The killer had, after all, tipped Rosalyn St. John to the fact that it was Lucas Hunter's ladyloves he was slaughtering, and why . . . because he wanted to *play.* As he was playing now? "I think it's far more likely that you're with a tabloid, disguising your voice in case I'm recording this call."

The answering sigh was electronic. But Galen heard the reaction loud and clear. Impatience. Disgust. So familiar to her even when disguised.

"Let me explain to you the reason for the electronic alteration. Our conversations *will* be recorded. By the police. Every sentence, every syllable, will be analyzed to death, as it were. And it's also my hope — which, in all candor, will come to pass since I happen to be calling every shot — that our discussions will be broadcast by KCOR. By you. I've decided to salvage your career, Galen. To make you a superstar. But not at the expense of destroying mine. I can't take the chance that one of your viewers might recognize my voice. Regrettably. Because you would like my voice, Galen. Very much. Most women do. Kay and Brynne especially did."

"The police will be recording our conversations?"

"You *know* they will. As an aside, my little gift for the taxpayers of New York, I'm alerting you in advance that tracing my calls would be a waste. I'll be using your cell phone, among others, and will be a moving target besides. But our conversations will be recorded. Must be. We really can't make you famous, can we, if our relationship is private?"

"Or make you famous."

"More famous, you mean. I'm enjoying a fair amount of notoriety as it is. I repeat, Galen, this is for you. I've already notified the police, a voice message on the hotline established expressly for information about yours truly. I just gave the evening operator at KCOR a similar message and will plan to inform KCOR's worthy — and not so worthy — competition as well."

"Given my track record, I think there's an excellent chance that your messages will be dismissed as a hoax. That *you* will be dismissed as a hoax."

"I'm the genuine article, Galen. Never doubt it. A fact the cops will confirm the moment you reveal the three magic words. *Not* the clichéd three, I assure you."

"The clichéd three?"

"You know. Surely. As a woman, you know."

As a woman. Those three words pierced as sharply as the other three, the magic three. *I love you.*

The piercing sharpness pricked her voice.

"So your magic words are?"

"At last! A glimpse of the investigative journalist in action. Aggressive. Proactive. And with an edge. Very good, Galen. *Very* good."

"And those words are?"

" 'Cross your heart.' You know that little ditty children say to each other? When they exact promises from one another? Cross your heart and hope to die and stick a needle in your . . . well, I assume you know the rest."

"Yes."

"Say it for me, Galen. The entire ditty. *Say it.*"

"Cross your heart and hope to die and stick a needle in your . . . eye."

"Very nice."

"You're a monster."

The electronic laugh was a monstrous roar. "But I'm *your* monster, Galen. All yours. Hark! What was that sound? A doorbell, perhaps? A sign that at least someone has taken seriously my messages? Unless you're expecting a late-night lover, that is. Whatever the case, I'd better go. We'll talk again. Soon. I promise."

SEVEN

The sound had not been the doorbell, but the intercom linking her apartment to the entrance nine floors below.

"Yes?"

"It's Lucas Hunter, Galen."

Galen touched the trio of numbers that released the distant dead bolt. "Come in."

The doorbell sounded far sooner than Galen would have imagined it could, as if dazzled by him and wanting to impress, the building's archaic and cranky elevator had carried him aloft with unprecedented speed.

He *was* dazzling, this elegance of shadow and stone.

Dazzling. And ominous.

Lucas greeted her with unsmiling gray eyes.

And a voice to match.

"You didn't look through the peephole to confirm that it was me."

"No. I didn't."

Had he truly slept, she wondered, in the five nights since she had seen him last? Did the gray-eyed panther ever sleep? Or was bed for him a place that nourished with passion not with dreams?

And when had the sensuous beast been nourished last?

"And there's no closed-circuit video between here and the front door."

"No. There's not."

She was quite glorious, he thought, in her baggy lavender warm-ups and pink woolen socks. And quite oblivious, it seemed, to the clash of hues with her fiery curls. Had she truly slept, he wondered, as he noticed the dark purple smudges beneath her eyes. And was bed for her a place of nightmares or of dreams?

Lucas's own nightmares haunted. "So you just let me in. Twice. With absolutely no proof that it was me."

"Yes. And yes. And it *was* you both times. Besides, I was expecting some law-enforcement type. In fact, if I'd had time to think about it, I would have known to expect you." *You.*

"So he's called."

"Yes. Just now. You think it's him?"

I know it's him. But Lucas remained fiercely focused on the more urgent matter:

Galen's terrifying disregard of danger. "I cannot believe you just let me in."

"You *mentioned* that." Her chin lifted a defiant notch. "It will never happen again. I promise."

Lucas smiled at last and glinting shards of silver illuminated the ominous gray. "Good. I sure as hell wouldn't want any cooperation with the police, especially when it comes to something as trivial as rounding up a killer." His smile vanished, but the silvery light glittered still. Then softly, an invitation to enchantment — and to death — he asked, "What did he say?"

"Cross your heart." Galen saw the truth in the harsh ripple of his strong jaw. The truth. And the fury. "It's him, isn't it?"

"Yes. What else . . . actually, would you just write down everything you remember?"

"Sure. It wasn't a terribly long conversation, but definitely a memorable one."

Memorable, Lucas mused. Like a wind-ravaged waif in turquoise fluff and matching mittens. No, nothing was as memorable as that — except for the lavender-and-pink vision before him now, with her sleep-starved eyes and naked hands.

Galen's hands were slender, as she was, and as she, delicate and long. And now the naked delicacy was fluttering beneath his appraising gaze, a nervous flight from lavender to fire.

"Thanks," Lucas said softly. "I'll get that from you tomorrow. In the meantime, do you mind if I look around?"

Galen frowned. "Do you expect him to come here?"

"No," Lucas admitted. "I don't."

"So I'm not his next victim?"

"That's right. You're not. Killing you would look to the watching world like failure on his part, an admission that you were getting perilously close to discovering who he was."

"But I might be the victim after next?"

Yes. *No.* "There isn't going to be a victim after next. Or even a next victim. We're going to get him, Galen. You and I. Which means, I'm afraid, that I really do need to see your apartment. It couldn't matter less if it's a mess."

Her apartment was not a mess, merely an uneasy standoff between what she did and who she was. Uneasy and quite crowded in the single room in which she dwelled.

Galen's studio apartment was *not* inexpensive. Au contraire. Its midtown location was a landlord's dream.

The accessories of a modern-day anchorwoman rimmed the outermost edges of the room. Computer, radio, TV, fax. And everywhere else, including nearly every square inch of her neatly made bed, were the ancient accoutrements of a seamstress.

Two irons, one large, one small, stood on the floor, glittering silver sentries amid the colorful mosaic of fabric and thread. And on the fabric-draped couch were the Barbies, some seated, some standing.

All clothed. Fully clothed. Modest even in the privacy of this design studio.

Lucas wanted to ask about the modesty of the dolls, to *know* about it. But the question he posed was more relevant to the reason he was here.

"Why the cardboard boxes?" There were four, emblazoned with a stylized *Mayflower*, its sails unfurled.

"I'm moving. At least I was."

"Moving where?"

"I'm not sure. Away from New York."

"And from KCOR?"

"Yes."

"Because of Sunday morning? Because of what you said? And didn't say?"

"You know what I said?" According to published reports, and since Sunday Galen had read every word, Lucas Hunter was a man possessed, consumed with the pursuit of his quarry and nothing else.

But at this moment he seemed consumed with only her.

"Yes. I know. I thought it was sensational."

"Thanks. It felt . . . right." And this, the gentle and approving caress of the hunter's eyes, felt wonderful. *Impossible.*

"But unpopular?" Lucas pressed softly even as fury churned within. He should have known what her courage had cost her. He *would* have known had he permitted himself such an indulgent distraction from the grim task at hand. But he hadn't, and . . . "They fired you?"

Her ballerina hands found again the tangled flames. "I fired myself."

"Why?"

"Because it's been obvious from the beginning that I'm simply not anchorwoman material."

Simply. She said it so simply, her failure at the job that was every reporter's dream. "Because?"

"Oh. Because I don't have the emotional range."

So simply. So dispassionately. An earnest assessment that pierced her soul. And his. "What the hell does that mean?"

"That I can't make smooth transitions from one story to the next with appropriate emotions to match."

"You have trouble making cheerful segues from 'fire kills a family of five' to 'Brooklyn housewife wins lotto'?"

"Lots of trouble."

"Maybe, Galen, you have too much emotional range."

"Oh! Well. Thank you. But . . . one couldn't say that Marianne didn't have emotional range. Or Adam. Or any of the hundreds of anchors who do this so successfully every day."

"I'm not saying that. Especially about Marianne. So I'll just say this about you. No other reporter in New York would have gotten the interview I gave you. No other reporter in the world." The sudden pinkness of her cheeks clashed wildly, enchantingly, with her hair. But she didn't seem enchanted, merely confused. Lucas returned to the police-business topic at hand. "When did you fire yourself?"

"Today."

"Who knows?"

"Only KCOR's owner John McLain." Galen's reeling mind spun to what else Lucas had said — "Especially about Marianne" — and the way he had said it: fondly. "Do you know John? Did you know Marianne?"

"Marianne and Fran and I knew each

other as children."

"In England?"

"No," Lucas said. "In New York. In a town called Chatsworth in Westchester County about an hour from here. I lived there until I was nine."

"And Marianne and Fran lived there too?"

"Yes." *As did pain . . . and horror . . . and the death of dreams.*

Galen saw the sudden shadow, deep and dark in his ice gray eyes. It was a glacial shadow, bitter cold — and edged, she thought, with pain.

The shadow vanished, Lucas vanquished it, as suddenly as it had appeared, and he replied to her query about John McLain.

"I met John several years ago."

Several years, Galen mused. And John and Marianne had been married for almost ten. Which meant that despite the fondness — and because of the pain? — Lucas Hunter had not attended the wedding of his childhood friend.

"What did John say about your firing yourself?"

Galen hesitated. And when she spoke, it was slowly and with care. "It wasn't what he said, but the way he looked. He should have been relieved. But he wasn't. Not at all. And

98

he refused to formally accept my resignation until Monday."

"To give you time to reconsider."

"Yes."

Lucas looked at the cardboard boxes, ready to be filled, even though it was only Thursday night. Galen wasn't going to change her mind. Didn't want to. She was eager, desperate, to leave the Big Apple.

"Maybe," he said, "you should leave as planned."

"I should?"

"Don't get me wrong, Galen. I need your help. Want it. But this isn't going to be pleasant." Lucas could keep her safe. Would. Absolutely. But he could not control the killer's words. "He may say some very disturbing things to you."

I need your help. Want it. It felt — to her foolish, lonely heart — like I need *you*. Want *you*.

"I'm staying, Lieutenant. In New York and at KCOR."

"Okay," he said softly. *Okay.* Galen would remain in Manhattan, and they would bring the killer to his knees, and . . . and Lucas did not want to talk, yet, about death. His gaze drifted to the small, crowded, color-ful couch. "You'll stay, and your dolls will stay."

"Actually, the Barbies were never scheduled to leave."

"Another" — *final* — "delivery of joy to
6-North? When?"

"I told Casey I'd be there at two Sunday
afternoon."

"That shouldn't be a problem." *No matter
what the killer has in mind.* The murderer
would not prevent the generous seamstress
from keeping her promise to Casey and the
girls. These dolls, this modest assembly of
color and shape *and joy,* would be delivered
right on time. "I hadn't realized Barbies
came in such variety. Such diversity."

"Barbie has definitely become politically
correct."

"It sounds as if you don't approve."

"I *do.* Of course. It's just that I never really
bought the 'destruction of self-esteem'
theory, the proposition that if a little girl
owned a doll who was beautiful and blond,
she'd set the same standard of perfection for
herself, only to face spiritual — or even literal — death when inevitably she failed."

"Literal death?"

"By starvation or plastic surgery or whatever other extremes she chose in order to
mimic the humanly impossible shape."

"What theory do you buy?"

"The one in which they're *dolls,* like any

other dolls. Companions, not competitors. And friends." Her shrug caused a dance of curls. "And I guess I just don't see what's wrong with any little girl, *every* little girl, having a pretty, stylish friend who's there for her *always*."

"Which Barbie is yours?" *Show me the friend who was your faithful companion as a little girl, even when promises were broken, and who is with you still, nonjudgmental where others have judged you so harshly, not disappointed in you ever, in any way. Show me, Galen. Introduce me to your blond, beautiful, plastic friend, and let's talk of dolls not death for as long as we can.*

But Galen made no proud and joyful introduction, and Lucas saw in her cloudy blue eyes what he had wanted to postpone. Loss.

Death.

"None of them."

"Where is she?"

Galen shrugged anew. But the flames did not dance. "I'm not sure. She was, is, my mother's. When I left her home, I left her Barbie behind."

Her mother's home. Her mother's Barbie. The mother's not the child's. This daughter, it seemed, this nomadic woman of cardboard boxes adorned with sailing ships was as homeless as he.

Homeless? Lucas Hunter? Yes. Quite homeless, despite the grand box in which he dwelled.

Galen moved then, away from him and toward her dolls.

But she halted before reaching the Barbies and for several moments merely stared at the glass-topped table. Then, with a long snowy finger, she began to trace a meandering path, a leisurely slalom between spools of thread which ended at a golden needle with an emerald tail.

Cross your heart and hope to die and stick a needle in your eye.

Her finger touched the needle's very tip. "Does he really . . . ?"

I don't want to tell you what he does. But the choice did not belong to Lucas. The murderer had already made it.

"Yes. He pierces their eyes. But only, Galen, after they're dead."

Galen's own eyes squeezed shut, tightly, briefly. Then, staring still at the needle, she asked. "How do they die?"

"He uses a knife."

"Yes. I know." *Viciously stabbed,* or variations thereof, appeared in every article she had read. "But how?"

"Galen."

"I need to know this. Please. I won't reveal —"

"I know that."

"So how do they die?"

How? Lucas echoed in silence. Horribly. Horrifically. Watching the frantic pulse of crimson and feeling its surprising heat, even as the shivering begins.

"He cuts their throats." *Quick. Painless. Terrifying.*

"Does he make a cross over their hearts? With the knife?"

"Yes. He does. After death."

"Does he do anything else?" she asked quietly, apprehensively, but needing to know.

"No, Galen. He doesn't."

She looked up, her voice urgent, her worried face framed with frozen flames. "He has no intention of getting caught."

"That's what's called the deluded arrogance of the megalomaniac."

"He certainly has the maniac part down."

"The deluded part as well. He's just made a monumental mistake."

"By calling me?"

"By calling you. We'll get him, Galen." *We will get him.* It was a promise, and a vow.

Lucas scanned the rest of her apartment, a visual perusal not a physical one, an unnecessary but somehow essential search for the personal artifacts of her life, the photographs of family, of friends — her absentee mother, the Barbie she had lost — and maybe a scented candle or two, and a community of merry figurines, and bright posters framed in gold.

But there was nothing. *Nothing.* Except for a book on her nightstand.

The book. So very, *very* personal for him. Was this what Galen chose to read before she slept? Before she dreamed?

As Lucas walked to the nightstand, he steadied his heart, his fury, his voice.

"Speaking with God," he said, reading the title, testing his fury, his control, and hearing nothing above the thunder of his heart.

Until she spoke softly from across the room. "Presumptuous, isn't it?"

Very, he thought. And so astonishingly pathologic. But that was Brandon Christianson: psychopath, murderer, and sorcerer of words designed to comfort, to inspire, to soothe.

Silence fell as her question lingered unanswered. His voice had been so cold, so dark, as he'd read the title. Contempt for the anonymous author, perhaps? The writer who offered not a biographical clue and who chose as his or her nom de plume the sign of the cross? Or was Lucas Hunter's pitch-black fury with God?

Or with her . . .

"I mean," Galen embellished hurriedly, "at least it seems presumptuous to me. It implies, to me, a remarkable degree of access."

"I agree."

Oh, *good*.

Lucas looked from the book to her. Galen saw coldness still, darkness still. But not for her. Not *because* of her.

But Lucas wanted something from her. The truth. More truth.

"Are the contents presumptuous as well?"

"I think so. But mine's clearly a minority opinion. It's been on all the bestseller lists for years and even renowned theologians have given it rave reviews."

"But you're not convinced."

"No."

"But you're reading it."

"Yes. KCOR's news director, Viveca Blair — well, I imagine you know her, too."

"I know Viveca." Brandon's cousin. The psychopath's cousin. "She has something to do with the book?"

"She gave it to me. She said it was possible that she might be able to get the author to reveal his or her true identity during an on-air interview with me. If that was something I wanted to do. Which I don't."

"No?"

"No. Not at all."

Lucas Hunter's expression was no longer either cold or dark. At least no more so than usual.

But still Galen shivered.

Even before he spoke.

"We're going to need a bigger place."

"We?" *We?*

"I need to be with you whenever he calls."

"Oh. Why?"

"Because with some killers, although certainly not with all, I'm able to sense things."

Sense? Things? "Emotions? Thoughts?"

"Sometimes. Yes." *And desire and lust.*

"And you know then who the killer is?"

"I get impressions, feelings, which in concert with other pieces of the investigative puzzle may lead to an arrest. The correct arrest."

Impressions? Feelings? "Do you see the killer?"

"No." Lucas hesitated, then admitted something he had never shared before. "I'm inside him, Galen." *I'm inside the devil.*

On the rare and long-ago occasions when Lucas Hunter had alluded even vaguely, to women he knew, about his gift, the reaction had always been a blend of fascination and alarm.

But even in the face of his explicit admission, his intimacy with evil, Galen's reaction remained interest not fascination, worry not alarm, and not a wisp of fear.

"Do you see the victim?"

"No." *It's too dark inside, a blood-red blur of frenzied madness.* "Never."

"And now," Galen said quietly, "you need to know if you'll be able to sense this killer."

"I already know that I can."

"Oh. Well. I guess that's good."

"You guess?" he echoed.

"Well. It's certainly good for the case. For the city. But not so good for you."

I'll survive, he thought reflexively. I always do. I always must. But very softly he confessed, "Not so good for me."

It was a confession and a warning. Not good for me, sweet seamstress, and sheer disaster for anyone who ventures near.

Which no one did, no one wanted to, no one dared. He would not permit it. Lucas gave his lovers pieces of himself, his fierce passion, his exquisite touch. But no more. Not his heart, not his mind, and not, never, the darkness of his soul.

His lovers knew to want no more. They sensed the danger, the blackness, the ice.

But now this creature stood before him, this tall pale vision in baggy lavender and tangled flames. Fearless. And worried *for him.*

"My sense of our killer is very strong," Lucas continued, confessing still, warning still. "Strong enough, perhaps, that I could simply listen to the recordings we'll make."

"But listening live and in person might be better?"

"Yes."

"So we need to" — *be together? all the time?* — "find a bigger place?"

"It's already been found," Lucas said, wondering when he had made the decision, if even before tonight he had been imagining her with him in his homeless home. "We just have to get you and your phone moved in by tomorrow night."

"Night. He's a darkness kind of guy."

"As dark as it gets. If you can fill these boxes tonight, I'll arrange to have them moved tomorrow."

"Okay. And do I go to work as usual in the morning?"

"Yes."

"And . . ."

"Yes?"

"I was wondering what I should wear."

"What you should wear?"

"At work. My clothes and my hair."

What should I wear, Lucas? The ghosts of similar queries echoed. Similar queries, but differently posed and by such different women. What's your *pleasure,* Lieutenant? Backless? Braless? Slit to the thigh? And Lucas, would you like my hair bound or free?

Such different women.

"I guess I don't understand."

"Well. Until Sunday I'd had a certain on-air look, thanks to Viveca, Saks, and Jose-Felipe. It was better. More New York. Everyone agreed."

"Did you?"

"Oh, I . . ." Galen shrugged, uncertain, as if she truly didn't know, as if she couldn't see herself at all. "Anyway, since Sunday I've regressed. I just wondered if you had a . . . sense of what would be best."

The man who could sense such evil had a clear vision now. Clear and lovely and stunningly pure. And it had nothing, he knew, to do with the killer.

"Wear what you've been wearing since Sunday." *Wear your curls, Galen Chandler. And your mittens. And your lavender warm-ups with your shocking pink socks. And don't forget, never forget, your impossibly turquoise coat.* "And in the meantime, Galen, don't open the door to anyone."

"Okay."

Lucas should have stopped there. But something ferocious stirred within. Ferocious, primal, possessive, male.

"Anyone," he commanded softly. "Except me."

EIGHT

How buoyant she felt on this Friday morning walk to work. How *safe*. The sky above Manhattan was dark. Gray. The color of his eyes. And it was as if he were watching her, protecting her, every step of the way.

Galen noticed the faces in the crush of humanity that jostled along Fifth, looked directly into oncoming eyes and was surprised by what she saw. Smiling strangers, sympathetic, *em*pathetic, as if there were others in this city of sophistication who had failed.

Galen arrived at KCOR shortly before nine. On this day, because Manhattan's Lady Killer had left voice messages all over town, Galen was greeted by a most interested foursome.

"Way to go, Galen," Wally observed, then shrugged. "That is, I guess way to go."

"You *guess?*" Viveca echoed. "This is the scoop of the century. Wally has it exactly right, Galen. *Way to go.*"

"Ditto, kiddo," Adam agreed.

"I'd say thank you, but it's really none of my doing."

Galen glanced at Paul, expecting amazement at least and skepticism of course. But Paul's expression was oddly muted, strangely thoughtful, and he said not a word.

"It *will* be your doing, however," Viveca insisted. "And we're all going to help you make the very most of it. We'll broadcast your taped conversations, of course, but maybe you could convince him to call in live? And if you could lure him into dropping the electronic disguise for even a *syllable —*"

"Hold on a minute, Viv," Adam interjected. "Convince him? *Lure* him? This man has slaughtered four women."

"Believe me, Adam, I *know.* Marcia and I were at Vassar together. We were *friends.* But Galen's his connection. His *link.* He wouldn't dream of hurting her." Viveca gazed at an approaching figure and when she spoke again it was so that he would hear. "Besides which Lieutenant Hunter will keep Galen safe. Won't you, Lucas?"

"Absolutely."

He wore black as always, and his gleaming midnight hair and his smoldering glacial eyes. He might have been in narcotics not homicide, an undercover narc fresh from an all-night stakeout. Fresh and *refreshed*, energized by a successful bust despite his own lack of sleep.

In reality, he was a panther on the prowl. And what energized Lieutenant Lucas Hunter? The impending kill.

"We're at your disposal, Lucas." Viveca embellished her offer with a brilliant smile. "We'll do whatever we can to help you nail the son of a bitch. If you'll come to my office, we can begin discussing the possibilities right now."

Viveca started to lead the way.

But she was stopped. Cold. By his ice-cold voice.

"I'll find you, Viveca. After I've spoken with Galen."

"Galen can join us."

"I'll find you, Viveca. After."

Viveca's smile became brittle. "Fine! *Whatever.* In the meantime let me introduce you to three of the other key players on the KCOR team. You know Adam, of course."

"Of course." Lucas's voice warmed with fondness. Adam was, after all, the husband — and brother-in-law — of the sisters Lucas had known as girls. He asked with concern about the sister who had always been the most fragile, the most frail . . . and yet was the sister, and the wife, who had survived. "How's Fran?"

Adam's deep breath spoke volumes about his own concern. "As well as can be expected. At least as well as anyone *except* Fran would expect. She's asking too much of herself."

"As usual," Lucas offered quietly. "Please give her my best, Adam."

"Thank you, Lucas. I will."

There was silence then, reverent beats of caring and respect, before Viveca spoke anew.

"This," she said finally, "is Paul."

Lucas's gaze shifted. "Yes. We've met."

"And Wally," Viveca added almost as an afterthought, as if in her estimation Wally was a most forgettable man. "Paul and Wally handle all the location shots for Galen and Adam. Either or both would be delighted to offer any camera or video-editing assistance you might need."

"Good. Thanks. We may need it. Now if you'll excuse us, Galen and I really do have some things to discuss. After which I'll see you, Viveca, and John, too, if he's around."

Lucas didn't wait for Viveca to acknowledge what amounted to a polite command. He turned instead to Galen, and they walked in silence to her office down the hall.

"Good morning," he greeted softly once the door was closed. "Did you get any sleep at all?"

Of course not. How could she? She had to pack, a task which took a pathetically meager amount of time. And she had to transcribe her conversation with the killer, also not a time-consuming process.

What had kept her wakeful was Lucas, thoughts of Lucas, worries and hopes, a spinning kaleidoscope that was sometimes brilliant, sometimes splintered, sometimes black.

Galen's brightest hope — and darkest worry — was that she *must not* let Lucas down. She must help him lure his prey from the shadows, to get the killer squarely in the hunter's sights.

At the moment it was she who was in the crosshairs, the focus of his intense, appraising gaze. And she was out in the open, fully exposed, her sleepless night nakedly revealed.

"It's obvious, isn't it?"

"No," Lucas said. "Just a logical guess."

It was a lie. It had to be. The circles beneath her eyes had substance and weight, as if the purple itself was laced with lead. Yet his eyes, dark-circled too, glittered true and clear.

Was it possible *ever* to discern in Lucas the pristine clarity of truth from the dazzling brilliance of lies? And if she could not reliably detect the little white fibs, those inconsequential triflings, how would she ever recognize the monumental ones, the falsehoods that slashed the soul?

"Well," she murmured, "it's not every night that one gets called by a murderer. Oh, before I forget, here's what I remember of the conversation."

Galen plumbed a front pocket of her turquoise coat and retrieved for him the two neatly folded sheets of paper.

"Great. Thanks. Did you also have a chance to fill the cardboard boxes?"

"Yes. And there's a suitcase, too."

"Okay. Good. If you'll just give me your keys, I'll take care of the move, and forward your phone, and lock the doors behind me when I leave."

"Oh. All right. Thank you." Galen reached into another pocket, realizing only too late, as her fingers curled around its familiar shape, what a pathetic symbol her key ring was — a miniature red apple that gleamed with all the excitement and optimism she'd brought with her to New York.

"I bet this is something else I'm not supposed to do," she announced as she twisted free the relevant keys. "Relinquishing my keys on demand."

Her remark was light, a bit of fluff to balm the foolishness she felt.

But Lucas's expression remained serious. And intimate. And hard. "You're not relinquishing them to just anyone."

"No. I . . . know." *Oh, how I know.*

His expression did not yield. "I'm having you watched, Galen. Followed. Whenever you go out. It's intrusive, but necessary."

"Would the killer really be so delusionally arrogant as to follow me around town?"

"I doubt it. But it would be an arrogance we'd be crazy to miss."

"Was I followed this morning as I walked to work?"

"You bet. By me."

No wonder she had felt *so safe.* "He didn't follow me to work?"

"If he did, I missed it."

It seemed impossible that Lucas Hunter could miss anything. Ever. And there was that other talent.

"But you wouldn't miss him, would you? You would sense right away if he were anywhere near."

"Not necessarily." It was a quiet confession, an apology almost. "It depends on what he's thinking, feeling, doing at the time."

"I see," she murmured.

But she didn't, not really, for she frowned.

"What?" he pressed gently.

"Well, could you be close to him, even speaking to him, and not know?"

"Yes."

There *was* apology this time in Lucas's soft confession. It had happened to him, Galen decided. And it tormented him. She saw the torment and the fury beneath the glacial gray: searing fire imprisoned in ice.

"Which is why," Lucas said quietly, "good old-fashioned detective work is so important. And why it's essential, Galen, that you neither inadvertently — nor advertently — elude the surveillance I've set up."

"Advertently? I shouldn't sneak off for a clandestine meeting with the killer, you mean? An interview in the flesh? That's really *not* me."

"I know," Lucas told the journalist who couldn't care less about personal glory, who had proven as much and so eloquently on Sunday at dawn. But to the seamstress who cared very much about little girls held hostage to sickness and to a hand grenade, he said, "But, just for the hell of it, describe for me the route you took from your apartment to the hospital last Saturday night."

"Oh." Her mind's eye conjured the path, the shortest and most dangerous distance between the two points. *"Well."*

Lucas saw with excruciating clarity the careless truth. She had been so concerned about Becca, so anxious to convey that concern, that she had disregarded entirely her own safety. "Oh, well?"

"That was a unique situation."

"Here's another. Our supremely arrogant killer wants to meet with you. He'll assume you're being watched, and that your calls are being recorded, and eventually he'll discover that you and I will be together every night. But he can still e-mail you, or pay some kid to hand-deliver a note. So what message does he send? How does he get you alone?"

"He doesn't. He can't. It's delusion on his part to believe that he can."

"Is it, Galen? What if he makes you a conspirator?"

"He's really not my kind of guy, Lieutenant." Galen met an expression that was fierce, unreadable, and unamused. "He's *not* going to make me a conspirator!"

"Even if he promises another death if you fail to comply? That you can save a life or doom it depending on your reply?"

"He wouldn't . . ." But of course he would. Happily. She could almost hear the glee in the electronic voice. *I'd be delighted to kill another of Lucas's ladies, Lucas's lovers, if you don't do precisely as I say.*

"Tell me, Galen, what you would do in that unique situation."

Meet with him. Of course. Conspire with the killer to elude the police. Galen knew it, and so did the panther with the smoke gray eyes. "I would call you right away."

Lucas Hunter did not smile. "Promise me."

The request, and the gaze that accompanied it, took her breath away . . . as if her willingness to permit him to protect her, to grant him that trust, mattered more to him than anything else.

"I promise."

"Thank you." His expression changed slightly. Hard still, and fierce in an entirely different way. "Are you seeing anyone?"

"Seeing anyone?"

"I'm trying to determine if I need to be even more intrusive by asking you to place your personal life on hold."

"I was planning to leave New York Monday afternoon."

"That doesn't preclude your leaving an

120

ICU full of broken hearts. Does it?"

Did he truly believe her capable of such romantic devastation? This man who was an expert, a master, of such things? His ferocious gaze offered the astonishing answer. *Yes.*

"No. I suppose not. But for the record I'm not seeing anyone."

The fierceness yielded then. And Lucas looked pleased. *Satisfied.* As a police lieutenant, surely, not merely — *merely?* — as a man.

"Here's the address." Lucas withdrew a slip of paper from his black-leather jacket. "It's on Sixty-fourth, between Lexington and Park, about six blocks north of where you're living now."

As Galen read the address, she envisioned the walks she'd taken, solitary strolls amid the elegance of the Upper East Side. There were no hotels, were there, anywhere in the vicinity of the address she held in her hand?

No. She was quite certain. There were only lavish buildings, the apartment *homes,* of Manhattan's glittering elite. Like the gray-eyed hunter . . . and aristocrat.

"This is an easy walk," she said. It was the truth, assuming one disregarded entirely the destination.

"Good. So I can expect you when?"

"Between seven-thirty and eight."

"Okay. I'll see you then."

It sounded like a promise.

It was a promise.

They would see each other tonight. In his home. And they would wait together for a murderer to call.

"This is an interesting turn of events."

The voice came from the doorway just moments after Lucas left.

It was a familiar voice, but as she turned Galen saw again the *un*familiar expression, thoughtful and concerned . . . about her. The look was so distinctly *not* Paul, at least the Paul she had known, that Galen assumed this was a trap, a pretense of worry that would be swiftly revealed once she'd taken the bait.

But such pretense wasn't Paul, either. If he was anything, it was direct.

Still, deciding the best defense was an aggressive offense, Galen readily and cheerfully concurred. "A *very* interesting turn of events. Who'd have thought I'd be clever enough to demolish my credibility so thoroughly that a serial murderer would feel compelled to rescue me? Out of the goodness of his heart? That's a bit too brilliant, isn't it, for the likes of me?"

"Maybe," Paul replied quietly. "Maybe not. More to the point, it's definitely not too brilliant, or too devious, for the stud. Be careful, Galen. I mean it. All kidding aside."

"Kidding?"

"Okay. Beyond kidding. I admit it. I've been a jerk."

"Why?" she asked, wary still, yet almost convinced.

"Why did I take my anger out on you? I don't know. You were convenient, vulnerable, *there*."

Galen saw what she had seen before. Contempt. But it was directed quite clearly at himself.

"Your anger," she echoed. "About?"

"Death. Murder. Marianne McLain's death was bad enough. Senseless *enough*. And eight nights later the truly senseless began."

Eight nights later. The night the Lady Killer first struck. With his middle-of-the-night massacre of the assistant DA.

"You knew Kay?"

"Yeah. I did. We met when I worked for the NYPD. Kay used my crime-scene photos for her various trials, and from time to time I made prosecution exhibits for her, collages to help the jury understand." Paul frowned, unfocused for a moment, as if

123

seeing a collage of memories of Kay. When he focused anew both his gaze and his voice were brittle, sharp. "Be very careful, Galen."

"I *will*," she assured him; wanting to re-assure. "And I'll be fine. As you've seen, the police are very much on the case."

But Paul was not reassured and bitterness twisted his mouth. "That's what I'm worried about."

"What?"

"Be careful, most of all, of Lucas Hunter. The lieutenant will do whatever is necessary to get this killer. Whatever. To whomever. No holds barred." His eyes seemed unfocused again. But what he said was not. "Lucas Hunter is ruthless, Galen. *Dangerous*. Mark my words."

NINE

Lucas was intercepted at the halfway point to Viveca's office.

"Lucas? Got a minute?"

"Sure, Adam. What's up?"

Adam waited until both were inside his office and the door was closed. "There are a few things you need to know. Things Viveca may not tell you."

"Or I may not give her a chance to tell me?"

"That, too," Adam conceded. "I'm well aware that there's still bad blood between the two of you."

Bad blood. Tainted blood. Demonic blood. Still. Always.

"You know why," Lucas said.

Even though Adam did not, Lucas was quite certain, know about his encounter with Viveca sixteen years ago. Still, that was an inconsequential chapter compared to the rest. And Adam knew the rest, and he was absolutely right. Lucas was not about to give

Viveca many chances to explain anything. Nor would he trust anything she had to say.

"Yes," Adam said solemnly. "I know why. And I hope that you know, Lucas, that we discovered Viveca's relationship to Brandon only *after* Marianne and Viveca had become friends. Good friends. Even then, and even though Viveca's hardly to blame for her cousin's psychopathic sins, it was very difficult. But we worked through it. All of us. Including Fran. And John. Which brings me to the point: John . . . and Galen."

"John and Galen?" *John and Galen?*

"And Marianne. As you may know, Marianne's final newscast was Thanksgiving Eve."

"I know," Lucas said. He had watched the telecast, made himself watch it, and he had witnessed the courage and the grace of the remarkable woman he had known as a girl.

"She'd insisted on working beyond what anyone believed was possible, much less advisable. We were certain she would die over that four-day Thanksgiving weekend. Fran and I planned to spend the holiday with Marianne and John at their home. Which was fine, with both of them, except that Marianne would have none of our death vigil. She insisted on watching TV, both as a diversion from her illness and as an escape, I suppose, from us. She clicked through the channels until she found one that appealed: Gavel-to-Gavel TV. Court was in recess for the holiday, but they were doing a recap of the trial they'd been covering, *North Carolina v. Vernon*. We all watched — watched the trial instead of watching Marianne. But when we did look at her, we saw a minor miracle, a final glowing spark of life. She lived for two more weeks. *North Carolina v. Vernon* kept Marianne alive, distracted, *happy*. The trial *and* the reporter."

"Galen."

"Galen." Adam frowned and added quietly. "Marianne died just hours after the verdict was returned."

Lucas's question was quiet, too. "And after naming Galen as her successor at KCOR?"

"I honestly don't know, Lucas. But there's no doubt that John's decision to hire Galen was emotional."

"And wrong?"

Adam drew a breath. "Let's say risky. Galen was a reporter, and a specialized one at that, accustomed to in-depth coverage of a single story at a time."

"Was she good?"

"As a reporter for GTG? Sensational."

"Does she know why she's here? How

much she meant to Marianne?"

"I don't think so. I certainly haven't told her, and I sincerely doubt either John or Viveca ever would. Galen's under enough pressure as it is."

"When did you last speak to John?"

"Yesterday morning."

"But not since? I assume that you and Viveca were notified of the killer's message to KCOR's evening operator as soon as it was left."

"Yes. We both were notified."

"So, given the profile of the Lady Killer story, not to mention John's commitment to Galen's success at KCOR, I would have imagined you would have let him know."

Adam hesitated. "I tried to. Viv and I both tried. But John wasn't home last night. At least he wasn't answering his phone."

Or his doorbell, Lucas amended. He, too, had made an attempt to speak with John McLain. But Lucas had wanted it to be a face-to-face conversation. The lieutenant needed to see, face-to-face, the man who, just hours before Galen received a call from a killer, had been distressed not relieved when Galen told him of her decision to leave KCOR.

"And," Adam added, "as of five minutes ago he hadn't yet come in today."

"Where is he?"

"I don't know." Adam's words were measured. And weighted. "John's in trouble, Lucas. With all he's overcome — and accomplished — in his life, he couldn't protect the only thing that ever really mattered to him. Marianne. Her death has devastated him. Truly. And, unlike Fran, John isn't facing how devastated, how impaired, he really is. Of course, it's hard to imagine John accepting the approach Fran has taken."

"Which is?"

"Sleeping, quite literally, around the clock. According to various experts, it's a viable and even productive way of getting through a trauma like this. Even during sleep, and even if such sleep is induced by pills, the subconscious is apparently absorbing the loss, dealing with it, handling it. It's escape, which is *not* Fran, and she fought it at first, expecting more of herself. But with Brynne's encouragement —" Adam stopped, frowned. "Brynne was Marianne's doctor, but she didn't vanish from our lives after Marianne died. She was there for Fran, emotionally, spiritually, medically. Fran doesn't know about Brynne's murder. About any of the murders. She's slept right through the horror. Which may," Adam said quietly, "be the greatest blessing of all."

"Yes," Lucas agreed. "It may."

"In any event, in the six weeks since Marianne's death, John has refused help of any kind. I'm quite sure he doesn't sleep, and I can't imagine he's finding escape, even though he . . . disappears."

"Disappears."

"For hours. Sometimes for days."

"How do you think John would react if Galen left?"

"Left?"

"KCOR."

"Oh." Adam shook his head, dismissing the possibility out of hand. "He'd feel as if he'd failed Marianne. Again."

"No John?"

"No John," Viveca affirmed. "He's away today."

Lucas waited.

But she clearly wasn't going to elaborate.

"So, Viveca, what do you want?"

"Whatever *you* want, Lucas. KCOR's committed to helping you get this criminal."

"And committed to ratings as well?"

"I don't deny it. And it's hardly a crime. This will benefit all of us — assuming, that is, you don't spoil the party as you've been *known* to do."

"Be very careful, Viveca."

The warning was stark. And thrilling. Like that autumn night sixteen years ago. "We would have had *quite* a party, wouldn't we, Lucas? I still can't believe, what were the odds, that some idiot I'd known in boarding school would show up and —"

"Expose you for what you were?"

"Which was *what*, Lucas? Someone with a strong allegiance to her family? You wrote the book on such loyalty, so how dare you?" Viveca's indignant challenge shifted to a provocative one. "I had you seduced, didn't I? *Admit it.* We were just seconds away from ending up in bed."

Lucas Hunter admitted nothing. "And then what, Viveca? A weekend of passion during which I would forget entirely Brandon's Monday morning parole hearing?"

His obvious skepticism infuriated her. And shouldn't have. Viveca Blair knew perfectly well how desirable she was. But her reply was a defiant hiss. *"Yes."*

"And when that failed?"

"As you mean it inevitably would?" His stone-hard gaze gave her the answer. She was in his estimation a mediocre seductress. "You really want to know my contingency plan?"

"Sure."

Viveca shrugged. "Why not? I had a little acid in my purse."

"Acid? For my throat or my eyes?"

"For your *brain*, Lucas. LSD."

He almost smiled at the notion. LSD would not have touched him, much less daunted him, not then, in college, when he had subjected his mind and his body to never-ending if sensual assaults.

Viveca saw the hint of a smile and was emboldened. "We would have been good together, Lucas. You *know* it."

"What I know is that I was twenty years old and stoned and drunk. Any woman would have done."

Bastard. "Just like now, you mean? Is that why the Lady Killer has such a vast selection of victims?"

The change on his face was subtle but real. And fearsome. Had Lucas Hunter not been in Australia at the time, Viveca might have wondered if he'd killed his lovers himself.

"Here's what's going to happen, Viveca. I'll decide what can and cannot be broadcast, and I will share that decision with Galen alone. I'll let her know by three this afternoon what I want said this evening. And Galen will not be interviewing Brandon. Not in this lifetime." Not in *my* lifetime. "No one at KCOR will."

Viveca implored to the heavens with her perfectly manicured hands. "Doesn't the First Amendment mean *anything* to you? No, of course it doesn't. Just another folly hatched by those renegade colonists."

"This has nothing to do with the First Amendment."

"Meaning it's deeper — or should I say more sacred? — than that? Lucas Hunter's personal vision of justice? The one in which Brandon would be imprisoned still, *always*."

No, Lucas thought. In my system of justice Brandon Christianson would be dead.

"My request is professional, not personal. As the station of record when it comes to Manhattan's Lady Killer, KCOR really cannot host another murderer."

"My cousin is *not* a murderer. It was an accident, Lucas. An *accident*."

"*It,* Viveca? You mean the rape and murder of a twelve-year-old girl?" Lucas's voice was as cold and as final as death. "Jenny was murdered. By Brandon. He wanted to kill her. Planned to."

"Fine! Believe what you want. You always do."

"It's what Marianne believed, and Fran. They were there, Viveca, on that winter day

133

in Chatsworth. They were Jenny's best friends. They know what Brandon did. And I can assure you, since apparently you don't know, that the horror of what happened, of what Brandon did, never goes away. If you felt even a whisper of loyalty to Marianne or Fran, you would not permit Brandon Christianson to set foot inside KCOR. Ever."

It was true, Viveca knew. And it hit a nerve. *The* nerve: her divided allegiance, with its conflicting passions and guilts, between her blood family, Brandon, and her KCOR one, Marianne and Fran and Adam and John . . . especially John.

When push came to shove, *if* push came to shove . . . Viveca clung tenaciously to that *if.* This wasn't the first time Brandon had told her he was ready to reveal all to his legions of admiring readers, to disclose his identity *and his past,* including his role in the accident, the tragedy, that had cost Jenny her life. Brandon wasn't concerned about the cost of such a revelation. He believed his words would be read and admired still, perhaps more. And Viveca believed it, too.

Brandon wanted to give the on-air revelation, with its stratospheric ratings, to Vivveca. To KCOR. But, Viveca knew, when, if, push came to shove, her KCOR family would win. She would tell Brandon thank you, but no.

Lucas was right. But it was not a concession that Viveca Blair was about to make. Not to him.

Her answer, which was a question, was a taunt.

"You're not big on forgiveness, are you?"

"Not for the unforgivable."

"It's supposed to be healing."

"Myth."

"There's still no *valid* reason to prevent an interview with Brandon."

"There's murder, Viveca, which should be reason enough. The Lady Killer wants to be the only bad guy in town. Anything that shifts the spotlight from him, such as an interview with *another* murderer, could provoke him to kill. On behalf of every potential victim —"

"Your *women*."

The muscles in his jaw contracted. But his words came without the slightest ripple. "I must insist that any interview with Brandon Christianson be deferred until this particular monster is safely behind bars. Or dead."

"Done," the voice was familiar to both of them.

"John," Viveca whispered. Then, in a

135

rush, she implored, "I haven't made *any* promises to Brandon. Truly. I've only told him that I'd give it some thought. I would never make such a commitment without checking first with you. You *know* that."

"Yes, Viv. I do."

John McLain managed a slight smile, a ghost of a smile, a faint curve in the face that was a mere ghost of what it once had been.

Lucas saw the pale yet vivid truth of what Adam had told him. John was barely surviving the death of his wife. Might not yet survive.

"Hello, John."

"Lucas. I . . . the note you wrote after Marianne died . . . it meant a great deal to me. But you wouldn't know that, would you? I've been meaning to write."

A thank-you note for a sympathy note? Lucas didn't know what the etiquette books advised. He knew only that it was not a failure for which John McLain should be beating himself up. Another failure.

"There's no need, John."

"Well. Thank you."

"Sure." Lucas's reply was solemn, quiet, calm. Nothing changed, neither his expression nor his voice, even as the topic did. Dramatically. "It seems that Galen won't be leaving KCOR after all."

"Leaving KCOR?" Viveca echoed.

John's sunken eyes didn't leave Lucas's solemn ones. "So she told you."

Lucas looked at the man who had lost everything there was to lose. Or so John had believed, until yesterday, when he learned he was about to lose the woman handpicked by his dying wife.

"Yes, John," Lucas said. "She did."

TEN

The building in which Lucas lived was sleek, shiny, and stretched twenty-two stories into the Manhattan sky. But its entrance was unprepossessing in the extreme, a single steel door amid the glossy granite.

It was a service door, Galen decided. Or a *servants'* door. And as such was logically equipped with an intercom, a video camera, and a panel of names encased in tarnished brass.

Hunter, L. was one of those names. Which meant she must be very near the awninged portico, the uniformed guard, the elaborate mirror-and-marble lobby that would be visible through a prism of finely cut glass.

Galen was about to walk on, in search of the grand entrance, when the steel door opened.

And there he was. *Hunter, L.* Steel and granite, too.

"You made it."

"Yes. I did." But you know that, Galen re-

alized. As Lucas had promised, had fore-
warned, her every footfall since leaving the
station had undoubtedly been protected,
chronicled, watched. The lieutenant had
probably received a radioed heads-up: *No
one's following her, sir. She'll be at your door-
step in less than a minute.* "I wasn't sure this
was the right entrance."

"It is. The only entrance. Please come in."

The lobby, for the residents' eyes only,
was tastefully subdued, *vieux* wealth not
nouveau, but nonetheless grand. Lucas gestured to the most distant elevator in an impressive brass bank. "Shall we?"

There were no buttons in this elevator, no
way to select a specific floor. Like a menu in
the finest of restaurants, where prices were
never revealed, this elevator was for a most
rarefied clientele.

Lucas Hunter's penthouse was on the
twenty-second floor. It *was* the twenty-
second floor.

The brass doors of his private elevator
opened onto the vast, vaulted space of living
room, dining room, and kitchen all in one. It
was a snow-white expanse, except for the
kitchen's glitter of stainless steel.

The relentless whiteness might have been
foreboding and stark. But in this elegant
sanctuary, the panther's extravagant lair,

Galen felt the peace and the purity of freshly fallen snow.

No traces of crimson splattered the plush white carpet. No hints of violence, of murder, at all. And there were no shadows either, only the brilliant shimmer of lights below and the sparkling bright heaven of stars above.

"This is beautiful," Galen murmured as Lucas took her turquoise coat. "Peaceful."

"I'm glad you like it. I hope you'll feel comfortable here."

Comfortable? Alone with you? "Sure."

"You're not the world's best liar, you know."

"Yes. I know."

"That's a compliment, Galen."

Oh. Well, then, perhaps it would be best to reveal a fairly pertinent truth: that she hadn't shared living space with another human being for over ten years. Galen was deciding how to make that revelation — without explanation — when Lucas spoke.

"This is going to be different, perhaps even difficult, for both of us. I'm accustomed to living alone, and I gather you are, too. But here we are, perhaps for a while, bonded by what I think we both agree is a worthy cause."

"Very worthy."

"So why not make the most of it? I for one intend to regard it as an adventure."

Galen looked from the vast private snowfield above the city to the man who'd just confessed he was accustomed to solitude. For Lucas Hunter, who knew intimately the most glamorous women of Manhattan, such solitude was clearly a choice.

And now he had no choice. The killer had taken from Lucas, from both of them, even the tiniest vestige of free will.

"You do?"

"Absolutely. Why not?"

An adventure. With him. Why not? Well, because there were adventures, and there were adventures. A transatlantic voyage on the *Titanic*, for example, could legitimately be regarded as an adventure. If only there hadn't been that iceberg.

And what of living in a world of snow with Lucas? It was both adventure and iceberg. *He* was. Thrill and terror.

Galen felt a shiver deep inside. The chill of the Atlantic at midnight? Or the gentle caress of ice gray eyes? Dangerous either way. But she smiled. "Why not?"

"Good. I thought you might set up right here."

Right here meant the snowfield, the vast living area of his home. And *set up* meant?

Galen saw the astonishing answer. The cardboard boxes labeled by her "Dolls/Fabric/Patterns/Thread" had been stacked by him in the middle of the snow. And beside the boxes stood her irons, large and small, like mother and child.

"You vacuumed."

"Did I?"

"Didn't you? After the boxes arrived?" And after, she realized, he had moved his furniture to mimic exactly the arrangement in her tiny apartment six blocks away.

He was welcoming her, wanting her, *wanting the monster.* Lucas Hunter will do whatever is necessary to get this killer, Paul had told her. Warned her. Whatever is necessary.

Including rearranging furniture . . . and vacuuming.

"How do you know it was me who vacuumed?"

"Footprints, Lieutenant."

"Ah." The homicide lieutenant tilted his midnight black head and studied her with intense gray eyes. "And something else."

"Yes," Galen confessed. "A professional vacuumer, a housekeeper for an upscale place like this, would have done a more symmetric job."

"Symmetric."

"Geometric. She, or he, would have left a pattern of triangles, rectangles, or squares."

"You have a great future as a detective, Ms. Chandler."

"Actually, Lieutenant Hunter, I had a great future as a housekeeper. Admittedly, my designs were occasionally over the top."

"What would you do here? Design-wise."

"Oh. Well, let me think."

Galen gazed at the whiteness, envisioning on the empty canvas an entire winter scene: children making snowmen, skaters on a frozen pond, toboggans in the distance, a one-horse sleigh nearby. It was a cheerful, lively, vibrant scene. But too cluttered, she decided. A happy yet oddly jarring intrusion on the pristine peace.

Besides, how could one improve on random drifts of snow fashioned by a panther?

"I guess," she said at last, "I'd let you vacuum first, just as you've done, and then I'd make a snow angel or two or three."

We could each make a few, she thought. Thin, vapory ones — mine, and strong, protective, stunning ones. Yours.

"Feel free," he said softly, in a tone that made her look from the snow to him . . . and made her ache in ways she had never known.

Thrill and terror.

"A living room cluttered with Barbies is probably already enough," she murmured. *Too much.*

Actually, Lucas thought, it would be very nice.

The thought, although surprising, in fact astonishing, was not new. It had arrived this afternoon with her boxes, and it came with an image so enticing — watching her sew — that Lucas almost committed an inexcusable invasion of her privacy by unpacking the carefully labeled boxes himself, lest she whisk dolls and fabric to her bedroom. To work there. To shut him out.

"I'd really like it if you'd set up here." It was a gentle command, and an even more gentle plea.

"Okay," Galen obeyed, and complied. "I will. If you agree to tell me when it becomes too great an adventure."

"I agree." *And it won't.* "Speaking of adventure, we have the uncharted frontier of food yet to explore. I took the liberty of looking in your refrigerator."

"Empty."

"Very."

"I grab things here and there."

"As do I. But I got some supplies anyway. Come."

Galen followed him to the kitchen where atop gleaming white granite lay a bountiful if eclectic buffet, from cereal to caviar and imported to the snow cave just for her. There were more selections, he told her, in the stainless-steel fridge.

"And we can also order in." Lucas gestured to a small but elite cluster of restaurant menus, Manhattan's finest, the five-star eateries where prices were never listed, at least never on the menu for the lady.

Lucas's ladies.

And now the lieutenant was implying that Jean-Georges would deliver. As would Le Cirque and Café des Artistes. Room service, penthouse service, just for him? Why not?

"We can do that tonight, if you like. Unless," Lucas added softly, "you're too tired."

"I really think I am. One of those breakfast bars and a cup of that tea would be just about perfect. But you should do whatever . . ." Galen shrugged.

And Lucas smiled. "I will. I'll do whatever. In the meantime let me give you the rest of the tour. After which you can have your breakfast bar and your tea, and crash."

Five rooms comprised the penthouse's other wing: two, with doors closed, at either end of the vaulted hall, and three, doors ajar, in between.

The first two of those three rooms were empty, carpeted with freshly fallen snow. When they reached the third, Lucas pushed open the door, a silent invitation for her to enter.

The carpet was pure white. But color abounded. And there was no peace.

A mammoth map of Manhattan, a tourist's dream, hung on a nearby wall, and there were file folders everywhere, brilliantly colored and neatly labeled, by some Lady Killer task force administrator — Galen assumed — someone who thought it made sense to cloak the Kay data in green, and the Monica data in violet, and the Marcia data in gold, and the Brynne data in the color that said it all: blood red.

"The war room," Galen murmured as she began to explore.

It was a technological epicenter to eclipse all others, this command post in the sky, this place where Lieutenant Lucas Hunter's private battle against murder was joined.

Four pins, the silver of his eyes, pierced the mammoth map, the battlefield itself, marking the places where the victims, his lovers, had lived, had loved, had died. There was a fifth pinhole in the map. But the shining silver itself had been removed.

Galen touched the tiny telltale indentation that had been made in an apartment building, hers, six blocks away.

"You're looking for a pattern." She spoke to the pinprick. She had seen a movie, hadn't she, in which the murderer chose his victims based on where they lived, so that when one connected the dots from crime scene to crime scene the constellation Aquarius was formed? "A design."

"Yes."

"But the only reason he selected me was because of my disastrous anchorwoman performance."

"So he said."

Galen met his unrevealing gray gaze. "But he's probably a world-class liar." *Too.*

"Probably."

Galen looked away, to one of the many colored stacks of folders with their neatly typed labels. This rainbowed stack apparently contained copies of the original handwritten crime-scene reports.

"I thought that everything — except, I suppose, the information on Brynne — had been entered into the task force data base."

"Yes."

"But you don't trust . . ." computers? Silly question. According to Rosalyn St. John, Lucas Hunter owned significant chunks of major software companies. Computers were reliable. Trustworthy. Human beings on the other hand . . . "You're reviewing the original documents in case you see something — or sense something? — the data processors might have overlooked."

"In case I see something," Lucas clarified. "As I told you this morning my ability to sense the killer is somewhat whimsical. Old-fashioned detective work trumps black magic every time."

Black magic, Galen mused. Sorcery in collusion with evil. The gift, she realized, which was also a curse.

She had heard, both last night and this morning, his ambivalence about his talent, his gift — the contempt he felt for the evil he pursued even as he was tormented by his limitations to do so. Lucas couldn't *summon* the evil; could neither invoke the magic nor control the curse. The evil came to him on its own terms, its own whims . . . and worse, on the whims of a killer.

It was a solitary torment, a private war.

Until now.

I need your help, he had told her.

"Is it permissible for me to look through the reports?"

"Permissible and welcome. As are any insights you may have." Lucas paused just a heartbeat, but a heartbeat for her. "There's

148

no point in your looking at the crime-scene photographs. You'll never forget them once you do, couldn't possibly, and you need to be able to talk to him, spar with him, play with him."

Spar? Play? Engage, perhaps, in a little witty repartée? Impossible. For her. With any man. Ghastly photographs or not.

"But *you've* looked at the crime-scene photos." *Studied* them. And, Galen wondered, if until this afternoon, when Lucas had readied the war room for viewing by her, the snowy walls had been papered with glossy eight-by-tens of his lovers, their hearts crossed, their throats slashed, their eyes pierced.

"It's my job," Lucas said.

"Mine, too. And if I don't look at them, because of the horror he has made of them in death, it's as if *they* were the monsters." *These brilliant and beautiful women you have loved.*

"There's only one monster, Galen."

"But seeing the photos might make me want to get him even more."

"Really? Meaning you need more incentive? The fact of the murders isn't enough?"

"Of course it's enough. It just seems that —"

"No," he said quietly, firmly, decisively.

"Your job, Galen, is to talk to him."

"Beginning tonight?"

"I don't think so. No."

"But you have an idea when?"

"About 3:13 Sunday morning." A faint smile softened the hardness of his face. "It's a fairly precise idea."

"Because that's when he murdered Brynne? Because you sensed . . ."

"Yes."

Galen shivered, an involuntary chill, so sudden she couldn't block it. Which meant that Lucas saw it, too, *felt* it, as if Galen were shivering from him.

The black magic *of him.*

Galen shivered, and Lucas withdrew. Without moving. He simply moved deeper inside himself, into that vast darkness, the icy emptiness of bloodlust, of evil, of death. "Let me show you your room."

As they left the war room, Lucas gestured to the double doors, sealed shut, directly to his right. "I'm here. And you're there."

There. At the far end of the hall. As far away from his bed as was possible in this snowcloud in the sky.

It was a significant distance. Indeed, were this snowy penthouse a five-star hotel, and each had been assigned its most lavish suite, their bedrooms would have been closer than this. And were they dwelling in her apartment building, at least ten units would have separated them. And were they neighbors, in any modest yet comfortable neighborhood one might choose, an entire house — a whole family — would stand between.

Yet here, under the vaulted roof within his lair, the vast distance felt so very close.

The journey to her bedroom was a trudge through snow as laden as the heavy silence.

But when they reached their destination, there was springtime. Pastel and lavender. The precise shade of her baggy warm-ups worn last night.

This was a brand-new spring, just-born on this January day, created by him for her, and with such care . . . except when it came to any thought of the expense required to conjure this magic in just one day. Lucas *had* conjured it. For her. So that she would feel comfortable on this adventure of enchantment and death.

Only enchantment bloomed in the pastel haven that was hers: the four-poster bed with its hyacinth canopy, the cushiony lavender chairs, the marble bath adorned with towels of lilac, of pink, of cream.

Lucas Hunter is ruthless. He will do whatever to whomever to get this killer. Paul's words, Paul's warning, haunted anew.

151

Whatever . . . enchantment. To whomever . . . her.

Paul's was an authentic warning, undoubtedly true.

But Galen spoke another truth. "This is lovely."

"It seemed like you."

Lucas's words were quiet, remote. And truthful? Who knew?

Who could ever know?

Galen looked away from his impassive face, needing to, and found the single telephone in the room. Lavender, portable, and, she realized, hers.

Elsewhere, in every other room, there had been two phones, a duet of lavender and snow, with portable headphones lying close by. But here, in her bedroom, the lavender was quite alone.

"Calls to my apartment have been forwarded to the lavender phones." *And your calls will come, as always, to snow, to winter, to ice.*

"Yes. The recording, as well as the probably futile attempts at a trace, will begin with the first ring, even before you answer the call."

"Slick."

"Useful."

"And the headphones?"

"That's how I'll listen. They're essentially a second extension which will engage automatically, too. No telltale clicks."

"Slick again," Galen murmured. "But he expects you to be listening, doesn't he?"

"Yes. He does."

"And yet he's not speaking to you directly."

"Too mundane," Lucas offered, even though he suspected a more disturbing truth. The killer would derive great pleasure, sinister pleasure, from commandeering Galen Chandler as his conduit. "There's something else, Galen. I think it would be best if I were with you, beside you, whenever you talk to him."

"So you can tell me what to say."

"No. Especially not in the beginning. I may at some later time ask you to mention certain things to him, to see what kind of response that evokes. But for now it makes sense to me, as much as any of this makes sense, that the closer I am to you, the closer I will be to him."

As much as any of this makes sense. Galen heard again his ambivalence about his "gift" — the talent and curse he could not control, the inexplicable magic that enabled him to lure murderers from their shadows to slay no more.

"For now," the magician was saying, "you need to speak to him as if I weren't there. I'll be nearby. I'll need to be. But I'll be very careful to do nothing to distract."

Nothing to distract? Galen imagined the scene. The Lady Killer's 3:13 phone call, awakening her from sleep, followed by her rush to Lucas, her feet bare, her bathrobe flying.

But wait. Manhattan's Lady Killer would not be awakening her from sleep. For how could she sleep, even in this hyacinth haven, with Lucas so close by?

How could she sleep, ever, when the thrill — and the terror — swirled within . . . when she wanted at once to laugh, to weep, to sing, to die.

And to dance.

Most of all to dance.

With him.

ELEVEN

But Galen did sleep, the kind of deep and peaceful sleep that came only when one felt absolutely protected.

Supremely safe.

Lucas didn't even attempt sleep until after midnight. He read police reports and studied crime-scene photos, staring at the mutilated images of Monica, Kay, Marcia, Brynne as he compelled remembrance of moments long since lost.

And all the time Lucas was so very aware of her, of Galen, in her bedroom down the hall. And so very aware — a restless, wondrous, tormenting awareness — of not being alone. In this place where he was always alone. Always wanted to be.

Alone. But not lonely.

Until now.

Lucas fought the restlessness, the torment and the wonder, only to be rewarded by the greatest restlessness of all, the astonishing feeling that Galen was calling to him from her dreams, wanting him to join her in a lavender sanctuary of pure peace.

Lucas surrendered to bed, his, and to sleep, lured by the promise of dreams even as he expected his usual nightmares, the potpourri of crimes, of corpses, he had seen.

But tonight's nightmare was entirely new. He and Galen were in the penthouse. And they were not alone. *Or were they?*

There was a killer in the penthouse. That was certain. But for endless moments it felt as if Lucas and the killer were one and the same. Lucas was inside him, feeling his heart, feeling his lust, seeing the penthouse through his eyes — and seeing finally, *finally,* an unfamiliar hand. The murderer's hand, not his own.

The foreign hand held a massive knife, gleaming and sharpened, and both hand and knife were intent on slashing Galen's translucent flesh, slashing *even more*, for already crimson droplets dotted the plush woolen snow.

The Barbies, too, were splattered with blood. And naked. And *immodest* in their nudity, even though the blood, there was so much, could have cloaked them entirely in glistening scarlet gowns.

Galen, too, was naked. But her hair was long, a luxurious fall of burnished flames so concealing that only now did Lucas notice she was nude. She draped herself in her coppery veil, her modesty more important than the blood that gushed from her neck, her heart.

Her eyes.

Even as she ran, and Galen was running now, she kept covered, kept modest, her luminous flesh.

She reached the elevator at last. Soon she would be free.

But the brass doors would not open! Even though she begged, pleaded, prayed.

She ran anew. To the kitchen.

But this wasn't *his* kitchen, this tiny closet in which she was trapped. This place was avocado, not silver and snow, and its cupboards, once cream, were gray.

There was *some* silver in this gray-green prison. A butcher knife on the counter beside the sink.

Galen saw the glittering weapon. As did the killer. And Lucas saw it, too, through the murderer's eyes.

Now the killer, that monster, was daring Galen to grab the shining knife, and to use it, to slash him, as he had savaged her.

In my eyes, the murderer goaded. Stab me in my *eyes.*

Lucas saw her hesitation, the temptation

and the horror, then heard her cry — *No. No!* — as she ran out of the kitchen . . . and into his penthouse again.

To the living room.

Where the naked Barbies lay. Bleeding. Still.

Galen's racing footsteps faltered, wanting to help her dolls, to arrange their abundant nylon hair over their small plastic bodies, affording them privacy, modesty too.

But she dared not stop. The killer was right behind her, feeling her fear, savoring it, and sensing and savoring the kill.

She ran to the white-brick terrace twenty-two stories aloft in the Manhattan sky. It was snowing, a blizzard of glittering crystals, but Galen wasn't cold. She was Venus, risen from the sea, and in moments the fire-haired goddess of oceans would become an angel of snow.

She would be carried to heaven on a cloud of snowflakes. All she had to do was step from the white-brick terrace into the crystalline swirl.

You *won't* be carried! Lucas shouted. You'll only fall. Only *die*.

But Galen did not hear his warning, for Lucas was inside the killer still, trapped too, a prisoner too. And now she was gazing at the killer, as if gazing *at him,* and Lucas saw hope, not fear.

Hope, as if her winter-sky eyes were seeing the glorious promise of spring. At last. Seeing — and believing.

For she was smiling now, happy . . . and almost free. From him. *From both of them.*

She stood on the low brick ledge, her arms spread wide. Unashamed of her nakedness? Almost free. Almost free? Perhaps. Yet the copper-gold curtain veiled her still, would conceal her even as she flew. As she fell.

And now she was making that choice, to fly, to fall. To leave him alone *and so lonely.*

Lucas awakened suddenly. Viciously. Pierced by a silent scream that echoed in the vast darkness of his ravaged soul.

Lucas did not reach for the swift illumination of a bedside lamp. That reassuring gold. He never did.

He merely sat in the darkness, forcing calm, forcing truth, banishing the phantoms of his nightmare even as he embraced the ghosts that were real.

No clock glowed in Lucas Hunter's bedroom, no bold, bright dial. But his watch lay on the nightstand.

Lucas knew without looking precisely what it would read.

3:13.

Was the Lady Killer on the prowl? Again? So soon?

No, Lucas realized. *He's just stalking me as I am stalking him.*

Or was it Galen who stalked his dreams? Galen. So fragile, so brave, so lovely.

So naked.

Time to get up. Beyond time.

Lucas showered and dressed with the practiced efficiency of a man condemned.

The door to her bedroom was ajar, more than ajar, halfway open. In invitation, or warning?

Lucas had to look. Had to. And what he saw was the place where Galen had slept, at the very edge of the canopied bed, as if in her studio apartment still, sharing her sleeping space with fabric and giving most of that space away.

Galen wasn't within. She would be sewing, Lucas told himself. Sewing, surrounded by her Barbies, keeping to her deadline, mindful of her promise to Casey and the girls.

But the cardboard boxes were still unpacked, the Barbies still hidden away. She would be in the kitchen then, her dinner of tea and a breakfast bar too meager for even her slender frame.

But the kitchen, too, was empty, its appliances ashimmer in the shadows like watchful ghosts.

Had Galen broken already the promise she had made? Had she vanished at 3:13 to rendezvous with the killer, lured by the murderer's threat that if she failed to do so another woman would die?

No, Lucas reminded himself, reassured himself, as he was caught, willingly captured, in the netherworld between reality and dreams. Galen *couldn't* escape for a clandestine rendezvous. The elevator would not open for her, not even when she implored, when she begged, when she prayed.

The reassuring if fanciful notion had a horrifying flip side. If Galen couldn't compel the shining brass doors to part, there was that other way, the only way, to keep her appointment with death.

It was a dream, Lucas admonished himself. A *nightmare*.

But his strides were urgent as he traversed the place where the naked Barbies had screamed and bled. And more urgent still as he neared the glass door that opened to the white-brick terrace.

It was snowing on the terrace. Snowing. The flakes fell gently, a crystalline mist, but several inches blanketed the ground, pristine testimony to the blizzard that had enveloped Manhattan during the few short hours while he had slept.

Footprints, tennis-shoe prints, marred the virginal purity of the freshly fallen snow. Running prints? Fleeing ones? No, Lieutenant Lucas Hunter told himself.

Galen had been walking not running, resolute and calm. Out the door and to the fountain, where she had stopped for a while before journeying, calmly still, around the fountain and beyond.

To the very edge of the terrace. Which was where he found her, bundled in her down-filled robe, luminous in the night black sky, the city lights aglow in the snowy crystals that adorned her curls.

There was, at the terrace edge, a low brick wall, an easy step up . . . and a lethal fall down.

But this was not the frantic woman of his nightmare, merely the enchantress of his dreams, and when she sensed his presence she turned to him, a pirouette of sheer grace, and she welcomed him, welcomed him, with shimmering blue eyes.

"Lucas."

"Hi. Couldn't you sleep?"

He looked so worried, this shadow in the shadows. His dark voice was shadowed, too.

"Actually," Galen said, "I slept very well until . . ."

Had her sleep been tainted by nightmares, too? he wondered as her words drifted off in a delicate frown. Had she dreamed, too, of gleaming knives and naked Barbies?

It seemed impossible that hunter and snow angel would share nightmares any more than dreams. Still, and softly, Lucas said, "Until you had a helluva dream."

Galen's frown deepened. "No. At least I don't think that was it." Her frown vanished, she forced it away, fueled by a compelling wish to reassure. And, she realized, by the truth. "In fact, I'm *sure* it wasn't."

She had awakened feeling so safe. Safe *still*. "I just woke up. At 3:13. And even though we're not expecting his call until tomorrow night, I decided to stay awake for a while, just in case. I looked out the window, saw the snow, and had to take a closer look. Did I awaken you when I left my room?"

Had tennis shoes on angel feet awakened him? That graceful exodus down the carpeted hall?

Hardly.

But had *she* awakened him? Yes. *Yes*. The image of her, so desperate, so needy, and so very determined to leap, to fly away. From him.

"No," the master liar lied. Then told the truth. "I usually get up about now. Especially when I'm working on a case. I would like to show you how to operate the elevator."

"Oh. Okay."

Her uncluttered surprise at the non sequitur was eloquent proof that no shared nightmare of recalcitrant elevators lurked in her subconscious. *Of course it didn't.*

"Is it terribly tricky?" she asked.

Lucas smiled at last. "Not tricky at all."

"Just your typical penthouse elevator?"

"Just that."

"Did you want to show me now?"

"No." The urgency had vanished. She was safe. "Are you cold?"

No, Galen thought, but did not say, for it was a truth whose time had passed. She *hadn't* been cold. At first. But the frozen crystals that had fallen on her hair were beginning to melt.

Her shrug spilled a trickle of icy liquid onto the nape of her neck. "A little cold, I guess. It's just so beautiful out here." She gestured toward the fountain, silent in winter, and to the barren bed beneath, its lush chocolate topsoil frosted with an icing of snow. Even in winter the tiered white fountain looked like a wedding cake, and when a bride's bouquet of flowers bloomed in pastel glory at its base . . . "Your garden must be spectacular in spring."

"Except for the snow I'm afraid this is pretty much the way it looks year-round."

"Oh."

"You were imagining what?"

"Well. The chattering fountain, of course."

"I've never turned it on. And?"

"Oh, you know, a zillion bulbs hibernating beneath the surface, just waiting to bloom." But he didn't know, this murder maven who lived in a world as colorless as ice. "Just a thought."

"It's a good thought." *For someone else.*

This time, as she shrugged, a single drop from a melted snowflake splashed from the tangled fire to her face, an icy tear that slid past sapphire eyes to trembling lips.

Lucas touched the tear, tracing its path and warming with his heat, with his fire, the chilled flesh where the droplet had been. He stopped the tear, seared it into a steamy vapor, beside her mouth.

"Your lips are blue."

"They are?"

"Very." He gazed for a moment, an eternity of longing, at her mouth.

His own mouth was solemn, at once sensual and hard, as he compelled both his eyes and his hand away. But not too far away. Just to the snow-misted flames, where with exquisite delicacy, impossible delicacy, he flicked from her frosted curls the tiny crystals which were destined to become ice-cold tears.

"Bedtime." His voice was soft, husky, harsh.

Hers was only soft. With wonder. "Bedtime?"

Lucas permitted his gaze to fall from shimmering crystals to shimmering eyes and saw spring, that bright, bright blue, with all its promise and its hope.

It was the same hope that had glowed with such brilliance in his nightmare as she'd stood on the ledge almost free, almost free. But she wanted to fly *to* him now, it seemed. To *him*, not away.

Bedtime.

For someone else. With someone else.

His hand fell from her curls and fisted at his side.

And she shivered. "But . . . you're going to be working on the case." *Our case.*

"I am." His voice was as cold as she felt. But then, for her, he smiled. "I want you to study the data, Detective Chandler. But I need to do some organizing, quite a bit in fact, before it's useful for you to even begin to take a look."

TWELVE

Lucas removed all crime-scene photos from the victims' files and locked them in the nearby file cabinet. Then he reassembled the files, collating the massive amount of data in a coherent, chronologic way.

That compulsive task complete, he shifted from death to life. To Galen. He read every spiteful word in *Start Spreading the News*, then viewed the videotapes obtained from KCOR and Gavel-to-Gavel TV — specifically, in the instance of GTG, Galen's coverage of *North Carolina v. Vernon*, the trial and the reporting that had provided distraction and happiness during the final weeks of Marianne McLain's life.

Galen had worn her Gavel-to-Gavel hair long, as in his dream, a cascade of fire that permitted modesty, allowed camouflage, but which, as Galen herself had explained, did not conform to Manhattan's standard of style.

Galen *did* look stylish on the KCOR

tapes. But so awkward, so oddly lost, as if ever mindful that her shorn hair could afford no privacy whatsoever in a nightmare of nakedness and knives.

Lost yet determined, intrepid in her resolve not to disappoint. But Galen was right. *Rosalyn* was right. As an anchorwoman Galen Chandler was pure disaster. Lovely, courageous, but disastrous nonetheless.

"What are you doing?"

The voice came from the doorway of the war room. Lucas turned, stood, and met confused, *betrayed,* blue eyes.

"Learning about you," he said softly. Indulging myself in enchantment in the face of all this death. *Justified* enchantment. "It's necessary, Galen. His decision to involve you may have been made before last Sunday."

It was true, she supposed. Any of her pathetically inept newscasts might have persuaded the killer to involve her once Lucas returned from cult siege down under.

But so what? The fact remained that she had been chosen because she was a total failure, the proof of which Lucas Hunter had now witnessed firsthand.

"When were you offered the KCOR job?"

"What? Oh." She shook her head, bewildered by what he was suggesting, that Manhattan's Lady Killer had chosen her even *before* she began to anchor the news. "John called me the morning after the verdict was rendered in the Vernon trial."

The morning after the verdict, Lucas echoed silently. The morning after Marianne died. "What did John say?"

"That he and Viveca and Adam had watched the trial and wondered if I might be interested in a job."

"And?"

"I was flattered, reluctant, surprised. Anchor work was so different from anything I'd ever done. But it was so important to John that I at least *consider* the possibility that I agreed to meet with them as soon as the sentencing phase was through. By which time I'd become persona non grata at Gavel-to-Gavel anyway."

She was doing it again, Lucas realized, describing herself objectively, analytically, with the journalistic detachment she was unable — emotionally — to use in describing anyone else. *Even a stranger.* "Because?"

"Oh, because my prediction of the jury verdict was correct."

"And," Lucas embellished, "at odds with what GTG's anchors, as well as other legal pundits, had forecast."

He'd seen enough of the tapes to know it was true. Galen gave the jury credit for being far smarter than the other analysts did — smart enough to understand the complexity of the science that was presented *and* to see the charmingly persuasive defendant for the sociopath he was.

And Galen had stood her ground against the other pundits, despite their far from subtle contempt.

"But you were right," Lucas said.

"The jury was right."

"So you came to Manhattan when?"

"On December twenty-first."

"And you accepted the job when?"

"On the twenty-second," Galen said quietly, knowing the significance of that date for him.

The Lady Killer's first murder was on that night, a killing that happened not by happenstance just hours after the news had broken that Lucas Hunter would be leaving for Australia in the morning. The Queensland standoff had reached a critical stage. The renowned hostage negotiator was desperately needed and had made the commitment to go.

Lucas learned of Kay's murder shortly before he boarded the plane. And five days later, when Monica was slaughtered, Rosalyn St. John received the killer's letter — *Lucas's ladies are dying* — and the torment for Lucas began.

Lucas Hunter had been chosen for torment by the killer.

And now, compelled by good old-fashioned and compulsive detective work, Lucas was trying ever so gently to determine when *and why* the killer had chosen her as well . . . and even though it was not Lucas Hunter's ever-so-gentle intent, for a staggering moment Galen felt just a whisper of the burden, the responsibility, he must feel.

"Maybe there *is* a link to me."

Lucas's smile was soft, surprised, grateful. "I doubt it. But for completeness' sake tell me how you got the job at GTG. You're not an attorney."

"No." *No.* "And it was a fluke. Remember my promising future as a housekeeper?"

"A future jeopardized because of a certain flare for designs?" *For snow angels crafted by the snow angel herself?* "I remember."

"Well. I kept my artistic impulses under tight control. I needed the job. I was living in Chicago at the time, working for a maid service. We worked as a team, two on every job. Our clients were wealthy. The team approach was a protection for all concerned."

"Unless both team members decided to steal."

"Or goof off. Which was the owner's other, and probably more major, concern. So she assigned her teams with great care."

"Incompatible types in which there was no hope of becoming conspirators?"

"Pretty much. In any event, she chose me as her own partner."

"I don't see you as either a thief or a slacker."

"Thanks. Neither did she. I was a hard worker, which meant she could relax a bit. And as the boss she could also relax the rules, including the otherwise verboten act of turning on the client's TV."

"Enter Gavel-to-Gavel?"

"Yes. I'd never even heard of it. But I became completely hooked, and when I realized the network was based right there in the Windy City, I went looking for a job. All the janitor, jani*tress,* slots were filled. But there was an entry-level position open on the production staff."

"From which you worked your way from behind the camera to in front of it."

"By way of another fluke. We were on location in Albuquerque when the trial reporter came down with staphylococcal food poisoning. It hit her suddenly, dramatically, and there was a key development that needed to be reported, something we had learned that the other media outlets hadn't — yet."

"So you became a trial reporter."

"So much for credentials."

"You reported what you saw, what you heard." And, Lucas knew, Galen Chandler also told the Gavel-to-Gavel viewers what she believed.

"It was a good job," Galen said quietly. "I really enjoyed it."

"Are you planning to go back?"

"No. There's that persona non grata problem."

"Not after this."

This. The Lady Killer's Manhattan crime spree and the monster's choice, for whatever reason, of her. "Oh, well, I can't *imagine* taking advantage of this. Besides, every other GTG reporter has a law degree. I don't even have a college one." She hesitated. Briefly. "Or a high-school one."

"You left high school on May ninth of your senior year."

"I can't believe you know that."

"However unlikely," Lucas said softly, "I have to be absolutely certain that the decision to involve you wasn't made before last Sunday. I can't, we can't, afford to leave any avenues unexplored."

We, we, we. "I understand. And agree."

"Thank you. So . . . you quit high school a month before graduation. Why?"

Galen hesitated again. More than briefly. "I was never a good student. I guess you know that."

Lucas did know. And he wondered if it was this admission that had made her hesitate before answering, or if it was something else entirely, a revelation that even the most sophisticated of computer searches might never retrieve.

But Lucas didn't push. He saw how invaded she felt already, how she wished for long flowing hair to wrap around her nakedness. She was concealed, of course — her literal nakedness quite hidden — beneath her baggy jeans, her oversized sweatshirt, her heavy woolen socks. But emotionally . . .

"I find it hard to believe you couldn't have been a good student had you wanted to be."

It was a gentle vote of confidence that was based, Galen imagined, on fact. If Lieutenant Lucas Hunter knew the precise date she left high school he'd undoubtedly seen the results of standardized tests she had taken along the way, the scores that belied,

175

sometimes dramatically, her mediocre grades.

"Not interested, I suppose."

"But you went to class."

Her eyes widened. "It never occurred to me *not* to. I went to class dutifully, day after day, and daydreamed."

Her head tilted with the confession, a gesture that would have cast a curtain of flames across her face, concealing that final nakedness, had not the fiery cascade been shorn to a tangle of curls.

"About what?" Lucas's soft query went far beyond legitimate, even far-fetched, police inquiry.

Let me see you, Galen. I know how lovely you are.

And she did let him see, her face exposed, her expression thoughtful, as quite suddenly she saw herself, an ancient image of herself as a girl. She was at school, gazing out the classroom window, mesmerized by an extravagance of daisies abloom in a meadow beneath a cloudless Kansan sky.

"About my mother. About her being happy."

"Which she wasn't?"

"No. She was lonely." *Even though she had me.* The harsh thought came swiftly, with conviction and with pain. But the thought, so familiar for so long, didn't feel quite right to the girl who gazed at daisies.

"Because she missed your father? I know they were divorced when you were two."

"She didn't miss him. Neither of us did. But she missed being in love."

"So you daydreamed about finding someone for her?"

The curling flames shook, shrugged, and concealed not a thing. Including her smile. "No. That was just going to *happen*. In the usual way. A knight on a white charger would come galloping across the meadow and sweep her off her feet. I daydreamed about her wedding dress, the one I would design and sew."

"And the flower-girl dress you'd design as well."

The smile became a frown. "Oh, no." But that was wrong. *No* was wrong. Because she *had* been part of the daydream. Galen had forgotten. She had made herself forget. But the girl she once had been remembered everything: the long-ago laughter, and long-forgotten love, between the lonely mother and her daydreaming girl.

Lucas saw the sudden sadness, the bewilderment, the *loss*. And he waited.

Tell me Galen. Let me see.

But she wouldn't. Couldn't. Not yet.

"Were there any subjects you did like?" he asked at last, knowing there was such a subject and even knowing its name. But the master detective had not a clue what *it* was. "Ones so interesting you never daydreamed at all?"

"Yes. Home Ec."

"Which is what?"

"You don't know?"

"No. If Home Ec was part of the curriculum at the boarding schools for boys I attended in England, it had a very different name."

"I doubt it was part of your curriculum. Of any curriculum for boys. And I'm not sure it was even routinely taught throughout the U.S., still, when I took it. But in rural Kansas, Home Ec — Home Economics — was alive and well. It was a course for girls, for the future wives, mothers, and homemakers we were to be. We learned to budget household expenses, and cook, and clean, and sew. I imagine that even in rural Kansas, Home Ec's long since been replaced by Health Ed."

"Health Ed. Which is what?"

"Oh, you know. Sex education, pregnancy prevention, AIDS."

"Ah. That. Why were you so good in Home Ec?" Lucas wanted to hear her confess: because I *loved* it, you see, the notions, however antiquated, of wifehood, of motherhood. Of home.

"I had an unfair advantage."

Yes, you did. You had your daydreams. "Oh?"

"My mother was, is, a teacher. Home Ec was her subject."

"So she teaches Health Ed now?"

"Oh, I don't know. I suppose she does."

"You're not in touch?"

"No. We're not." Galen lifted her chin. "Is there anything else you need to know about me?"

Yes. So much. So many enchanting indulgences. "No."

Galen looked from his too intense gray eyes to the neat stacks of colored folders in the war room. They were arranged differently, she realized, since last night's tour. And there were new documents on the desk, bright white downloads from the Internet.

Galen recognized the top copy at once. *Manhattan's One-Trick Pony,* the shoutline read, snagging eager readers to peruse further Rosalyn St. John's most scathing critique, the three-week report card — her searing F — of the high-school dropout with such mediocre grades.

Galen Chandler, Rosalyn asserted, had

179

only one trick to her repertoire. Her *reportage*. Ploddingly, trudgingly, she could chronicle a trial. *One* trial, mind you, at a time. But when it came to doing anything else, the odd canter, the occasional whinny, the slightest prance, the flame-colored pony miserably failed. She could not even walk and chew gum — *munch hay* — at the same time, much less report story after story on the evening news.

Galen looked from the glaring white censure, which Lucas had obviously read, to the rearranged stacks of rainbowed files.

"Where should I start?"

"In the living room."

Her heart began to ache. "The living room?"

"Unpacking the cardboard boxes."

The neatly stacked containers, he meant, of fabric and dolls. What else, Galen chided herself, did she expect? Lucas knew so much, too much, about her. Too much and the truth: she could sew. Period. It was her aching heart that spoke to the rainbows of death. "You were going to permit me to look at the files."

"Would listening to them be all right? I thought, if it's agreeable to you, that I'd read aloud to you while you sew. You do, as I recall, have a promised delivery to Casey tomorrow afternoon. Galen?"

Look at me, Galen. Let me see.

She obeyed at last, at least, this silent command, and when her worried, wary eyes met his, he smiled.

And to the bright, complicated woman who daydreamed about making wedding dresses, Lieutenant Lucas Hunter said, "For the record, Detective Chandler, I am quite confident that you can listen and sew at the same time."

THIRTEEN

Once upon a time four beautiful young women took Manhattan by storm. Modern women. Sexy. Savvy. Confident. Strong.

First there was Kay, the brilliant prosecutor with the future that could be as dazzling and distinguished as she liked. Politics, if she chose. The White House, if that was her pleasure. As First Lady? Of course. Any man would want smart, stunning, glamorous Kay. A President could be hers. But so could the Presidency.

Then there was Monica, the ultra-sophisticated model with the girl-next-door smile. And heart. Monica was over thirty, and her modelling career was still sky-high, and there wasn't the slightest reason to believe it wouldn't remain stratospheric forever.

And then there was Marcia, whose innovative interior designs routinely graced the pages of *Architectural Digest* and who was a welcomed guest in the homes of Manhattan's most discriminating and discreet. Indeed, it was for those valued friends and valuable clients that Marcia placed winning and often preemptive bids at the renowned auction houses of London and New York.

And last but surely not least was Brynne, physician and scientist, the dedicated oncologist who nurtured her patients' souls even as she waged unrelenting war against the ravages of their diseases.

It was a spectacular fairy tale . . . until one by one throats were slit, hearts were crossed, and unseeing eyes were pierced.

There was not a glimmer of a happy ending in this fairy tale — unless one decided that swift death was preferable to lingering heartache, that only in death could the pain of being jilted by the black-haired prince be mercifully ended at last.

Had Lucas come close to choosing any one of these remarkable women as his bride? It was a question Rosalyn St. John posed to her readers, and for which no one had a reply. Including Rosalyn. She hadn't even known until the killer's letters that these four glittering stars were Lucas's loves.

But that was the ferocious privacy of the man. And had he been involved, intimate, with all four women at once? No, Rosalyn surmised. That was definitely *not* his style. Not the hunter who was so focused, so intense. The lieutenant worked hard. And played hard. One lover at a time. Midnight liaisons of passion. And then good-bye, *adieu*.

To at least three of the four.

But had Lucas been seeing one of them still?

Rosalyn St. John didn't know, nor did any of her readers, and Galen couldn't tell as Lucas read to her from their colorful files.

He mourned them all. Would avenge them all. She heard that promise in the quiet darkness of his voice.

"Show me what you're doing."

It was a soft command, and it spoke to an irrelevance, surely, amid the chronicle of glamour and of death.

But it felt to Galen like a fairy tale in itself.

They sat on the snowy carpet, facing each other, separated by the distance of their jeans-clad legs, and between them, in that denim-bordered space, were the fairy-tale kingdoms — his of pictureless police reports, and hers of fabric and dolls.

Flames blazed in nearby granite, and tea and scones shared the glass-topped table with needles and thread, and every hour the snow-white clock on the mantelpiece would chime.

And now the storyteller wanted her to show him what she was doing, and he was gazing at her with the intensity of a lover, as if at this fairy-tale moment she and the doll clothes she was making were all that ever mattered . . . and all that ever would.

"Oh! Well. It's nothing."

It was hardly *nothing*, Lucas knew. Her slender fingers, so graceful and quick, were creating magic, creating happiness, for the Sarahs and Beccas of the world.

"You begin with a pattern," Lucas himself began, the storytelling lieutenant revealing what he had deduced from good old-fashioned detective work — observation — about this once upon a time. "I get the impression these particular patterns are home-made. Galen Chandler originals."

"The gowns and robes are replicas of what the patients wear."

But not the other outfits, Lucas knew. Not the imaginative ensembles proclaimed by Casey to be works of art, the clothes worn by the Barbie when girl and doll were ready to go home. But the notion of Galen Chandler originals seemed to embarrass her, as if her A-plus performance in Home Ec, in home*making*, was trivial in the extreme.

"Okay," Lucas said. "Let's get technical. You pin the patterns to the fabric and cut the pieces, the shapes, you need. That I get. But then, by what can only be described as magic, you figure out which pieces need to be joined."

"It's *easy*."

Lucas arched an elegant brow. "I'll accept as a given that there's some logical way, as yet unclear to me, to look at the pieces and decide. So. You have two pieces that belong together. Then what? Show me."

"Well." Her slender hands moved as she spoke. "You pin the pieces together like this, right side facing in, then stitch the seam a quarter of an inch from the edge. Here. You try. You'll see just how easy it is."

With that, the burgundy velvet of a fairy-tale gown crossed from the land of dolls to the land of death. And there was a gold-tipped needle, too.

Lucas held needle and velvet in the hands that could flick snowflakes off of soggy curls, a caress of sheer delicacy, and could vaporize snow-crystal tears into the winter night air.

Such talented hands. But now oddly clumsy. And his smile, that devastating smile, was wry.

"This is *not* easy."

"I took Home Ec and you didn't."

"I think," Lucas Hunter said, "it's more basic than that. Something primal. Mysterious. Elemental. The sort of male-female distinctions we're supposed to pretend don't exist."

He was talking about something in the chromosomes, ancient and enduring, a remnant of the genetic message that impelled women to tend the home, the cave, while their men hunted and preyed.

A sexist observation? Perhaps. But at this moment, in this fairy tale, it felt sexual, not sexist. For there he was, this incredible male, quite unable to sew. And he was saying, this incredible male, that she, gifted seamstress that she was, was the other half of the primal equation, as consummate a woman as he was a man, as exquisitely — enchantingly, mysteriously — female as the extraordinary women whose savage murders were the reason she was here in this fairy tale. The *only* reason.

Lucas held the needle, and the velvet, still.

But Galen felt the sharpness of another needle, a searing hot phantom that pierced and plunged.

Her eyes closed briefly, tightly, and when they opened she saw with clarity the true distance, the vast distance, between the kingdom of death and the kingdom of dolls.

"They were all so remarkable. Kay and Monica and Marcia and Brynne."

"Yes," Lucas said quietly. "They were."

Galen drew a breath. Then remembering his torment and wondering if perhaps this private man might want to talk, she said in a rush, "You must have loved —"

"No."

No? *Of course no.* Except in Home Ec, and in fairy tales, love was *not* a prerequisite for sex.

"I wasn't involved with any of them."

"Involved?" Galen echoed by mistake, as if she were so naive she'd never heard of liaisons of passion, of pleasure, of lust.

"Sexually," Lucas replied. Then, clarifying further with words that had no meaning for him, but might have meaning for her, he embellished, "Emotionally. Romantically."

"But . . ."

"It was an assumption that Rosalyn, and maybe the killer, made."

"But did you know them?"

"Yes. But not well, and, except for Kay, not in any public way. If we can figure out how the killer made the connection between the other three and me, we'll know exactly who he is."

Lieutenant Lucas Hunter was talking about good old-fashioned detective work. And *we*. Did he mean the NYPD *we?* Or the improbable team of seamstress and hunter?

Galen had her answer as Lucas placed the needle and velvet beside him, in his kingdom still, and handed her four snowy white sheets of paper.

There was writing on the snow, in a primal, masculine script: the victim's name at the top, one page for each woman, with notations, clues, below.

"These are summaries," he said, "of my association with each of the four. As you can see from the first, Kay and I worked together on a number of cases over a period of years. They were murder cases mostly, high-profile and amply reported. Kay was an aggressive prosecutor. When she went after a conviction, she got it, with tough sentences to match. Most of the criminals she put behind bars are there still, or dead, and I haven't yet identified anyone, imprisoned or free, with either the access or the patience to discover my links to the other three women who were killed."

Lucas paused, which was her clue, Galen realized, to move to the next white page.

"You and Monica met last March," she said as she read. "On a United Airlines flight from Denver to JFK."

"I'd been consulting on the Boulder murder, and she'd been in Aspen on a shoot. We talked throughout the flight and went our separate ways when it landed. She called me a few weeks later, a follow-up to our conversation, to tell me she'd decided, as she'd been inclined to do, to call it quits with her lover of two years."

The date, place, and time of that phone call were recorded on the sheet labeled *Monica*. April twelfth, in his office at the precinct, at 7:15 P.M. There were no more words on the paper, just stark, empty white. Galen looked up. "You didn't see her? Date her?"

"No." Lucas paused, as if considering a clarification, then repeated softly, quietly, "No."

After a moment Galen looked from his suddenly too intense gaze to the third sheet of paper he had given her. "And Marcia came here, to the penthouse, four years ago last September."

"At my request. I'd just closed on the purchase and needed someone to oversee the changes I had in mind. I knew exactly what I wanted. But it was a big job. Beginning with gutting the place. It wasn't much fun for her, from a designer's standpoint. I wanted a minimalist look."

"And a white one."

Lucas nodded. "She tried to convince me at least to choose a warmer white." A faint smile of remembrance, of fondness, touched his lips. "It was a battle, among others, that she lost. But Marcia enjoyed the fight. And even after the renovations were complete, she'd send me brochures from time to time, photographs of pieces that were going on various auction blocks and which would not, she insisted, overly clutter the look. That's how I got the mantelpiece clock. Marcia saw it, liked it, and thought I would, too."

Galen looked at the white antique that chimed on the hour. Simple. Pristine. Pure. Like freshly fallen snow. "Which you did."

"Which I did."

Clock, with a date two years ago, was the second to last notation on the page entitled *Marcia.* Below, with a date last May, was a single word.

"Peacock," Galen murmured.

"It was porcelain, and old. Marcia had previewed it for a client from Long Island who was out of the country at the time. But he'd heard about it and wanted her to bid for it until she either won or the price became ridiculously steep. Marcia loved the piece and knew there'd be aggressive bidding. She wanted some input on how high she should go. 'You're British, it's British' was her justification for calling me. But I think she also knew how much I'd like it, too. I stopped by Sotheby's to preview it the following evening. I went by myself. Marcia wasn't there. And I spoke to no one. I called her later at home and told her to bid until the peacock was hers. If her client wasn't happy, I said, I'd buy the piece myself. She left a voice mail, here, a few days later. Her client loved it, wanted it, kept it."

There were no more words on the *Marcia* sheet. Which meant Lucas hadn't seen or spoken to her again. But still Galen asked, "Your penthouse never appeared in *Architectural Digest*?"

"Hardly. Nor did Marcia use me as a reference for other clients, nor did she ever, at least not anywhere that I can find, make mention of the work, minimal as it was, that she'd done for me."

That was Marcia. All there was.

And then there was Brynne.

The dates, the *only* ones on the fourth and final sheet, were between November and April seventeen years ago. And the place?

"You knew Brynne in college."

"Yes. She was dating one of my housemates. She was around the house a lot, and we acknowledged each other in passing, but we never really talked until a party that spring. I was outside, by myself, and she joined me. 'You drink too much,' she said. That was her opening line."

"Was it true?"

"Sure. Among other excesses."

"Why?"

"Because she was pre-med, and two years older than me, and most of all because she came from an alcoholic family. It worried her that I could drink so much and appear so sober."

"I meant," Galen said quietly, "why did you drink, and other excesses, so much? Too much."

Was her question too much? No. His gray eyes glinted, faintly amused, as he replied.

"Part of it was my age, nineteen, and the fact that I'd spent the nine years prior to college in boarding schools in England, the sort of places for future kings where discipline *was* king. Sex was fiercely discouraged, as were alcohol and drugs."

"And the other part?"

The amusement vanished and the gray turned dark. But still he replied. "The usual. Drugs and alcohol were a way to escape. To escape," he repeated softly. "And I suppose, maybe, to daydream."

"Do you still drink and use drugs too much?" *Do you still daydream?*

"Not drugs. Not since college. And as for drinking too much? Yes. Sometimes. Between cases."

Between cases? According to Rosalyn St. John there was no "between cases" for Lieutenant Lucas Hunter, at least not, according to her impeccable sources, for years. There had been a time, in the beginning of his pro bono work for NYPD, and any other law-enforcement agency who needed him, when he would insist upon having time between cases. It was a time during which, Rosalyn reported, he would simply disappear. There would be occasional sightings in Venice, in Paris, in the south of France. With women. Ravishing ones.

But it had been years, Rosalyn St. John insisted, years since the sensual hunter had disappeared.

"Between cases," Galen echoed. "Which is when?"

Lucas smiled. "It's been a while." *Since I've dreamed, since I've daydreamed, since I've escaped.* "Drinking to escape, much less to daydream, isn't really something to aspire to."

"Is that what you told Brynne?"

"No. That would have been conceding far too much. I admitted that, although she might have a point, I was sober enough — no matter how much I'd had to drink — to see what she, despite her abstinence, could not: that my housemate wasn't right for her."

"And that you were?"

"No, Galen." *Even then I knew I wasn't right for anyone.* "Not at all."

"But you and Brynne became friends after that?"

"No. She broke up with my housemate about a week later. I never saw or spoke to her again."

"Even though you both lived in Manhattan?"

"Even though."

"Could the housemate be the killer?"

"Could. But isn't. He actually turned out to be more sane, and more moral, than I ever imagined he would be. It's not him, nor is it anyone else who lived in that house."

"So the killer may be someone Brynne knew, someone to whom she mentioned your name at any time over the past seventeen years." Galen paused, frowned. "Or she may not have known him at all. She may have merely mentioned you to someone who knew him, or someone who knew someone who did. But *somewhere* in that grapevine, there's someone who actually does know him. Is that what you think?"

Lucas looked at her, this bright seamstress who made such flawless seams . . . including this one. "Yes, Detective Chandler, that's exactly what I think."

"And the same applies for Monica and Marcia."

"Yes."

"Did *they* know each other? The four women?"

"Not that I've been able to determine."

Galen sighed.

And Lucas smiled. "We'll get him, Detective."

"I know." *You will get him.* "What about the killer himself? His relationship to you. It feels so . . ."

"What, Galen?"

"Personal."

"You're right. It does. But it may not be personal at all. He may regard himself as a professional of sorts, a murderer who merely wanted to get my attention. And to play. Cat and mouse. Hunter and prey."

"What does he want now?"

To play with you. "I guess we'll find out tonight."

"Should I ask him?"

"If you like."

"I'm so afraid I'll say something wrong."

"You can't possibly. He'll be controlling the conversation. He'll tell you only what he wants to tell you, and he'll get you to say only what he wants you to say. Tell him the truth, Galen. Whenever you can. And be expansive. Keep him on the line. Reveal whatever he wants to know about what we know about him. Nothing is off-limits. You'll do fine."

FOURTEEN

"Did I awaken you?" the disguised voice wanted to know.

"No. I was awake. Expecting your call."

"You haven't been up all night, I hope."

"No." *Just for thirteen minutes.* "Just since three."

Her alarm had been an unnecessary precaution. An internal clock had awakened her with time to spare. She had changed from pajamas to warm-ups, then sat in darkness at the edge of her bed.

Now she was moving, opening her bedroom door, walking toward Lucas, who was walking toward her. He was dressed, too, and wearing the headphones.

"Where are you?"

"What do you mean?"

"I mean," there was controlled impatience in the electronic voice, "where *are* you? What hotel? I trust the lieutenant has you ensconced in someplace swank."

"Actually, Lieutenant Hunter has been

kind enough to allow me to stay in his home."

"A little advice, Galen. *Don't lie to me*."

"It's not a lie."

There was an electronic pause, an electronic silence. "My, my. The lieutenant is really pulling out all the stops. Is he there, too? *Right* there?"

"Yes."

"And is he listening?"

"Yes." Galen glanced at Lucas, so close to her, yet so far away.

His eyes were closed, his concentration intense, as he listened to the evil, felt it, *channeled* it. Galen imagined the evil flooding him, filling him, swamping his heart and searing his veins.

It was a ghastly journey. But it had purpose and destination, and every minute she kept the killer on the line, the closer Lucas drew.

Be expansive, Lucas had told her. Spar and play.

In a voice she did not recognize, Galen Chandler began to do just that.

"I'm *so* glad you called. I have a million questions for you."

The murderer's distorted laugh was low and mean. "Let's do my questions first, shall we?"

"Oh. Well, sure. Lady killers first."

"Nice, Galen. I'm *so* glad you agree. Let's see. Where to begin? Oh. I know. How about my favorite subject? *Sex.* I'm in the mood to hear *everything,* from your first time to your last. By which I mean your most recent. I wonder, and I truly demand to know, if your latest sexual escapade occurred earlier this very evening."

"What? No. And this" — Sex. *Sex with Lucas* — "is really none of your business."

"Here's the thing, Galen. I'm the killer, remember? I hold every single card. My business is whatever I want it to be. Which, at the moment, is you. And sex. Our catty Rosalyn may believe you're frigid. How else to explain your rigidity on air? But I simply don't agree. I'm a fan, you see. Your *greatest* fan. But even the most loyal devotees have demands, and I must demand details now. The devil being, as they say, in those details. The devil and the *delight.* So, Galen, let's begin with your deflowering. Give me everything. The journalist's full bouquet. The who, the what, the when, the where. In a cornfield, maybe, amid all the husks? And, last but not least, I need to hear the *how.* How *was* it? Bloody? Painful? I'm hoping for something out of the ordinary. But even the routine will do. No embellishments, please.

Not that you would. Your journalistic integrity is beyond reproach. Just the truth, Galen, that's all I ask."

The truth. The truth. I can't.

She was trembling, shivering, and walking toward the living room, toward the Barbies, away from Lucas.

From them both.

But they followed her. Both of them.

"Do you know what happens if you deny me, Galen? Our fifth lady dies. Tonight. She dies. *You kill her.* So start talking, my pet. And do not tell me lies. Deceit like denial is punishable by death."

When Galen reached the living room, the venue just hours ago of enchantment and fairy tales, she looked at the Barbies on the snowy white couch.

Each doll was already dressed in her striped bathrobe and cottony gown. But the dolls' hair still needed to be done, and Galen needed to swaddle each one in a tissue-paper cocoon, and lay each carefully in the Bloomingdale's shopping bag which, over scones and tea, Lucas had promised to carry for her, with her, to the hospital.

"Galen." The electronic voice crackled with impatience.

Enchantment and fairy tales. Scones and tea.

Dolls and death.

Galen abandoned the Barbies and crossed to a windowed wall far from the fantasy of fairy tales. And the reality of Lucas.

Galen looked outside. To darkness.

"I haven't . . . There's never been a first time."

"Oh my God. You *are* extraordinary. I knew it! A twenty-nine-year-old virgin, and all mine. I wonder how Lucas is reacting to the news? No, don't tell me. Let's pretend he isn't there. This is just between the two of us. *Especially* the first time."

"What?" Galen whispered to glass so shimmering it was a flawless mirror.

In the distance, and so clearly, she saw the panther. He stood beside the fireplace, where no longer there were dancing flames.

But Galen saw fire nonetheless, the glitter of molten silver, of searing fury, in the stone-hard granite of his face.

"You heard me, Galen. We're going to do it. *Do. It.* Right now. It's not *ideal.* You'll have to pretend that your hands are mine. But don't worry, I'll talk you through it, every devilishly delightful detail."

Galen focused beyond the mirror — and the fury and the fire — into darkness. *"No."*

"You're denying me?"

"No. Not *really.* It's just that it's too soon.

We barely know each other."

"Bravo! The bashful virgin. All right. I'll play along. For a while. But I warn you, Galen. When I decide the time is right you must do everything I tell you. Agreed?"

No. No. No. "Agreed."

"Oh, and Lucas? Are you there? Don't touch her, Lieutenant. *She is mine.*" When it spoke again the electronic voice sounded immensely pleased. "I think that's enough foreplay for one night. So on to my promise, Galen Chandler, to make you a star. Your ascension to the Emmy-award-winning heavens will begin with a one-hour special, a recap of the killings, the investigation, and, since such celebrations are in vogue, of the victims and their lives. I'm toying with the idea of insisting on an appearance from the lieutenant. A little up-close-and-personal about his lady friends. He *owes* you an exclusive, after all. But let me get back to you on that, all right? There's time. Your special won't be airing until Wednesday evening, by which time all of Manhattan will know to watch. Plan for an *entire* hour, by the way. No commercials. And nothing else, either. Which reminds me, my starlet. You won't be covering any *other* news. I'm your only story."

"Of course."

"Good. Oh, and one last thing. I fear your virginal undergarments are utilitarian at best. As baggy, perhaps, as your bag-lady clothes? That *won't* do, Galen. Not for me. You'll need negligees for our private tête-à-têtes, not to mention for the *big moment,* and I need to know you're wearing something truly special, deliciously erotic, for your telecast on Wednesday night. Only I will know. But I'm the only one who matters, aren't I? You're going on a shopping spree, Galen. Today. You'll go to Ophelia, of course."

"Ophelia?"

"Don't tell me. You've never even *noticed* the lingerie boutique adjacent to KCOR? Well, no matter. I'm quite sure Lucas knows where it is. Take the lieutenant with you, Galen, and let him help you decide. He's undoubtedly an expert on such things. In fact, my precious virgin, the thought of you alone with Lucas . . . Don't touch her, Lieutenant. *Don't you dare."*

"You're sick."

"No. I'm *Lucas."*

"What?"

"You have to call me *something,* don't you? 'Lady' isn't quite right. And 'Killer' is over the top. And we're going to be *lovers,* after all. So call me Lucas. Touch me, Lucas. Kiss me, Lucas. Yes, Lucas. Yes, yes, *yes."*

FIFTEEN

Lucas could not see her, not even in the mirrored wall of glass. Her head was bent, her face shadowed.

But he could see himself, so clearly.

Lucas. His name. And the killer's. And at this moment, *still,* they were one. The evil flowed, flooded still, freezing his veins, flogging his heart, icing his soul.

They were one.

And now, as he neared her, Galen looked up and saw too, and so clearly, the image of him reflected in glass.

And Lucas saw? Luminous blue eyes that searched, that sought. *But did not fear.*

And the evil ebbed.

He said, "You're off the case."

And she said, "There's something I need to tell . . . what did you say?"

"I said, Galen, that you're off the case."

No. *No.* She turned. "I realize this is a problem, Lucas. That *I'm* a problem. But I can do this. I *can.* I mean, I wouldn't really have to . . . I could just pretend, couldn't I? Granted, I'm not the world's greatest liar. But the killer doesn't know that. And there are movies that might be helpful, and with coaching, perhaps from Viveca —"

"What the hell are you talking about?"

"My . . . inexperience."

His voice was a caress. "How can you possibly think that's why I want you out of this?"

And hers was a whisper. "Why else?"

"Because it's hideous for you. You shouldn't have to be involved."

"But I *should*. Because it may be about me after all. He may be someone I know, someone I *knew*, years ago."

"The man in the avocado kitchen."

Her expression, and her voice, were bewildered. "How do you know about that?" *How can you possibly know?*

"I had a dream, a nightmare, last night. I saw you and the kitchen and a butcher knife."

It was *her* nightmare, the one that had haunted her for eleven years. But there had been no haunting last night, and she had felt so very safe. "Is that something you sense? Too? Nightmares? Dreams?"

"No," Lucas said softly. "Never before." *Never until you.* "Maybe it's because you al-

206

most told me about him yesterday. Didn't you? When I asked why you quit high school a month before graduation?"

"Yes. I did. Almost. But I decided it wasn't relevant. *He* wasn't. Couldn't be. But now . . . his name is Mark. He was my mother's boyfriend. They began living together when I was fourteen. They talked about marriage but decided against it. They'd both been married before, and it hadn't worked well, and everything was good between them, wonderful, just as it was. Mark made her very happy, which made me happy, and he was kind to me, too. I didn't have a lot of friends, any friends, when we met. I was a bit of a scarecrow. Mark made me feel special."

Scarecrow. Was that the name her classmates chose for the too tall, too skinny, flame-haired girl who daydreamed of happiness and wedding dresses for her mother?

Yes, Lucas thought. His voice was so gentle for that taunted daydreaming girl. "Too special, Galen?"

"Yes. Mark would wander into my room when I was dressing and would take great offense when I'd ask him to leave." It was Galen who began wandering then, needing space, needing distance, for the confession she must make. "He was my *father*," he said.

The father I'd never had. How could I imagine his motives were anything but pure? That made me feel guilty, of course, and prevented me from locking a door I'd never locked before. *I* was the one with hang-ups, Mark said. *I* had been abandoned by my father. He insisted it was normal, in fact necessary, for fathers to monitor their daughters' physical development, so they'd know when to start worrying about teen-aged boys. Mark would come into my room, whenever he pleased, to look at me, to *stare* at me. And to make comments."

"About?"

She was with the Barbies now, standing in front of the couch where they were assembled in the nightgowns and bathrobes she had made. "My . . . shape. Shapelessness. How skinny I was. How immature even at fourteen. And he'd comment about my clothes, too. How . . . baggy they were. He didn't touch me. Why would he? He never, then, did anything sexual at all."

"But it was all sexual," Lucas said softly. Sexual. And sadistic. Mark took pleasure in embarrassing her, humiliating her. Just as the Lady Killer did. "You know that now."

"Yes. And subconsciously I must have known it even then. I avoided Mark as much as possible and spent more and more time away from home."

"Where did you go?"

"Oh," she murmured. "Well. I'd go for walks in the cornfields when the weather was good, and in winter I'd go to the bowling alley, or the library, or the grocery store. That's where I met Julia. At the grocery."

"Julia?"

"Yes. Julia and her sister Edwina. Winnie." *Our sweet, sweet little Win.* Galen reached for a Barbie, one with long black hair, and spoke gently to the tiny face. "They'd come to the store to get tapioca pudding for their great-aunt Anne — Gran — with whom they lived and who wasn't feeling well on that December day. Julia was a year younger than I, and Winnie was just six months old. Julia was holding her, talking to her, when a woman approached with her young son, wanting him to see the baby. But when the woman saw Winnie, she shrieked at Julia, *screamed* at her. 'How dare you take that *thing* out in public? It's disgusting, indecent. You should be *ashamed.*' "

Galen stroked the doll's raven tresses, a cherishing touch. "Julia *wasn't* ashamed, of course. When she looked at Winnie, Julia saw love, only love, even though to the rest of the world Winnie looked . . ." Galen faltered.

"How did she look?" His voice was a soft caress. "Can you remember? Or did you see Winnie only as Julia did, as a precious little girl?"

"That's how I saw her," Galen whispered. "That's who she was. But she had developmental anomalies — skeletal and neurologic — that were quite apparent and very severe. The doctors hadn't expected her to survive at all, not even for a few days."

"But she was six months old when you met her."

"Yes, and her amazed doctors had stopped predicting how long she would live. But she would never walk, they said. And that was true. And they weren't certain, either, that she'd ever be able to see. But Winnie *did* see, and in a palette of colors that was all her own. In Winnie's world the daylight sky was green, and at night it glowed golden with an aquamarine moon, and the cornfields were her favorite of all colors, turquoise blue."

Turquoise blue, Lucas mused. Like a certain billowy coat with mittens to match.

"And Winnie's Christmas trees were fuchsia?"

"Yes. My mittens were a gift from Winnie

to me, knitted by Julia and Gran."

Gran. Their great-aunt Anne with whom, Galen had said, Julia and Edwina lived, and whose name Galen spoke with such fondness that the issue of the girls' absentee parents was, Lucas decided, quite moot.

Besides, Galen was speaking again, with remembrance, with love.

"For a while everything was perfect. I lived at home, my mother's home and Mark's, but I spent most of my time with Winnie and Julia and Gran. And then . . ." Her frown forecast the impending loss and her voice quavered with its sadness. "Gran died. She was almost eighty-two, and her death was sudden and peaceful, but it was still devastating. It was devastating when she died, in March of my senior year, and devastating still, two months later, on that night in May."

"May ninth."

"Yes. May ninth." Bitterness replaced sadness as Galen described the losses, even more losses, that were to come. "It was early evening when I returned from Julia and Win's. They always went to bed early. Julia had adapted her sleep pattern to Winnie's, to what Winnie *needed* it to be. I expected to be alone in the house. My mother was taking a night class and Mark was working the evening shift. Or so I thought. I was in the kitchen getting a glass of water when he appeared. In uniform."

"Uniform?"

"Mark was a cop. *Is* a cop."

"Terrific," Lucas muttered.

"He'd actually worked the day shift, a last-minute trade, after which he'd stayed to complete the paperwork on a case. He said he hadn't seen me for a while. He meant naked. I *still* looked like a scarecrow, he told me, at least in my baggy clothes. But I was eighteen, so surely I'd matured underneath. He wanted to take a look. I told him he was sick, *perverted,* that I understood that at last. I was going to tell my mother, I said, and the sheriff. Mark merely laughed. *I* was the pervert, he said. It was my friendship with Julia, with *Winnie,* that was truly sick. Mark knew all about it, had discovered it at the time of Gran's death. Since then he'd made a habit, a nasty game, of driving past Julia's, very slowly, to smirk and stare. *I* was the pervert, he insisted. And besides, he taunted, who would believe that *he* would look twice at a girl like *me?* But he was going to do me a favor, he said. As unappealing as I was, he was going to make me a woman — right then."

"There was a knife on the counter."

212

"Yes. Mark dared me to reach for it, to protect myself. I *started* to. I even saw myself stabbing him. It was an image so terrifying that I pulled my hand away. See? he goaded as he unbuttoned his shirt and unclasped his belt. I *wanted* him. I always had. He was kissing me and opening my blouse when my mother walked in."

There it was, Lucas realized. The killing frost. The icy end of the hope and the promise of spring.

"And?" he asked gently of the wintry blue eyes.

"And she was in her bathrobe. I guess she'd been asleep. She hadn't been feeling well and must have decided not to go to her night class after all."

"And?"

"And the moment Mark saw her he started to explain. He'd come home, missing her, wanting her, because some tragedy he'd seen that day, a car wreck on the interstate, had made him realize how precious life, *love*, really was. But she wasn't home, at least he'd believed she wasn't, and there I was, and I'd been *coming on to him* for a while. He'd resisted my seduction until that night, when he needed *her* so much. It wasn't an excuse, he said, and he wouldn't blame her if she tossed him out."

213

"But she tossed you out instead."

"I left before she had the chance."

"So you don't know."

"Don't know what?"

"What she would have done."

"Of course I know." Galen's reply was swift, bitter, harsh, and it came with a familiar thought: She would have believed Mark *whom she loved*. Mark, not me.

"But you hadn't ever told her about the times Mark came into your room, had you?"

"No." *No. Because she wouldn't have cared, wouldn't have —*

"Because she was so happy," Lucas said. "And you didn't want to make her *un*-happy."

His soft words stunned her, jarred her, and then so gently transported her back to the daydreaming girl who had stared at daisies . . . and who remembered all the laughter, all the love, before Mark. That girl, that loving and beloved daughter, was remembering more now, the way she'd pretended that everything was *fine,* so her mother wouldn't know, couldn't possibly suspect, what Mark did when she wasn't around.

The daydreaming girl had kept that secret from the mother with whom once she had shared so much. *Everything.* But the sharing had changed, *she* had changed it, because of Mark. It was she, Galen, who had withdrawn from the closeness. To protect her mother's happiness? Or because she blamed her mother for allowing Mark into their life?

To protect. Perhaps. In the beginning. But eventually she *had* blamed Bess Chandler for Mark. It was a hidden resentment that smoldered and seared, and which remained as secret as all the other secrets Galen kept, including the most treasured one of all: the world, *her* world, with Winnie and Julia and Gran. Once, before Mark, Galen would have so joyfully shared that secret world. Once, before Mark, mother and daughter would have sewn together the clothes Galen made for Winnie, the special clothes for special Win.

Lucas watched in silence the emotional storm evoked by his suggestion that Galen had kept hidden the truth about Mark because she hadn't wanted to shatter the happiness that Bess Chandler had found. It was a wintry storm, turbulent and dark. Yet Lucas saw amid the desolate blue the most delicate wisps of wonder.

And of hope.

"Galen? Was that why you didn't tell her?"

"I . . . maybe."

"But you left that night."

"Yes. My mother and Mark were still in the kitchen. He was talking, *explaining,* still. I threw some clothes and my mittens into a knapsack and left the house."

"And went to Julia's."

"That's where I was going. She lived across town, and I was *almost* there when Mark screeched to a halt beside me. He got out of his car, grabbed my wrists, and laughed at my fear. He'd seen enough in the kitchen, he told me. Enough to know that I was a scarecrow still. He wasn't interested after all. Besides, he gloated, my mother was waiting for his return, wanting him more than ever. But she wanted something else, he said. They *both* did. They wanted me to leave town and never return. And if I didn't leave right then, and if I ever tried to contact Julia *in any way,* Winnie would be institutionalized. He'd make sure of it. And it would be easy. Julia had been educated at home by Gran until Winnie was born. But the lessons stopped because of Winnie, because caring for Winnie was all they did, all they wanted to do. Julia was a truant, Mark said. And she was only seventeen. He could and would notify the appropriate authorities. Julia would be compelled to return to school, and Winnie would be placed in an institution far away, where I knew, and Mark knew, she wouldn't survive for very long. If I didn't do exactly as he said, he'd see to it that Winnie died abandoned and alone."

"So Mark made you abandon Julia instead." And at a time, Lucas realized, when Julia needed her friend so much, when Gran's death was still so difficult for them all.

"Yes. He did. He drove me to a bus station two towns away from where we lived, bought me a one-way ticket to Chicago, and waited until the bus and I were gone."

"You didn't have a choice, Galen. You had to leave for Julia, to protect her and Winnie."

"Yes. I know. But Julia doesn't."

"You never told her?"

"No. Not even after Winnie . . . died." Galen didn't even know when that immense loss had occurred. She hadn't dared make the phone calls that might tell her when the end was near. Galen knew only that she hadn't been there for Julia when her friend had needed her the most. And to simply reappear years later . . .

"You need to talk to her."

Hope, so delicate and so brave, shimmered anew. "I do?"

"You do. Absolutely. And I imagine Julia needs to talk to you as well." The hope of spring glowed in her winter blue eyes, and its glorious promise glittered bright silver in his. "And then there's your mother."

"My mother?" Galen echoed. But the hope did not fade. The glittering silver wouldn't let it.

"Your mother. I wonder if you should talk to her, too. Tell her what Mark did to you. And find out, perhaps, what would have happened if you hadn't left, and what's happened since. Is she still with Mark? Do you know?"

"Yes, I do know. And she's not. A few years ago, when I knew that despite all Julia's love Winnie could no longer possibly be alive, I called the sheriff's office and the school. I didn't identify myself and no one asked. Mark had moved to San Diego, the clerk said, to join the police force there."

"And your mother?"

"She's still in Kansas teaching school." Just as, Galen mused, she had been doing *before* Mark, when every mother-daughter secret was shared, and there were daydreams of wedding dresses and daisies, and there was such laugher and such love.

"So?" Lucas asked softly, as if knowing her dreaming, her daydreaming, thoughts.

"So maybe," Galen heard herself say, "maybe someday I should talk to her."

Lucas smiled. As did she.

And then, because *someday* wouldn't happen, couldn't happen, while there was a killer on the loose, the smiles faded, and they turned once again to the solemn topic at hand: the potential suspect Galen had known.

"Did you ever report what Mark had done?" Lucas asked.

"Yes. Six months ago. I wrote to San Diego's chief of police. I'd been with Gavel-to-Gavel long enough to know about the presumption of innocence. I knew no action could result merely from my claims. But I expressed the hope that my allegations would be placed in context should similar accusations occur."

"Did you sign your name?"

"Yes."

"Was there any reply?"

"No. Nor did I expect one. But my letter might have been shown to Mark."

Yes, Lucas thought. You might have been betrayed by yet another cop.

"And if so, Mark would have been angry. Enraged." Galen drew a breath. "And Mark knew that I sewed — and the killer uses needles — and tonight the killer alluded to

Kansas cornfields and to the baggy clothes . . . underclothes . . . I wore." *Wear.*

"And," Lucas added quietly, "both Mark and the killer are sexual sadists. But you made the decision yesterday not to tell me about Mark."

"Yes."

"Because?"

"Because I can imagine an angry Mark coming after me, stalking me, terrifying me, and I suppose even killing me. But this is so elaborate. So calculated. So controlled."

"And," Lucas said, "because establishing a connection between the victims and me would probably require having spent some time, maybe years, in Manhattan. Which, as far as we know, Mark hasn't done."

"No. He hasn't. So," Galen concluded quietly, "you don't think it's him."

No, Lucas realized. He didn't. Despite the significant coincidences — the needles, the knife — and the more trivial ones, the Kansas cornfields and baggy clothes. The latter were easily dismissed, a combination of conjecture and information provided by Rosalyn St. John. But the former were more troubling, more persuasive. Except that Lucas wasn't persuaded. He didn't think the killer was Mark, didn't *feel* that he was.

"No," he replied. "I don't. Which isn't to

say I won't pursue it, won't establish with absolute certainty that Mark was in San Diego, preferably on duty, for at least one of the nights. But this isn't about you, Galen. This isn't your fight."

"You still want to fire me."

"I want you off the case," Lucas said. "Yes. For you."

Silence fell. With thunder. The frantic thundering of her heart. He wanted her gone. For her. For her.

The snow-white clock began its 4 A.M. chime, a pristine carol of joy, a reminder of enchantment and fairy tales.

And torment and death.

The antique timepiece that Marcia, his murdered designer, had known that Lucas would like.

Galen spoke when the chiming stopped.

"I'm staying, Lieutenant." *For you. To help you avenge this senseless slaughter, and to end — for you, for you — the torment.* "I'm hooked, you see. I really want to see this adventure through."

She was chugging straight for the iceberg, full speed ahead, and she didn't care. She could handle it. Would. But it was best for the moment not to define *it* — to submerge entirely, for example, the specter of speaking *about* sex with the killer named Lucas, much less pretending to engage *in* same.

"Okay?" she asked.

"Okay. For now."

For always, Galen vowed. For as long as it takes and as difficult as it is. Full speed ahead.

But there it was *already,* a floating glacier looming large, and so daunting that her gaze skittered from Lucas to the glassy mirror. And Galen Chandler saw herself. A gawky scarecrow in baggy warm-ups.

"Do you think it's necessary to make the purchases the killer wants?" she asked of that glassy reflection. *To purchase, at Ophelia, sexy and explicit lingerie?*

"Not necessary, but better," the sleek, elegant, sensual man replied. "Best."

"The concept of keeping to a minimum the lies I'm compelled to tell?" *This* isn't a lie, her mirrored image, that gangling eyesore, seemed to say. This is *you.* Please remember that when you start thinking about fairy tales.

"Right. Galen?" He moved. At last. But it wasn't to close the distance, as he'd been so tempted to do. Lucas moved instead to block her view of whatever it was that made her so confused. But her confusion only deepened and she looked at the floor. "You won't need to wear the items. But having something to look at, to describe to him, will make the dialogue easier. We'll deliver the Barbies to Casey at two as promised, then swing by Ophelia en route to Riverside Drive for your interview with Janet Bell."

"My interview?" Galen looked up. At him. "Who is Janet Bell?"

"Kay's best friend. She was in Paris when Kay was murdered and didn't even know of Kay's death until she returned. By which time my connection to the case and the victims was known. Still, Janet's statement to the investigators seems excessively hostile. If they wanted to know *why* Kay was murdered, she said, why didn't they simply ask me? It may mean nothing. She was obviously upset. And still is. She won't talk to me. I've tried."

"And you think she'll talk to me?"

Galen saw a new mirror then, and such a different one, impossible really: her reflection it seemed — *hers* — in the glittering silver of his eyes.

"If she'll talk to anyone, Galen, she'll talk to you."

SIXTEEN

Manhattan, on that Sunday afternoon, was a winter wonderland.

Lucas and Galen were on foot, everyone was, on foot or sled or snowmobile or skis. Or paws. Manhattan's canine citizenry frolicked as gaily as their owners, bounding through drifts, their muzzles bearded with snow, their eager yaps in gleeful harmony with the laughter of children.

Families flocked to Central Park. Human ones with their pets and an ever-growing population of families made of snow. The snowpeople came in all sizes and shapes, with adornments from button eyes to apple ears to a Sunday *Times* tucked beneath a frosty arm.

There was much gaiety in the winter wonderland. But the man who walked beside her, carrying the bountiful sack of tissuewrapped dolls, neither saw the happiness nor heard its splendor.

Or maybe to him the joy spelled only torment, a harsh reminder of those not destined to enjoy this spectacular day because of their association, however remote, with him.

Or maybe . . .

"Are you feeling him?"

Him? Manhattan's Lady Killer? No, Lucas mused. But he was feeling this day and remembering the killer who had stolen his soul all those years before and who stalked his heart still.

"No. I was thinking about something else entirely." *Someone else.* "Sorry."

Lucas found a smile for Galen, and for Casey as well when they dropped off the dolls at precisely two. And his expression was serious, but not so faraway, as they neared Ophelia.

Manhattan's Lady Killer was not entirely correct. Galen had noticed, subliminally, she supposed, the lingerie boutique. Noticed and dismissed.

Not that Ophelia was tacky in the least. Here was a place of class, of style, a destination for the modern woman, confident in work and in play, a woman who celebrated her femininity, its power and its mystique, and who chose to share both with the man — the men? — she loved.

Galen's assessment of Ophelia was made from the spacious foyer. Her legs, those skinny denim-clad limbs beneath her cavernous turquoise coat, would have to move, boldly and decisively, to survey the merchandise on display.

"Why don't we divide and conquer?" the solemn voice beside her asked. "You begin over here."

Galen felt herself moving, suddenly so graceful in her baggy jeans, guided in this impromptu ballet by a gentle hand on her back.

She *felt* his hand, its strength, its heat, despite her turquoise coat and the layers beneath . . . as if she, a modern woman, wore only the most courageous wisp of silk.

The place Lucas chose for her was a venue for brides, for wedding days and marriage nights. Traditional ones. One-fashioned ones. In every shade of white.

Galen didn't touch. At first. But eventually the workmanship, or maybe the dream, irresistibly beckoned her. Her mittens came off and she felt the softness of a satin gown, a wedding-night gown, embroidered with roses of ivory on cream.

Would the groom, she wondered, see the loveliness of the roses, those delicate blossoms of hope? Would he admire the hand-stitched petals before he eased the gown from his trembling bride?

Trembling? Yes. But the modern bride, the Ophelia bride, would tremble with eagerness not with fear. And that confident celebrant would shimmy out of the gown herself, leaving a pool of satin and roses at her feet.

Lucas, too, was irresistibly beckoned by the dream. But he watched from a safe distance, a necessary one, moving closer — and breaking the spell — only when the piercing ache became a desperate one.

"Galen."

"Lucas! I'm afraid I haven't gotten very far."

"That's okay. I think I've got what we need." The same hand that had carried a shopping bag of Barbies, and had guided her to this place of roses and brides, held now an ivory-colored sack. The paper, it seemed to be parchment, was as upscale as the boutique, and as discreet, and so richly textured one could not begin to discern the garments within. *Ophelia* did not appear on the opaque parchment, only a small bouquet of wildflowers etched in gold. "Are you ready to go, or would you like to browse some more?"

"No. I'm ready." Galen gestured toward the ivory parchment. "Should I carry it?"

"No. I will."

And he did, as they returned to the winter wonderland and walked toward the apartment building, and Galen's unscheduled interview, on Riverside Drive.

"Ms. Bell?"

"Who is this?"

"Galen Chandler. From KCOR?"

"I *know* who you are. Are you alone?"

"No. Lieutenant Hunter is with me."

The voice in the intercom hesitated briefly, then resumed with a brittle edge. "I'll speak to you. Only. Agreed?"

"Yes. Agreed."

Galen looked at Lucas as a loud buzz signaled the release of the latch.

"I'll wait right here."

"Outside?"

"Sure." The silvery glint in his eyes sent a glowing reminder of the sensual fires that burned within, the smoldering heat that would keep him warm. "I'm fine, Galen. Happy. Take as much time as you need."

Galen needed excessive amounts of neither time nor coaxing. Kay's best friend was eager to talk.

"I can't *bear* seeing him."

"Seeing who?"

"Lucas Hunter."

"You know him?"

228

"*Of* him. That's all. But it's *enough*. I very much wish I'd never had a reason to hear word one about him. But I did have a reason, and, as a result, I know *all about* the bastard who flew to Australia just hours after Kay was killed. *I* feel guilty about not being here. For her. And I didn't even know she'd died. But Lucas knew, and *still* he left."

"He had to leave," Galen countered quietly. "He'd made a commitment."

"Commitment? Lieutenant Lucas Hunter? *Please.*"

"The cult leaders threatened to kill the children on Christmas Eve. And Lucas had no idea that Kay's murder had anything to do with him. How could he? Yes, he and Kay had worked together on a few cases, but —"

"*Worked* together? Is that what he told you?"

"Yes."

"And you believe him? *Of course* you do! I don't know why I'm surprised. Lying *and sex* are what Lucas Hunter does best. Lying. Sex. And murder. Let's not forget that. He very nearly murdered Kay with his cruelty and his *lies.*"

"I don't understand," Galen murmured, even though she was so terribly afraid that she did.

"Kay was *in love* with him. And according

to Lucas, the *real* lady-killer, he was in love with her, too. Oh, yes, Galen. Lucas Hunter said the three magic words. Again and again and again. I love you, Kay. Marry me, Kay."

The three magic words, Galen echoed silently. Not the killer's ghastly three, *cross your heart,* but the ones of true, of traditional, magic.

"But you know what?" Janet asked. "It was a lie. All of it. Lucas *admitted* as much when he was through with her. And Kay was devastated. *Destroyed.* I was so afraid she wouldn't make it, that even strong, brilliant, talented Kay could not survive. But she did. She soldiered on. And at last, *at last,* her life was finally getting back on track. She'd met someone *wonderful.* She wouldn't tell me who, except that it definitely *wasn't* Lucas. She would not, she assured me, be that foolish ever again."

Janet paused, and even though the faux journalist was reeling from the revelations, Galen managed a reflexive query. "Did you ever find out who it was?"

"No. But . . ."

"Yes?"

"Well. There was something forbidden."

"Meaning he was married?"

"Maybe."

"Or?"

Janet shrugged. "Or maybe *he* was a *she*. Some prominent man's socialite wife. And why not? After being so hurt by Lucas, why on earth would Kay get involved again with another male?"

"Do you think her new lover might have killed her?"

"What? *No.* Is that why you're here?"

"I'm here to listen to whatever you have to say." *No matter how much it hurts.*

"Kay spent her life putting criminals behind bars. She could spot a psychopath a mile away — except, of course, for Lieutenant Lucas Hunter. But she definitely wouldn't miss spotting *another* one."

SEVENTEEN

"That didn't take long." *Look at me, Galen.*

But she didn't. Wouldn't. "No. It didn't." *The truth is so easy, Lucas. For everyone but you.*

"Meaning Janet wouldn't talk?" Lucas asked gently. *I'm not disappointed, Galen, if she refused. You haven't failed.*

Galen heard the gentle persuasion of the master seducer. And looked away. Toward the river that was a glimpse of gray through skeletal limbs of winter-bare trees.

"Meaning she would," Galen told the ice gray water. "Happily. Expansively."

"And did you learn anything useful?"

Oh, yes. So much. Too much. "Not really. Janet just wanted to vent. To grieve. She did say that Kay had had a new lover before she died." *A new lover, Lucas, unlike the old one, the man who doesn't care and tells such lies.*

Did that old lover, that purveyor of the blackest magic, care now? Would the revelation that Kay had found someone else evoke

the slightest trace of jealousy, or even a soupçon of regret?

Galen drew her gaze from the icy Hudson and saw nothing. *Nothing*. Only the granite of his face and his watchful gray eyes, as calm as a drowning sea, its currents lethal yet unseen as it waited to consume anyone foolish enough to take the treacherous plunge.

"Did she say who?"

"No. She doesn't know. The relationship was forbidden somehow. A married man, maybe. Or a married man's wife. Whoever it was, it wasn't sinister. Kay was deliriously happy." *At last. Without you.*

"Which doesn't mean that her lover, or her lover's husband, couldn't be the killer."

"No," Galen conceded. "It doesn't. I guess that's something you'll have to pursue."

"Yes," Lucas said quietly. *I will.* "Anything else?"

Just everything else. "Nope."

She was lying, he knew, and now she was walking down the snow-covered steps, away from the river and toward the park.

They walked in silence for three blocks.

"I have a little news," he said, then. "I got a call from San Diego while you were inside. Mark has iron-clad alibis for two of the four

nights. He doesn't know, by the way, about the letter you sent. But he's in big trouble. Internal affairs is investigating a number of allegations of misconduct."

It might have been good news. Once. But now it was simply news — which the one-trick pony would be unable to assimilate, given the other devastating news of this day.

She didn't have the emotional range, *hadn't* had it, even before her heart had shattered.

"So Mark's not the murderer. Does this mean I'm off the case?"

"If you want to be."

Yes! *No.* I *don't* know.

They walked in silence as heavy as the snow until just ahead, beneath trees aglow with aquamarine lights, stood the Tavern on the Green.

"Are you in the mood for a drink?" Lucas asked softly as the glassy edifice loomed inviting and golden and near.

A drink? With Lucas? Who *didn't* drink, or so he had said, when he was working on a case.

And who, during those rare times between cases, would drink too much. To daydream. To escape.

Or so he said.

What would it be like, she wondered, to

drink too much with Lucas Hunter? What lies, what daydreams, what escape?

And what excess? The pretense, perhaps, that they were like everyone else within the shimmering gold, flushed and vibrant lovers at twilight on this wonderland day.

"No," she replied at last. "I'm really not in the mood. But why don't you go ahead? I can walk the rest of the way by myself. It's safe. There are people everywhere."

It was true, and it was safe, and she wanted to go. Alone. And Lucas almost said yes. Because she wanted so desperately to flee. From him.

And he wanted not to imprison, but to protect.

He answered her with apology in the bitter cold air.

"I'm not in the mood, either. Let's go home."

Home.

The word taunted. Pierced. All the way home.

As Lucas took her coat, to hang in the foyer closet, he handed Galen the Ophelia sack.

The expensive parchment was crushed where he had held it, crumpled where his powerful hand had fisted and clenched.

His voice when he spoke seemed fisted too. Clenched. Too. "I bought what I thought the killer would choose. These items aren't my taste, Galen. And not yours. Just his."

"Slick."

It was far from the light, wondrous, wide-eyed *slick* she had whispered when he'd explained to her the state-of-the-art electronics of their snow and lavender phones. This *slick* was wary and wise, an informed assessment of the ruthless hunter who had every angle covered just so, including an intimate knowledge of the killer's erotic tastes.

"I told you why we should make these purchases."

Galen stared at the crushed parchment. "Yes, you did. To minimize the lies. Always good advice."

"Does that mean you're going to tell me what else Janet said?"

She studied the golden wildflowers. "It means you could tell me. The truth. About your relationship with Kay." *And with Monica and Marcia and Brynne.*

"I told you the truth. Kay and I worked together on a number of cases over a period of years. She prosecuted. I testified. The State of New York won."

Galen looked from delicate flowers to

slate gray ice. "Janet had a different version."

"There is only one version, Galen. But please tell me hers."

"She said that you and Kay were lovers."

"We weren't."

"And that you asked her to marry you."

Lucas drew a slow, deep breath. "No."

"And that you were forever telling her how much you loved —"

"No." His eyes were cold, clear, true. "What I've told you is the truth. The only detail I haven't shared, because Kay asked me to forget it ever happened, was a phone conversation we had a year ago on New Year's Eve. She was interested, she said, in me."

Interested. Was that a euphemism for *in lust? In love?* The sort of euphemism an honorable gentleman, discomfited by sullying the reputation of a lady, especially a dead one, might choose to use?

And was the master liar speaking the truth? Or was this yet another lie?

"And you said?"

"That I was flattered, of course. But that I was already involved with someone else. Which," Lucas Hunter confessed quietly, "was a lie."

"*Great.* Why?"

"Did I lie? Because the lie seemed more palatable, and maybe even more plausible, than the truth."

"Which is what?"

"That for quite some time I'd confined my sexual relationships to between cases only, and only when I was out of town."

What? Just how gullible did he think she was? Did he truly imagine that the virgin from Kansas, who excelled in Home Ec and never even took Health Ed, knew so little about sex — well, so little about his alarming sexuality — that she'd believe he would *or could* simply impose such austerity, such celibacy, whenever a killer — or a playroom of captured girls and Barbies — just happened to be nearby? "Don't lie to me now, Lucas. *Please.* It's too demeaning. For both of us."

"I'm not lying."

"So you have what, one-week stands every once in a while?" *Far away from Manhattan and in between drinks?*

"Something like that."

"But . . ." *that's so lonely, so empty.*

"It's just sex, Galen. Sex with women I'll never see again."

She could almost imagine it. The aristocratic playboy jetting off to the south of France to meet women as rich and sophisticated as he, and having sex with them, just sex, on his own terms. Sun-steamed and champagne-drenched and safe.

So safe. As safe as one could get, with no intrusion whatsoever on his privacy or his heart.

There was just one problem with this lie.

"It's been years since you've taken time between cases."

"Yes."

"*Years.*"

"That's right," he said softly. "It's been years."

She looked down, away, at the crumpled parchment, ever more crumpled, in her hands. "How did Kay respond to your . . . lie?"

"She believed it, laughed, and asked me to forget she'd ever called. Chalk it up, she suggested, to a dreary social life and too much scotch. Which I did. I've told no one. Until now."

"Did you see Kay again?"

"All the time. We were colleagues. It was as if the conversation had never happened."

So what Lucas Hunter was saying, among even more implausible things, was that Janet's version, *Kay's* version, was entirely

239

false . . . a fantasy created from whole cloth not by a naive seamstress but a brilliant prosecutor.

Was smart, savvy, sophisticated Kay that hopelessly deluded? That desperately in love? It seemed far-fetched. And yet Galen Chandler knew without a doubt, and with an ache that made her want to scream, that a woman might fall very hard for the gray-eyed sorcerer — especially a skinny scarecrow whose successes, such as they were, were merely flukes, and whose lonely heart had been imagining such wondrous things in the glittering gray. Like longing, like tenderness, like desire.

Illusions, surely, *de*lusions.

As she was being deluded even now.

Oh Lucas what do you want from me?

"It's very important, Galen, that you believe me."

I want to. So much. And maybe the part about Kay *was* true. But that other part, that this sensual male animal had been without love — without sex — for years . . .

"Well," he said softly. "Think about it, and let me know."

I don't need to think about it! I believe you. Of course I do.

"Okay," she murmured. She gestured with the parchment-and-wildflowers sack.

"Well, I'd better go put this in my room. And . . ."

"Take a hot shower? And maybe a nap? For the rest of the night?"

It had been a long day, beginning with the 3:13 A.M. call from the killer. At Lucas's insistence she had returned to bed but not to sleep, and once she had officially awakened for the day she had spent the entire snowy morning reading the rainbowed files of death as she began to plan the hour-long special that would air on Wednesday night.

At noon and together, she and Lucas had spoken by phone to Viveca, informing her of the killer's request for the special telecast. KCOR's news director embraced the request with sheer joy, and with suggestions that were, with few exceptions, summarily vetoed by Lucas.

Between the end of the conversation with Viveca and one-thirty, when they left the penthouse, Galen had combed and ribboned the Barbies' hair and wrapped the dolls in their tissue-paper cocoons. She readied herself, too, for the winter-wonderland afternoon that ended with the twilight of ice.

"I am tired," she confessed.

"Sleep well, Galen."

She nodded her thank-you and walked

from marbled foyer to the carpet of snow, the wintry trek that would lead to spring, the illusion of spring, in her pastel bedroom.

The journey in this winter gloaming was particularly stark, barren as it was of fairy tales and dolls.

Galen was halfway across the living room when he spoke.

"Galen?"

The rawness of his voice stopped her. Staggered her. And when she turned she saw the staggering rawness in his eyes. "Yes?"

"I've never been in love with anyone."

She almost ran to him, the gray-eyed iceberg. Full speed ahead. He stood there holding her turquoise coat, as he had been holding it all this time, not crushing it, not crumpling it, even as she'd challenged his lies.

Lucas Hunter stood in the foyer, smoldering and raw. And utterly still. With glacial calm.

It was, the maritime historians maintained, the calmness of that night which doomed the *Titanic* to its watery grave. Had the Atlantic not been so still, had there been waves, the captain might have seen eddies of foam where ice caressed sea . . . might have seen the glacial danger before it was too late.

"Neither have I," Galen said softly, seeing the danger despite the calm and knowing, even as she turned and fled, that it was — for her — already too late.

Far too late.

For the second she murmured the first lyric, *Neither have I*, a joyful chorus deep within started to sing the rest.

Until now.

Until you.

EIGHTEEN

Until now. Until you. Until now.

Until you.

The chorus echoed, a steady refrain, defiant and strong and sure. The lyrics were there as Galen took the hot shower Lucas had advised, a steady heartbeat amid steamy raindrops, even as reason imposed stern commands.

Okay, fine. You're in love with him. You're not the first, nor will you be the last, and you're in impressive company. Witness brilliant, successful Kay. But let's get a grip, shall we? This fantasy is supremely foolish and absolutely trivial compared to the issue at hand — murder.

Remember? *Murder.*

She *would* get a grip. All she needed was a little sleep.

Which would happen soon, she realized, as she emerged exhausted and floating from the steam.

She would float to her bed and curl beneath its plush comforter like a springtime bulb slumbering beneath the snow.

She'd be a rather gangly bulb. If such things existed. A sprawling mass of angles and points.

Such things *did* exist, a floating memory asserted. Remember the lessons of Home Ec? When Kansas schoolgirls learned to plant the gardens that transformed houses into homes?

Tulip bulbs were round, smooth, like chestnuts without their shells. And hyacinths, as embryos, were onion-like, with layers of purplish peel.

But then there were the baby daffodils: gangly, awkward, like her. Fine. She'd be a daffodil bulb. The point, reason reminded her fatigued and floating brain, was to get into bed and *go to sleep*.

There was just that one obstacle, that crumpled parchment sack. It lay where she'd tossed it in the center of the bed. *Fine.* She'd simply toss it onto the floor, to be opened an infinity of refreshed and infinitely reasonable moments from now.

Except that now she was unfurling the ivory edges that had been so harshly crushed by his strong — and gentle — hands.

And? She noticed the vivid colors only in passing, and the scant cut of satin and silk.

Not my taste, Lucas Hunter had told her. And not yours.

But quite definitely her size, the same scant and far from womanly size in which the scarecrow made utilitarian purchases for her meager breasts and bony hips. *Exactly* her size. Even though these garments weren't to be worn, were merely to be props to assist her in making silk-and-satin descriptions to a killer.

Lucas Hunter had seen the truth beneath her baggy clothes, and had found bold and sexy items which were not his taste, and not hers, but which existed in her size . . . and maybe, had she thought to look, she might have found bridal lingerie in her size as well — there, in that place of embroidered roses, where he had wanted her to be. Her taste. And his?

Until now.

Until you.

Her bedside phone began to chime, to scream. And why not? The electronic voice need not wait until she slept to awaken her from her dreams.

Galen stared at the phone, its soft lavender suddenly foreboding, drew a steady breath, and answered.

"Galen?"

"*Julia?*"

"Yes. Hi. It's me."

"Hi. *Hi.* I can't believe . . . how *are* you?"

"Worried. About you. I was just watching the news on FOX. Apparently there's some killer who's terrorizing New York? And who's calling you?"

Calling *us,* Galen amended with a jolt.

She'd been on the verge of curling beneath the plush comforter, not to slumber but to talk, to *talk,* to her long-lost friend.

Instead she opened her bedroom door to the image of Lucas walking away. The headphones were in his hand, discarded already, eloquent assurance of her privacy. He turned at the sound behind him. Briefly. Before turning away.

But Galen saw so much in that moment, so very much from the man from whom she had so recently fled. Lucas was happy for her, understanding what this phone call meant, *wishing* it for her. And there was something else, wasn't there, in his ice gray eyes?

Loneliness, and longing, as if *he* had hoped to be the one to give her such joy.

You're getting delusional again.

"Galen?" Julia asked into the lingering silence. "Is it all right that I called? In one of the newsclips, from a KCOR broadcast last Sunday, it looked as if you were wearing the mittens."

"I *was* wearing them, and it's *wonderful* that you called," Galen enthused quietly as she shut the door. "FOX really had a report? Lucas didn't phone you?"

"Lucas? You mean the police lieutenant? No. He didn't. Did you want him to, Galen? Did you ask him to?"

"No. I didn't. But Lucas knew how much it would mean to me to talk to you. I *had* to leave, Julia. And I couldn't even say good-bye."

"I know."

"You *know?*"

"Not the specifics. But it was because of Mark, wasn't it?"

"Yes. How did you find out?"

"He came to the house. Looking for you. More than once. Many times."

"Threatening you?"

"He threatened you, too, didn't he? Threatened you with us?"

"Yes. He did. He said if I ever tried to contact you . . . Well. I thought of clever ways to send messages to you. At least they *seemed* clever. But what if I was wrong? It was too great a risk. And too selfish. My peace of mind in exchange for Winnie's safety."

"I know, Galen. That's why I never called the sheriff, not even from a pay phone and with a disguised voice. I just didn't dare. I hated myself for not doing it."

"The sheriff? Hated yourself? Why?"

"What if you were dead? What if Mark had *killed* you? I allowed myself to believe that he wouldn't keep driving by the house, looking for you, if that's what he'd done — even though that would have been the *smart* thing for him to do if he had."

"It never occurred to me that you'd worry about that."

"You knew you were fine."

"I was alive," Galen countered. "But I wasn't fine."

"Will you tell me what happened with Mark?"

"Yes," Galen said softly. "If you'll tell me, Julia, about our sweet little Win."

They talked for hours.

Hours.

And as soon as they said good-bye, with promises for future chats and more, Galen left her bed to find him.

Him.

I do believe you, Lucas. I *do.* I believe you, and trust you, and you were *so right.* I needed to talk to Julia, and she needed to talk to me.

Winnie had lived until she was seven, the little girl who was never supposed to live at all. Her death six years ago had come just twelve days before Julia turned twenty-one. And in the years since Winnie's death? Julia had been working nights and weekends for a physician's answering service. She worked from home, from the house where she and Winnie and Gran had lived. Julia's life since Winnie seemed isolated to Galen, and terribly alone. And Galen sensed that Julia knew it too, was *beginning* to know.

Galen decided, on her journey from lavender to war, that she would tell Lucas all about Winnie and Julia, and about her own plans as well. She was going to return to Kansas. Sometime. She needed to see Julia and maybe even, *yes,* her mother.

Would Lucas care about the emotional journeys she planned to make?

Galen believed he would.

I believe you, Lucas. I *do.*

"Hi," she greeted from the war room door.

Lucas turned. And stood. "Hi."

He looked tired. And lonely. Alone with death.

"We've been talking all this time."

"That sounds good."

"It was. Very good."

He did care. She was right to trust him. She felt the resilient chorus on the verge of song, and with symphonic accompaniment this time — for she heard in the distance the mantelpiece bells.

She would get a very firm grip on her delusions. She *would*. Later. When this was all over. After Lucas. For the rest of her life. But for now, as soon as she managed a steadying breath, she'd tell him all about her conversation with Julia.

Lucas spoke first.

"There's something I need to tell you."

"Oh?" *Oh, no.* Galen's heart ached as she anticipated the confession she did not want to hear. Kay and I *were* lovers, Galen. And yes, I even said the three magic words. That's standard operating procedure for me. What can I say? I'm a bastard.

"Will you come with me to the living room?"

Galen nodded even as her racing heart flooded with dread, drowning already in the revelations to come.

The truth at last.

They were *all* my lovers, Galen. I just didn't want to tell you. I wasn't sure you'd understand. Your Midwestern naïveté, you know, your Kansan — no wait! Those were the killer's words, the *killer's* taunts. Not Lucas's. Never Lucas's.

The snowfield was barren still. But there was something new, a spot of color like a cluster of crocuses, on the glass-top table in the center of the room.

It was a photograph. Of Kay? Galen wondered as she drew near. A crime-scene shot, perhaps, a portrait of death from which the lieutenant had protected her once, but which was designed to convince her to help him still, despite all his lies.

Galen needed no such graphic inducement. Her heart was already drowned. I'll help you get him, Lucas. Why not?

Galen sank onto the couch without so much as a glance at the photograph.

"This was taken twenty-seven years ago today," Lucas said.

Today, Galen echoed in silence as she took the photograph from his hand. A day *like* today, she realized as she looked at it. A winter-wonderland day.

Far from a crime-scene photo, here was a snapshot of four children, three smiling girls and a solemn boy. The girls were on the verge of becoming little women, teetering on that delicate cusp. But they were still girls, rosy-cheeked and eager, and so proud of the snow castle beside which they stood.

The boy was younger. How young? Galen knew precisely. Lucas was thirty-six now, and the photograph was twenty-seven years old, so the boy — Lucas — was nine.

And beautiful. And solemn. He stared at the camera, not smiling, not laughing, and ashen not rosy.

He looked at once shell-shocked and searching, battered and brave, and desperate in a quiet, private way.

"This is you."

"Yes. And Marianne." Lucas pointed to the tallest of the three girls, the one who looked even then like Grace Kelly. Marianne stood beside the second tallest girl, blond too, patrician too, and delicate and frail. "And Fran."

And the third girl? The lovely original of freckles, of roses, of joy? "And she is?"

"Jenny." His voice was a whisper of love. "She's Jenny."

Galen whispered in reply. "Your sister."

"Emotionally. Yes. But Jenny was six when we met, and I was three. My mother is Helena Sinclair."

"As in . . ." Galen paused. Encapsulating entire lives into tiny little sound bites was not, after all, her forte, as Paul had so accurately observed. And Helena Sinclair's *entire* life wasn't even the issue. The celebrated British actress was alive and well and dazzling still, enthralling audiences even as she bewitched an ever-changing series of younger leading men.

"Yes." Lucas smiled faintly. "As in all of that. My father was an earl, married and much older than she. His affair with Helena was far from his first. But this time his mistress became pregnant."

"By design?"

"Not at all. Helena's first husband had left her with all the money, and the only title, she would ever need. What Helena wanted, all she ever wanted, was the unfettered freedom to pursue her career."

"Unfettered," Galen echoed quietly, even as other echoes — Lucas's allusion to his mother by her given name — thundered. "Without a child?"

"Without a child. The earl, however, was not so sanguine about aborting his flesh and blood. Not that he had any intention of welcoming his bastard son, he had two legitimate ones already, into his home. He merely believed I had the right to be born and that he had no right to prevent it. Helena was philosophical, and shrewd. The earl would assume full financial responsibility for me, the best in nannies and schooling that money could buy. His surname but not title would be mine, as would a substantial fortune to be held in trust until I was of age. Helena had a final demand. For herself. She wanted the earl to wield his immense influence and land her a leading role in an upcoming production on London's West End. She had the talent. She merely needed the break."

"Which her pregnancy provided."

"Yes and no. The earl died playing polo four months before I was born. The provisions for me were all in place. But he hadn't yet spoken to his West End friends."

"Oh." *Oh.* Galen had assumed that Lucas and the earl had become father and son after all, and that at some point, after Helena had vanished to pursue what became an illustrious career, certain man-to-man, aristocrat-to-aristocrat, revelations had been made. But if the earl died before Lucas was even born . . . "How do you know about conversations before your birth?"

"Helena told me."

"That she'd wanted an abortion?" *That she wanted to be rid of you — you — sight unseen?*

"Sure. It was nothing personal. How could it be? Neither was our relationship personal after I was born."

"How old were you when she told you?"

"Almost eighteen. A week away from inheriting the fortune she'd insisted be mine."

"So Helena wanted credit, gratitude, for making you rich? Even though, if left to her

255

own devices, you wouldn't have existed at all?"

It was a rush of outrage. *For him.* As if Galen truly believed the astonishing proposition that it would have been a great tragedy had he never been born.

"She didn't want my gratitude, Galen, and I very much appreciated her candor. It gave me insight into the man, the father, I had never known."

"And made you like him?"

"I guess so. Yes." Lucas paused, frowned. Then he said, very softly, "What I really want to tell you about, Galen, what I need to tell you about, is Jenny."

Jenny. Jennifer Louisa Kincaid. Beloved daughter and only child of playwright Lawrence and ballerina Isabelle . . . who died during her daughter's birth.

Lawrence absented himself from Broadway after Isabelle's death, absented himself from everything save the care and nurturing of his little girl.

Father and daughter lived in Chatsworth in Westchester County, an elite enclave of power and wealth within commuting distance of New York. It was there, at the estate called Bellemeade and while Jenny was sleeping, that Lawrence penned his tour de force play in memory of wife.

Pirouette was in essence a one-woman show. And when it came time to cast the virtuosa role? Lawrence chose the actress who'd been stunning London theatergoers for the past three years: Helena Sinclair.

Six-year-old Jenny Kincaid and three-year-old Lucas Hunter met six weeks later. And the die was cast. He was *hers,* this serious little boy who rarely spoke but knew so much — an ancient knowledge, it seemed, solemn and wise. Lucas had been raised by an ever-changing cast of nannies, all of whom were terrorized by the exacting Helena and not particularly enamored with their mostly silent charge.

Lucas was silent. As was Jenny, at least in the strictest sense.

She'd been born deaf, and mute.

But Jennifer Louisa Kincaid was a chatterbox with her hands. A whirling dervish of charm, of grace, of joy.

And Jenny could be quite bossy with her surrogate baby brother, issuing admonitions, elaborately signed, directed at him but reminders mostly for herself. Lucas! We need to wipe our muddy shoes! And — with hands on her hips between the dancing signs — if we eat *all* this Halloween candy, Lucas, we're going to get really, *really* sick!

Jenny chattered with her ballerina hands, Isabelle's hands, and she danced as her mother had, and spun and twirled. But Jenny would stop, everything would stop, when Lucas had something to say.

To sign.

Years later, Lucas Hunter would learn to speak the Queen's English, beautifully, flawlessly, with elegant, eloquent diction and style. But that would always be his second language.

Jenny's was his first.

Lucas signed, and Jenny signed, and Lawrence signed.

And although Jenny never mouthed words herself, she became a wizard at reading lips. Her vision was eagle-eyed, and Jenny Kincaid took impish but never intrusive delight in recounting conversations that no one else could hear.

Do you hear, she would sign, what I see?

For six years Lucas lived at Bellemeade. Lucas, Jenny, Lawrence. And Helena? She would have been quite happy to become the mistress of the grand estate, Lawrence's mistress, but it wasn't to be. Lawrence was in love with Isabelle. Still. Always.

So Helena Sinclair lived in Manhattan, and for those six idyllic years Bellemeade became her son's only home.

Lucas would remember forever the brilliance of that time, the exquisite clarity of a world so bright, so sparkling, so pure.

Jenny was a dancing star, a golden sun from a galaxy of joy, and he was a minor but grateful moon spinning in her exuberant orbit.

They were a family at Bellemeade, and they were part of a larger family, too, the cloistered community of Chatsworth, of privilege and of wealth, where everyone felt safe.

Eventually Lucas Hunter had three big sisters. Jenny and Marianne and Fran. It was Lucas who enabled Jenny's friendship with the other girls. Neither Fran nor Marianne signed, nor did they need to. Jenny read her friends' lips perfectly, signed her reply, and Lucas spoke aloud precisely what she had said.

Lucas Hunter's world was perfect, sparkling and clear, and so blindingly bright, perhaps, that the darkness remained hidden until it was far too late. Lucas sensed the darkness, the evil, two days before the brilliance shattered . . . that last week in January when Jenny was twelve and he was nine . . . and when the snow fell so pristine and so pure.

Lucas had no idea what the darkness was,

what it *meant*. Years later, he would become an expert at this, too, this language that was neither Jenny's nor the Queen's. But then, at age nine, Lucas knew only how it felt, this monstrous invasion of his soul.

The incursion came with pain, talons that pierced his heart, and with fear so cold it froze his blood, and with feelings that had no name. Not then. Lust, rage, madness, pleasure. He would know those names. Later.

Later. Lucas would not have believed, then, that there would be a later. He was certain he was going to die. He wanted to. *Deserved* to. For the unnamed feelings should not be permitted to live.

The feelings came that first time late at night. And in moments that felt like forever they were gone. But they returned the next night, piercing, clutching, *longer* this time, long enough to taint him, to change him, forever.

By daylight the evil was in retreat. But even on this winter-wonderland day, its shadow, its stain, remained. Lucas accompanied Jenny to the "park," the vast meadow between the mansions where the Chatsworth children played. She insisted that he come. Not to translate. She and Fran and Marianne could manage alone. But Jenny wanted Lucas with her, as did Marianne and Fran, to share this perfect day.

Besides, the three girls told him, they could use his help in building their castle of snow.

But Lucas didn't help. He merely watched, remote, detached, and wary. He was a stranger in this foreign land, this pristine place of laughter and joy. He stood, watchful and still amid the gaiety — watchful, on alert . . . for what?

Lucas didn't know, would not know until it was far too late, wouldn't realize until too late that it was the monster himself, his talons of evil carefully hidden, who stood before him and urged him to smile.

The camera was Fran's, but it was Marianne who suggested the photograph. And it was Brandon, *Brandon,* who took it.

Brandon Christianson was sixteen, a golden heir in a dynasty of power and privilege, a family of such prominence that in the minds of its many glittering members the rules that governed others simply did not apply.

Shortly after taking the photograph Brandon and his friends announced a new game, their game, that everyone was going to play. The park was a pagan village, and they were conquerors on skis, plunderers in the snow.

The sheer recklessness of their skiing had already wreaked havoc on the serenity of the day. But now there was purpose, destruction, in the marauding teenage quartet. They slalomed between the snow families, beheading with their poles, leaving preteen sculptors in tears even as they swooshed and whooped toward the ultimate prize: the snow castle with its pleading princesses and its solitary nine-year-old guard.

Lucas fought valiantly to keep the marauders at bay, positioning himself in front of the castle and grabbing at ski poles even as their wicked spikes pierced his skin.

Marianne and Fran joined the fray, as did Brandon's own sister, who was Jenny's age. For a while the winter air was filled with the soprano cries of girls, and the raucous laughter of adolescent boys, and the thud of sculpted snow being savagely whacked.

Then there was silence. For Jennifer Louisa Kincaid had something to say. To sign. She stood before Brandon, her hands a frenzy of impassioned rage and mesmerizing grace.

Jenny's eloquent tirade might have gone on forever. But Brandon's mother intervened. It was left to the beleaguered women of the Christianson clan — even those bound by marriage alone — to make amends for the arrogance, the entitlement, of their male children. And men.

Patricia Christianson invited marauders and victims alike to share hot chocolate and cookies in the ancestral home.

Jenny accepted only because Brandon's little sister was her friend and was so mortified by what her brother had done that she feared Jenny and Marianne and Fran would never forgive her. *Ever.* That was why Jenny accepted the invitation, as did Marianne and Fran. The only reason. It was most assuredly not because of Brandon's apology before the demolished castle.

It was there, before the snowy ruins, that Brandon reached for Lucas, who was too startled to move, and ruffled his hair as he praised his courage.

"You're a fighter, kid. A real fighter."

Was it Brandon's ruffling touch that drove Lucas away? Did Lucas feel as Brandon touched him the talons of evil piercing his soul?

No. *No.* Brandon's evil was in hiding still. Or was it?

It was a query that would haunt Lucas always, for maybe it was *he* who was in hiding — from the evil — *he* who was so fearful that he denied its malevolent access to his soul at the one time, of all times, when such access would have mattered most.

Had Lucas sensed the evil, had he *permitted* himself to sense it, he would have stayed with Jenny. Never left her side. Protected her until she was safely home.

As it was, Lucas returned alone to Bellemeade.

And when the evil visited him anew, more powerfully than ever before, somehow, somehow, Lucas compelled his frozen limbs to run to Lawrence, to the firelit study where the playwright worked.

And did Lucas scream his frantic message to the man whose hearing was as perfect as his?

No. He signed. As always. He signed.

Jenny needs us. Hurry. Please!

Lawrence did not question the command. Not then, and not after.

Then all that mattered was Jenny.

And *after* nothing mattered at all.

Man and boy raced into the winter twilight, past the ravaged snow village to the Christianson estate. Hot chocolate flowed, and a third batch of cookies was warming in the oven, and Marianne and Fran had closed ranks around Brandon's still-troubled little sister, and Brandon and his marauding comrades were watching TV.

But where was Jenny?

At Bellemeade, Brandon replied with a shrug. He had escorted her home personally an hour ago. She had wanted him to, permitted him to, proof that she had forgiven him after all.

Jenny was *fine*, Brandon assured. Fine, and at home.

Liar! Lucas signed the silent scream.

Then he was running once again, outside, into darkness. Lawrence followed, and Marianne and Fran. And eventually everyone did, including Brandon.

They followed Lucas in the darkness, to the darkness, for he was following an invisible trail that only he could see . . . a trail that led to torture, to rape, to death, in the boathouse by the frozen pond.

Twenty-seven years ago.

Today.

NINETEEN

"Brandon killed her," Galen whispered in the silence that fell in the snowy living room of the penthouse in the sky.

Her words were spoken to a panther. Lean. Taut. Ravenous for the kill.

"Yes. He did."

"Oh, Lucas. I'm so sorry."

"So am I. For Jenny."

Oh, so am I. For Jenny, and for you. "Did he confess to the murder?"

"No. Never. Not to murder. And he assumed only minimal responsibility for what he claimed had occurred. It was Jenny's idea to go to the boathouse, he said. Jenny, the twelve-year-old innocent who had been flirting with him since Christmas and had succeeded in seducing him on that January day. The only crime Brandon Christianson ever admitted to was poor judgment fueled by raging adolescent hormones. Jenny died by accident, he said, by *mistake* during a sexual game they both wanted to play."

"That's . . . grotesque."

"Yes. It is."

"But he didn't get away with it." *He couldn't have, please, not for what he did to Jenny, to Lawrence, to you.* "Did he?"

"That's a matter of opinion. He's still alive."

"But he went to prison," Galen insisted. "You told the police that it was premeditated murder, that you'd sensed it, *felt* it, two days before."

"Brandon went to prison, but not because of me. I didn't tell anyone, then, about what I'd felt. I'm not sure I even could have. And my testimony, the words of a nine-year-old boy consumed with guilt, wouldn't have carried much weight."

"Consumed with guilt?" For not recognizing the gift, the curse, that even now was impossible to define? For not knowing as a child that the shadow of evil could lurk in the glitter of even the most brilliant light? "You shouldn't have felt guilty."

"Nor should you," Lucas countered softly, "when Mark forced you to leave Julia and Winnie with neither explanation nor good-bye. But you did. Crime victims do. Fran and Marianne blamed themselves for permitting Jenny to leave alone with Brandon, even though it was what Jenny wanted. And Lawrence . . . well, I'm not sure in what way Lawrence imagined himself to be responsible for her death. But he did. Everyone did. Except Brandon."

"But Brandon *did* go to prison."

"Yes. And without the trial that would have been a spectacle unworthy of the dynasty. The family's eagerness to avoid publicity gave the prosecutor powerful ammunition in the plea-bargain process, as did the aversion to attaching *murder*, of any degree, to the Christianson name."

"So he pleaded to manslaughter," Galen deduced, with the informed frown of the Gavel-to-Gavel reporter she had been. Depending on the state, and the judge, the penalties for manslaughter ranged all over the map, from trivial to . . . "What did he get?"

"Twenty-two years."

It was, Galen knew, a significant win for the state. A significant win, a substantial sentence, unless you happened to be the twelve-year-old girl who died. Or the loved ones who survived.

And there was that *other* problem, that fine print, the joke that was perpetrated on victims' families everywhere. "When was he eligible for parole?"

"After nine and a half years."

Galen recalled what he had told her about the nineteen-year-old who drank too much — and other excesses — in reaction, in part, to where he'd spent the years before. "During which time you were in boarding schools in England."

"For most of that time. Yes." In fact, Lucas's incarceration had begun even before Brandon's had, at the moment of Jenny's death. And when it came to being shipped off to England within days of the murder and at Helena's behest, there was no plea-bargaining at all, no request for mercy, least of all from him. Lucas attended the most elite of boarding schools, austere confinements of discipline, which he welcomed, and of sound, of speech, which he did not.

"When I was seventeen I got a letter, out of the blue, from Fran. She included the photograph, and the sobering news that the parole hearing was little more than eighteen months away. I'd been thinking about college, followed by law school, although I hadn't actually considered applying over here. But suddenly that made sense. It was at the initial parole hearing that I revealed for the first time what I'd felt during the days before Jenny's death. I hadn't planned to, hadn't made any plans at all, except to express my strong belief that Brandon should not be released. The conventional wisdom was that he would be. He was a model prisoner, a college graduate by then, working on an advanced degree."

"And except for drinking too much, and other excesses, you were a model student."

"Hardly." He'd been a poster child for self-destruction, imposing punishments far more harsh than any civilized, if severe, disciplinarian would have ever doled out. "For some reason, however, the parole board listened to me. Maybe it was my accent, which was quite pronounced back then."

Or maybe it was your passion, Galen thought. Maybe you told the parole board about Jenny's dancing hands and sparkling eyes. "They denied parole."

"Yes. With the next hearing set for the following year." *Enter Viveca.* But there was no point, Lucas decided, in mentioning Viveca's attempt to seduce him, or drug him, into failing to appear. For the moment, until the Lady Killer was subdued, he and Galen and Viveca needed to work as harmoniously as they possibly could, and given Galen's ferocious indignation about the mother who would quite happily have aborted him . . . "It was a significant year for Brandon, although he didn't know it, and for me. I'd spent quite a bit of time helping the local police solve a murder."

"You sensed the killer."

"Yes. Which meant a homicide lieutenant testified to the parole board that what I'd said the year before was undoubtedly true."

And over the ensuing years, Galen realized, there were more testimonials from law-enforcement officers, all of which kept Brandon Christianson precisely where he belonged.

"Brandon served his full term, didn't he?" *Because of you.*

"Yes. He did."

Served. Her own word echoed. Jenny had been murdered twenty-seven years ago today, and Brandon had been imprisoned for twenty-two years, which meant he'd been out, *free,* for almost five.

"And since his release?"

"He's been on his best behavior. He divides his time between Marbella and Greenwich."

Marbella was fine. *Spain.* But Greenwich? "He lives in Connecticut? He's that close?"

"That close. But when Brandon's in residence in Connecticut, he keeps pretty busy writing what I assume will be his next spiritual bestseller."

"Oh *no*," she whispered with comprehension. And horror. "Brandon wrote *Speaking with God*." Brandon Christianson, Jenny's killer, was the anonymous author who had chosen, in lieu of a nom de plume, a golden sign of the cross. "That's *despicable*. He's . . ." There were no words. Only a quiet query of hope. "Is Brandon the Lady Killer?"

"I wish he were, Galen." His ice gray eyes, ravenous for the kill, told her how much. "But he's not."

"You're *sure?*"

"Positive. He's been partying on the Costa del Sol since mid-December, before Kay died, and from the moment Rosalyn received the killer's first letter until after Marcia was murdered he was under police surveillance over there."

"He could have eluded the surveillance," Galen insisted, suddenly ravenous, too. She wanted an end to Brandon Christianson, something quite decisive and very final.

"He could have. But he didn't. And there's more. I know how Brandon Christianson's evil feels inside me. The Lady Killer is someone different, Galen. Someone else."

Someone else. Another monster. Not the

one who'd caused such destruction to Jenny. And to those she loved.

"Are you and Lawrence still close?"

"I'm not sure we ever were, except in our feelings for Jenny."

"But . . ."

"Besides, even within families, the survivors of violent crimes — especially the murder of a child — often withdraw from one another. They care about each other still, often more fiercely than before, but it's difficult for them to spend time together. So much, everything, has changed. They feel great guilt that they survived and the loved one didn't, and they are haunted by what they might have done, could and should have done, to prevent the death. I told you I don't know in what way Lawrence feels responsible for Jenny's murder, but I'm very certain that he does. I'm quite sure he feels he didn't protect her enough, that he permitted her to get into a situation in which, had she been able to scream, she might not have died."

"But to protect her absolutely he would have had to cloister her at Bellemeade, within the mansion, and he would have had to forbid her from going outside to play with her friends — perhaps from even *having* friends." Galen stopped abruptly as she remembered Jenny's friends and *why* Jenny had them: because of the solemn boy who was her personal translator and enabled the lively chatterbox to expand her horizons far beyond the walls of Bellemeade. "Are you saying that Lawrence might blame you?"

"No. He would never do that."

"Blames himself, then, for permitting you . . ." *into his home?*

"No. He wouldn't do that, either, because in essence that would once again blame me."

Galen heard the fondness, the respect, the loss. "Have you seen him?"

"Sure. Lawrence spoke at every parole hearing."

Like you. "You must have spoken to each other then. He must have thanked you for being there."

"We spoke briefly, sometimes. There wasn't much to say. We always sat next to each other," Lucas added quietly. "I'd almost forgotten that. But he never thanked me. Nor would I have expected him to. Any more than I would have thanked him."

Because you were family, Galen thought. Jenny's father. Jenny's brother. And father and son? For those six years of chattering silence and shimmering joy?

Galen looked again at the photograph, the

winter day when the brilliance shattered, and at the image of Lucas sensing evil, but too young, too innocent, to understand, yet searching still, wanting desperately to know what it was and so ready to protect the ones he loved.

Lucas would have died for Jenny had he known. For Jenny. And for Lawrence.

Had he known.

Galen looked up to the adult version of that fearless little boy. He was a panther now, fearless still, always, and in complete control even now, at this moment, as he sensed evil anew.

Galen saw the change in his dark gray eyes, the cold determination, the calculated calm, and the reassuring smile *for her* even as the unspeakable horror was filling his veins . . . and several heartbeats before her lavender phone began to ring.

"Galen," Lucas urged softly, moving to the headphones even as he remained focused so gently on her. "You need to answer."

But I don't want to! I want to talk to *you,* Lucas. Only you. And if this is the night the killer wants me to pretend to make love to him . . . I *can't.*

"Galen." His voice was soft still. But it had become a command.

Which she obeyed, as she must. She returned the photograph to the glass-top table and walked the short impossible distance to the phone.

"Hello?"

"Galen," the electronic voice cooed. "My pet. You sound annoyed. Did I call at an awkward time? Notice I didn't say *intrude.* I'm not the intruder, Galen. Never forget that. I'm your savior, your *lover.* May I assume you're wearing something deliciously erotic? Something in purple satin with gaping windows of lace?"

It was so close, too close, to one of the purchases Lucas had made. In her size. But not in his taste. Or hers.

Only the killer's, precisely the killer's, as Lucas had so precisely known.

Galen didn't search for Lucas. She looked instead at the snow-white carpet, pristine and pure. Her taste. And his.

"No," she replied. "I'm not."

"*Excuse* me? We had an agreement, my love."

"For the one-hour special on Wednesday night."

"And for bed, Galen. To wear for me in bed. To be wearing *for me* when I call."

"I'm not *in* bed."

"No? Well, all right then. I won't murder anyone — tonight. Especially since you already may be somewhat annoyed by the change in plans."

"Change in plans?"

"There won't be a one-hour special, after all."

"Oh. All right. May I ask why?"

"I was hoping you would. I've decided that the entire Lady Killer production needs a little more tension. Did you ever see *Jaws*?"

"No."

"You should. It's a masterpiece, Galen, the marriage of undisputed genius with a quirk of fate. The mechanical shark wasn't ready, apparently, when the filming began. But Spielberg transformed bad luck into brilliance. Since he couldn't provide shot after shot of carnivorous shark, he created something far more frightening, the *promise* of said shark. The ominous music. The swimmers splashing in terror. The rippling pools of blood where the feasting had taken place. And all, by the way, beneath deceptively calm seas and summertime skies. You see how that creates tension? That's what *we're* going to do, Galen, you and I. I'll lurk beneath the surface, playing hard to get with the terrified world, while you play hard to get with the lieutenant. Feel free to drive him crazy. That's what *sexual* tension is all about. But do not let him touch. I want *our* production to be the masterpiece of all masterpieces."

She was clutching the phone so tightly that her hands were the color of the carpet. "Our production?"

"Is that an edge in your voice? Sexual tension already? Or just annoyance with me? Most women would die — literally — for the chance to be locked up, locked *in,* with Lucas Hunter. That's what's going to happen, Galen. Beginning right now. Deliveries will be permitted. But no *visitors.* And if either of you leaves, even for a moment . . . well, the great white shark has another meal. You'll be bride and groom in a honeymoon suite, but without the honeymoon. Until I say so. At which point I'll personally direct every delicious detail over the phone. Lucas will be my surrogate. In *every* way. Touching you, exploring you, invading you, *knowing* you."

"That's . . ."

"What, my pet? Sick? Brilliant? Impossible, perhaps? Do you think the lieutenant might be unable, or unwilling, to perform the deed? How precious you are. How naive. You may not be his *first* choice, Galen. But you're his only one. And you will become ever more desirable — may I say irresistible?

278

— with each celibate day. *Especially* if, my one-trick pony, you prance around in your Ophelia attire. I believe you *can* prance, Galen, and you *must* if you have any doubt at all about the lieutenant's interest in you. You must do everything you can to make him want you. You do not, *do not,* want to see the bloodbath that will result if the two of you don't, *can't,* do precisely what I say. So torment him, Galen. *Drive him wild.* But do not let him touch you until I say it's time. *So.* That's all for now. Back to my watery depths. I'll surface when I get hungry for blood. *Or sex.*"

TWENTY

The ice storm engulfed Manhattan late Monday night. The ice storm *outside*. Within the penthouse the storm began on Sunday, the moment the Lady Killer ended his call.

"Get some sleep," Lucas commanded. His voice was cool, the storm's first zephyr.

Then he left the room, a man possessed. Obsessed. Racing with solemn purpose and stunning calm against the invisible, impossible clock.

It was a solitary pursuit. A private dash against madness. A personal war.

Galen's only task was to stay out of his way.

Which she did. But she would wander close to where he was, unable to resist. She'd stand in the hallway outside the war room, her footfalls silent in the snow, and listen to the sounds within.

Often she heard only silence, the hush of his concentration, the intensity of his thoughts, then the sound of his strong lean fingers on computer keys as he searched the Internet, the universe, for clues. And sometimes she would hear his voice, the tone not the words, occasionally harsh, occasionally gentle, always in control. He was issuing commands, she assumed, to police officers, and speaking with quiet compassion to the families of the women who'd been slain.

Lucas received phone calls, too. His ice white phones rang around the clock. Occasionally there was a double ring, the signal that someone stood outside the steel door twenty-two floors below. Lucas could view the intruder from a monitor in the war room and could enter a code from there to release the latch.

Most visitors were cops. They came bearing documents that were, Galen imagined, either too unwieldy or too intricate to fax, including on one occasion something rolled in a yard-long black plastic tube. A poster, perhaps. Or blueprints.

The cop-couriers never set foot inside the penthouse. They remained within the elevator even as they delivered their packages to Lucas, or to her, or simply placed them on the marbled foyer floor.

Galen happened to be in the kitchen making tea when the elevator door opened to Paul. She had known someone was coming. She had heard the double ring followed by the sound of the elevator's swift ascent. But Paul?

He had a delivery apparently, something within a document-size manila envelope, something she would have retrieved from him had not Lucas appeared. The two men exchanged a few hushed words. Hushed because of her? Galen doubted it. Neither seemed to have noticed she was near.

Then Paul left, and Lucas returned to the war room, and that was late Monday afternoon.

The storm hit, outside, a few hours later. The Tuesday morning world awakened to destruction, a blanket of ice that coated roadways, crumbled trees, and froze even the air.

Power lines sagged and snapped throughout the northeast. Residents of the Big Apple, however, were lucky. Most were spared the loss of light and heat. The temperature within Lucas Hunter's penthouse remained balmy, a thermostat setting, Galen guessed, that had been established for her comfort, a level far higher than the man of ice — with fires ablaze within — could possibly need.

The penthouse was balmy. But Galen was

so cold on this Tuesday. From the storm within. She curled beneath her comforter, a gangly and shivering daffodil, and she shivered still, despite the showers she took.

Galen emerged from her room at twilight, in pursuit of tea so hot she could barely hold the mug.

She had planned a direct journey to the kitchen. But she veered, was compelled to veer, to the windowed vista of the terrace and the icy beauty that shimmered there.

Icicles adorned the wedding-cake fountain, glistening and clear, save where they were touched by the pale golden rays of the winter sun. There, where sunglow caressed crystal, Galen saw rainbows.

Rainbows. Within the icicles. Pastel promises frozen in ice.

"I miss the Barbies."

The words, the softness, came from behind her and across the room. But Galen felt the heat, his heat, and the chill within began to yield to a melting joy.

"You do?" she asked, gazing still at rainbows. You miss the Barbies? The fairy tale? The improbable enchantment of scones and dolls?

"I do." He was closer now, his voice softer, his fire hotter. "I'm very sorry, Galen, about the past day and a half."

It was a gentleman's apology, urbane and polite, as if she were his neglected house-guest. Or his abandoned bride.

But, a voice within reminded her, a sharp remnant of unmelted chill, you are neither. And the enchantment of scones and dolls? Kindly remember the main topic of that fairy-tale day. Death. *Death.*

Galen, who was not an abandoned bride, abandoned the ice-frosted wedding cake with its promises of rainbows. She met the cool, polite eyes of a gentleman . . . and the glacial gaze of a hunter.

"You have a killer to catch." Galen saw something else then, as far away from rainbows and fairy tales as one could possibly get. "You know who he is."

He might have been annoyed, this ice-man who could not be read but who had permitted her to glimpse the truth. If so, Lucas's annoyance with himself remained frozen deep within.

What Galen saw, for her, was a silvery glint.

"Yes, Detective Chandler, I do know. It would be best, however, if you didn't know even that, much less who he is."

"Because I'm not the world's best liar," she murmured. "Because I might inadvertently tip him to the fact that I know — or, more significantly, that *you* do."

"We have to catch him literally in the act. *Before* he murders but *after* his intent is abundantly clear. Indefensibly clear. Anything less, even compelling circumstantial evidence such as finding your cell phone in his possession, and he'll walk. And if he senses we're on to him, he'll go to ground — or, in his delusional scenario, swim out to sea. Perhaps forever."

"I know nothing, Lieutenant. Absolutely *nothing.*"

"Good."

His faint smile was devastingly sexy, and it only became more devastating as it made the transition from sexy to sexual. Too devastating. And accompanied by an expression so fierce, so searching that Galen might have looked away. Had his ferocious gray gaze not imprisoned her.

"What, Lucas?"

A lean finger touched her cheek, a caress of unbearable gentleness. And stunning heat. "I've missed you, too. Even more than the Barbies."

"You have?"

"I have." His finger found a curl, flame touching flame, and moved it with exquisite care from her eyes. "Too much."

"Too much?" Like drinking too much,

you mean? An excess which enables you to escape, and to dream? Escape with me, Lucas, *dream with me.*

"Too much." The confession was fierce. Primal. Ancient. Male. And shattering, for he withdrew his touch, and with it the heat and the dream. "This might be a good night to give Jean-Georges a try."

The gentleman, this impeccable host, was suggesting room service, penthouse service, delivered by Manhattan's best despite the icy streets.

Galen hadn't eaten. But she wasn't hungry, merely ravenous, and so very bold.

She drew his hand — the heat, the dream — back to her face.

"Tell me what you want," he said softly as his thumb grazed, so gently, her trembling lips.

"You," she whispered. "I want you."

And Lucas wanted her.

He kissed her carefully at first, and with such care, and then devouringly, as she kissed him in reply, with welcome, with passion. And springtime. And joy. And need. Such need, for both of them, for more.

And then, *but* then. Lucas tasted her worry even before she drew away. And as he searched her shimmering springtime eyes, he saw worry and worse. He saw fear.

Lucas cradled her face in his hands as if holding the most precious of treasures. "Galen?"

"What about . . ."

"We won't do anything you don't want to do. Not anything. And I'll stop, I promise I will stop, whenever you say. When*ever*." Lucas touched the lovely lips that were damp from his passion. "We could spend the entire night kissing."

Galen frowned slightly and knowingly, needing more than kisses, as did he. Wanting more. "We could?"

His laugh was soft, husky, low. "Sure."

She shook her head, a dance of flames. "I wasn't worrying about that."

"No?"

"No." *This is what I want, this night with you. This impossible dream.* "It's just that we're not supposed to be . . ."

"Doing this? Because a psychopath warned us not to? This is about us, Galen. You and me. No one else. Nothing else. Just us. Okay?"

"Okay."

"And Galen, if you tell me to stop, I will stop. No matter when."

"I won't tell you to stop." *Not ever.*

And she didn't, in her bedroom of hyacinths, as he made love to the gangly daffodil in the canopied bed where once — long ago — she had been so cold.

She was blooming now, that awkward bulb, blossoming before his eyes . . . because of his eyes, his mouth, his hands, his voice, his touch. For it was wonderingly, cherishingly, that Lucas made love to her, all of her, every meager patch of translucent flesh.

He loved her breasts as if they had been created just for him, and he had been searching for these breasts, only these, all his life. And he had been searching, too, for her bony hips, and her too long limbs, and her pointy nose, and her huge blue eyes, and her brave, eager, ravenous mouth.

"Galen," he whispered as he loved her. Galen, Galen, *Galen*.

She was his, and always had been, and she felt, and she knew, the desperateness of his search for her. But now she was found. And his. At last. His.

Finally, finally, he possessed her, claimed her, as she wanted so desperately to be claimed. And it felt to her like being home. At last.

Home. At last. With him.

Lucas possessed her still in the lavender darkness when Galen felt the greater darkness, the horrific blackness, come to him. His strong sleek body changed in a heartbeat. Lover no more. Merely panther. Merely hunter. Motionless but on alert as he listened to a thunder only he could hear.

"He can't call now," Galen whispered, she implored, even as the phone began to ring. "He *can't*."

Lucas left her, a motion of swift, sure power as graceful as the one that had claimed her, and which hadn't hurt her. Not then. But as he left her now, she hurt terribly, a deep, depthless, ache.

"You need to speak to him, Galen." Lucas's voice — was it truly the same voice that had whispered *Galen?* — was hauntingly calm. "Tell me when you're ready."

There was only the one phone, hers, and no headphones. But Lucas no longer needed the intimacy of headphones, that stereo of evil. He knew who the killer was.

Galen's speakerphone would do.

Lucas was standing, a naked shadow poised to depress the speaker button on the phone. He seemed to know precisely where that button was, even in the darkness, as if he had made certain *in advance* that he knew.

"Galen?"

"Yes. Okay." She sat up, unaccountably clutching the comforter to her breasts, covering the nakedness he knew so well and had wanted so much. "I'm ready . . . Hello?"

"Are you bleeding, Galen? Hemorrhaging?"

"I beg your pardon?"

"You just *couldn't* resist him, could you? Don't bother to lie, Galen. I know. A woman like you, especially like you, could not possibly resist a man like him."

"No. You're wrong."

"I'm not wrong, my pet, and it's a little late for 'no,' don't you think? That might have been the thing to say to Lucas. But you couldn't, could you? You were too weak, too *needy*. But don't worry. I'm not upset. Everything's gone precisely as planned."

"As planned?"

"You didn't really believe I cared about your career, did you? Good God. Maybe you did. Your pathetic naïveté knows no bounds. Well, Dorothy, we're not in Kansas anymore. It was a *game*, that's all, part of the bigger game between the lieutenant and me. You were merely a piece, *the* piece, as it were. But now the game's over. At least for you. And for the Lady Killer's next victim, of course, your victim, Galen. The woman who dies because of you."

But she won't die! Lucas won't permit it! He knows who you are!

But the killer cannot know that, an inner

290

voice reminded her. You cannot let him know. "You can't kill someone just because we . . ."

"Because you *what,* Galen? *Made love?* Is that what you think you and Lucas Hunter did? Think again. Better yet *ask* him while I'm carving up lady number five. Speaking of which, I really can't spend any more time with you, Galen. I have a woman to kill."

The dial tone came, then Lucas's hand disconnecting the call. Galen looked up. To him. Lucas. *Who was dressed.* Who had gotten dressed even as he listened to the killer's words.

Now Lucas was placing a call, which was answered on the first ring and amplified as the murderer's call had been.

"I'm here, Lieutenant," the male voice, a cop's voice, said.

"And you've got him?"

"You bet."

"Where is he?"

"In the park, heading your way, just like you predicted he'd be. We'll know in about a minute whether he turns right or left when he reaches Fifth — assuming, that is, he doesn't kill himself on the ice. He's moving pretty fast."

"Are the teams in place? In*side?*"

"Yeah."

"Was there a problem?"

"Just the usual surprises. The husband wasn't home at the Lexington location and the wife wouldn't let us in. She'd seen too many warnings on TV, wouldn't open the door for strangers, even ones, especially ones, claiming to be the police. The guys on the scene encouraged her to phone 911 and she ended up talking to me. The team's inside now. She's making coffee for them while they wait."

"And the problem at Park?"

"The adjacent unit wasn't quite as empty as we expected it to be. The owners had given keys to selected neighbors in case of emergency, for which the ice storm apparently applies. The fellow who's stranded by the storm and spending the night had no problem, however, with letting us in."

"The sharpshooters?"

"Are exactly where they need to be."

"And the prosecutor?"

"Right here, in the van with me."

"And you are where?"

"Just pulling, *sliding*, into the alley behind your building."

"Okay. I'm on my way."

On his way. Galen saw his eyes, glittering in the shadows, anticipating the kill.

Lucas looked down at her. Touched her.

Cupped his hands around her face.

"It's almost over, Galen. Almost over."

That was his good-bye, that solemn vow.

Wait! Don't leave. Not yet. Please.

But Lucas Hunter was gone.

Long gone.

The question was had he ever been there at all?

The answer — *was* it the answer? — came in a flood of emotion, a wash of tears, of sobs, so drowning that Galen had to struggle simply to breathe.

Maybe this was normal, her thoughts gasped in harmony with her lungs. Normal. *Natural,* the nourishing rain that always spills on a deflowered virgin, especially one whose lover has to leave her, has to, at the time when she needs his reassurance the most.

Maybe this gasping deluge had nothing whatsoever to do with the deep, the depthless, ache.

But of course it did. Her tears, and her brain, had simply taken a little time to catch up with her shattered heart.

The sobs stopped as abruptly as they had started, and she became so purposeful, this creature without a heart, this Arctic explorer, alone for the first time in the snow and about to embark on the final adventure.

To invade. To intrude.

To violate.

As she had been violated.

Betrayed.

Galen pulled on her bathrobe and went to the war room. In search, perhaps, of the smoking gun? The battle plan on snowy white paper written in Lucas's unmistakably masculine script?

Identify the killer. That would be step one. Essential, and accomplished apparently during the two-day ice storm within the penthouse. Had it been good old-fashioned detective work that cracked the case? Or had it been black magic? Had Lucas managed to control what he had never been able to wholly control before? Had he manipulated his gift, his curse, to find the answer *now?*

Get everything in place. That would be step two. Which quite obviously had been accomplished as well. There were SWAT teams at two locations, and sharpshooters, too, just in case. And there was at least one more cop, plus a prosecutor, in a command-post van. And Lieutenant Lucas Hunter was also in that van, calling every shot.

Seduce Galen — no, let her seduce you. That had been the easiest step of all. Simple. Effortless. The final step in a plan so straightforward, so remedial, that there would be no telltale note.

But there might be other discoveries to be made within the war room, the clues so carefully hidden from the dispensable Detective Chandler . . . clues that would reveal not only the identity of the killer but of his potential victims, too; the two women who Lucas had decided were the most likely targets tonight.

Galen found the second answer first, the blueprints of the buildings on Lexington and on Park, and the names of the women who dwelled within. Rosalyn St. John lived at the Lexington address. The gossip columnist was an eminently logical possibility, Galen mused — a deduction commensurate with even her elementary detective skills.

But the other name came as a surprise. Viveca Blair. Did that mean, she wondered, that the killer was somehow connected to KCOR, *at* KCOR?

Yes. For here were folders, manila not rainbowed, a stack which seemed to include dossiers of KCOR's every male employee, with no one exempt, not even the station's grieving owner or its famous anchorman star.

The top folder was Wally's, a slim file which consisted in fact of only a single photograph, *the* photograph carried so proudly by Wally, the picture of his pretty wife and cute kids. This wasn't a wallet-sized photo, however, but an eight-by-ten, and there was a note attached from Paul directing Lucas to look at the information on the back: the copyright held by a commercial photographer and the names of the professional models who had posed for the shot, the kind of perfect family portrait that appeared in for-sale picture frames and wallets around the globe.

This wasn't Wally's family. Not Wally's. Not anyone's. But did this falsehood, this pretense, mean that meek, mild Wally might actually kill?

True, Wally had been devoted to Marianne and devastated by her death just eight days before the Lady Killer's spree began. And true, Wally had been routinely demeaned, discounted, by Viveca. And Wally had looked so awful that Sunday morning, when he said he'd been up all night worrying about the hostages and feeling the anguish of the girls' parents, for what if one of the captured girls had been his precious Annie?

But Wally had no precious Annie. Which meant, Galen supposed, that Wally had no alibi for the time when Dr. Brynne Talbot was killed.

Wally fit perfectly the profile of a serial killer. The quiet loner. The good neighbor. Who would imagine he would spend his lonely nights committing murder?

Not me, Galen decided. I wouldn't imagine it. I won't.

Nor would she have to, not for long, for now she was opening the second folder, the one assembled about Paul. Paul, of the dual personalities *at least,* and who had taken crime-scene photos for the NYPD — a fascination, perhaps, with death? — and who had admitted knowing Kay. Knowing her quite well apparently, for here was a photograph of Kay, nude but far from dead and very lovely . . . as was the other nude photo in Paul's folder. The one of Monica.

Monica. Paul had known her, too. Had he been involved with Kay, with Monica, with both? Or had he merely *wanted* to be, only to be rebuffed? And had each woman, as she posed for her photo, spoken glowingly, so glowingly, of Lucas?

That hostage-crisis night, when Paul had taken off instead of waiting in the midnight chill with her, he'd announced that he was going to spend the night making some woman very happy. Had he meant, a macabre joke, Brynne?

Then there were Paul's other words, the

warning that had been both prophetic and sincere. Lucas Hunter will do whatever is necessary to get this killer. Whatever. To whomever. He is ruthless.

Would such ruthlessness include deflowering a virgin to provoke a killer? *Of course it would.*

But the timing had been so perfect, right on cue. Had Lucas neglected to mention that his communication with evil went two ways? That he could *transmit* to a killer as well as receive?

Maybe. But such sorcery need not be invoked. Lucas had known from the start that the game was between himself and the killer. He had known, *both* players had known, that when the killer warned him to stay away from Galen, Lucas would do the reverse.

Had Galen been a better liar — or a woman with any sexual experience at all — Lucas could have just had her pretend they'd been to bed, and maybe even *were* in bed, whenever the killer called.

But Galen Chandler wasn't either of those things.

So the moment the pieces were in place, the SWAT teams on alert, Lucas Hunter had done what was necessary. The sacrifice of a virgin was not, after all, such a very big thing. Not for a primal hunter, an elemental male. Lucas had even performed the sacrifice in its most ancient way: by ripping the still beating heart right out of his victim's, his virgin's, chest.

But the hunter had gotten his prey. Mission accomplished. Game over. Time for her to go.

Which she would.

Soon.

Galen left the war room without reading farther down the stack of KCOR files. The killer's identity would be breaking news and then old news soon enough.

She had just one more stop, the final intrusion, before returning to the room of hyacinths and snowfall and love and lies.

His bedroom. Galen needed to see it. To see perhaps the photographs of his lovers. Kay and Monica and Marcia and Brynne. Nude photos, artful and exquisite, and taken by Paul.

But there were no photographs in Lucas's bedroom. No color at all.

There was only snow. Frigid and foreboding.

Here, Galen realized, were the greatest truths about Lucas Hunter. The only ones that mattered.

He was solitary, and private, and glacial.

He was the ice . . . and the storm.

TWENTY-ONE

She moved slowly, weighted and waiting, as if there were an imaginary deadline measured by wisps of hope.

Lucas will call, the wisps promised. He'll tell you it's over — for Manhattan's Lady Killer — but not for the two of you. *I'll be home soon,* he'll whisper. *Home, Galen. To you.*

Despite her weighted limbs and shattered heart, it took very little time for the bag lady to pack. What remained of the contents of the cardboard boxes fit nicely in a Bloomingdale's shopping bag that had been folded within. The scraps of fabric went in the bag, as did the thread, the patterns, the needles, the pins. The irons, mother and child, nestled amid her clothes in her suitcase.

Items another woman might have put in a purse went into her turquoise coat instead, in its innermost pockets with their Velcro seals. Money. Credit cards. Bankbook. ID.

There. She was packed. And moving ever

closer to her departure. Her suitcase and shopping bag, with her coat draped across, stood in the marble foyer. But there was more to do. Slowly. She stripped the sheets from her hyacinth bed, gathered her pink and cream and lilac towels, and placed the soft pastel bundle in the wash.

She wiped the snowy granite kitchen counters, a futile search for scone crumbs that were not there, and in the event that there was already news flipped on the kitchen TV.

There *was* news. Live. Breaking. On every channel.

Galen selected KCOR.

"We're awaiting official confirmation of what we believe to be true, that Manhattan's Lady Killer is dead."

Reporting for KCOR was Marty, who'd been officially assigned to cover the hospital hostage crisis that Saturday night, and whose dossier had been among the KCOR stack she did not read.

The killer wasn't Marty.

And what about the cameramen whose files sat at the very top of the stack? Their faces would not be visible, but she might be able to tell from the quality of the shots. The artlessness of Wally, the artistry of Paul.

Galen wanted *both* men to be outside the

building. And alive. And not responsible for the horrific crimes. Both of them. Safe and sound and sane. Wally, who'd been so nice to her. And Paul, who had tried to warn her, to protect her, as best he could.

The camera panned back as she watched, a reverse zoom that anyone could do, and revealed the scene. Lights flashed from a battalion of police cars and were reflected, their intensity all the more brilliant, by the ice-laden street. The building illuminated in that flashing glow was on Park. Viveca's building. Just six blocks away.

Lucas was so close.

Lucas.

A shadowed silhouette emerged from the building. Tall and elegant and lean. But not Lucas. And not someone, either, with information to disclose to the assembled press. The silhouette remained behind the yellow crime-scene tape until he vanished from sight.

But now there was another man, and he was stepping over the yellow ribbon and approaching the bouquet of microphones. He wasn't Lucas, or even a cop, but the prosecutor, the assistant DA who'd been in the van that had skidded into the alleyway below the penthouse in the sky.

The killer was dead, the prosecutor confirmed. Yes. Dead. And *yes,* definitely the Lady Killer. Was anyone else injured? No. No one. Although, the attorney noted, the intended victim was naturally upset. But she was fine. Unscathed. No, he would not reveal her name. Or the killer's. That name, the murderer's name, would be released in due course. There was the legal, procedural red tape to be attended to first. And of course the formal notification of family.

Family. The killer had *family.* Did that, Galen wondered, exclude Wally then and there? Was the faux family in the photograph the only family Wally had? She would not have wished that loneliness for him. For anyone. Yet she found herself hoping that Wally was an orphan, and Paul, and John, and — John McLain *was* an orphan, wasn't he? The self-made billionaire who'd been born with nothing, less than nothing, and who had created so much, only to lose the one thing that had ever mattered? But Marianne's sister was alive. Fran. Did a sister-in-law, once the sister was dead, qualify as family still?

Galen flipped off the TV. The identity of the killer was not a guessing game she wished to play.

Besides, the wisps promised, Lucas will tell you *so gently* when he calls.

303

Lieutenant Lucas Hunter was busy now, tending to the red tape of this, his, spectacular triumph. Far too busy even to *think* about making a call.

And she had things to do, anyway. More penthouse projects to attend to. Slowly. There were the Ophelia purchases, the actress's props that weren't her taste or Lucas's. The X-rated garments were in their crumpled parchment sack, in the foyer, beside her suitcase and bag. The gold-etched parchment and its contents could simply be dropped in the brass-handled chute, a free fall that would end in the subterranean trash bin twenty-four floors below.

But maybe she should shred the garments first. Lest there be tabloid scavengers in pursuit of Lady Killer memorabilia. Or maybe she should take the lingerie with her. The fabric was expensive and could be used for making clothes for dolls. It was something to ponder while she vacuumed, which she really *should* do, exemplary houseguest that she was. Maybe she'd make a snow angel or two. Or maybe an entire flock.

Or maybe, some terribly non-wispy voice suggested, just a massive snow-white skull? The voice became even less frothy as it issued the command. *Stop* it! It's *over*. And you are leaving, you *must* leave — now.

Galen looked at the snow-white clock on the mantelpiece. 11:29. Thirty-one minutes until midnight. The wisps reached a compromise with reason. At precisely 11:59 she would call for a cab, Cinderella summoning her pumpkiny coach, and by the clock's final chime of midnight she would be in the elevator descending to earth, and then she'd be on her way to the airport and then to Kansas, to visit Julia, and maybe, maybe, her mother.

The phone rang. Right then. At 11:29. Lucas's ice white phone. But that first sound, the one that gathered every valiant wisp into a billowy cloud of hope, was only *half* of the ring, for now the double ring, signaling a communication from just outside the building's thick steel door, was achingly clear.

"Hello?"

"Ms. Chandler?"

"Yes?"

"This is Sergeant Doyle, ma'am, from NYPD. The Lady Killer is dead."

It's over. I know. Oh, how I know. "Yes. Thank you. I saw the report on TV."

"Lieutenant Hunter asked me to come get you."

"Oh?" *Oh.*

"He'd like you with him at the scene."

"I'll be right down."

"Wait a moment, Ms. Chandler. There are some things the lieutenant needs from the penthouse. He said you'd be able to show me where they are."

"Oh, yes. Of course. Hold on while I release the latch. Once you're in, take the last elevator on your left."

Galen walked as she spoke. There was a code, she knew, that could open the heavy steel from any of the penthouse's snowy phones. But she didn't know what it was. So she walked to the panel in the foyer and pressed the button beneath the closed-circuit TV.

She might have turned the monitor on. But she didn't.

And did warnings sound in her brain as the latch released twenty-two flights below? Did she hear echoes of her own words, her own admonitions spoken from the anchor desk at KCOR to the women of New York? Be very sure to get *visual* confirmation of whomever you're letting in *before* you open the door. Do this *always*. Even if the voice is familiar. And if he's a stranger, especially one posing as someone you should trust, don't let him in at all.

No warnings sounded. Or perhaps they were merely muted to silence by the wispy cloud of joy. It *wasn't* over. Lucas wanted her with him. He'd sent someone to traverse the six blocks of icy sidewalk with her, protecting her even though Manhattan's menace was dead and even though she could quite easily have flown.

Alarms would not have sounded.

And even as the man stepped from the brass elevator into the marble foyer and the seamstress saw his overcoat of pure cashmere — a sharp contrast to the turquoise fluffiness she'd donned during the elevator's swift ascent — Galen felt more curiosity than concern.

Wealthy police officers existed. Witness Lucas. And Manhattan's Lady Killer was dead. Besides, she realized, this stylish man was the elegant shadow she had seen leaving Viveca's building, having been dispatched by Lucas to her.

Still, her journalistic instincts told her he was not the police sergeant he claimed to be. Not the sort of man accustomed to saying "ma'am."

"You're not Sergeant Doyle."

"No. And I apologize for the ruse. It's just so damned cold outside. Too cold for an elaborate explanation through an intercom."

"Who are you?"

"My name is Brandon Christianson."

"Brandon," Galen whispered, backing away, every instinct, survival not professional, on full alert.

"I see," he said quietly, "that Lucas has told you about me."

"Yes." *Yes.* She had backed as far as she could, as far as this wall of the foyer would permit, into a corner from which he could easily overtake her should she try to escape. She was trapped. But Brandon Christianson, *murderer,* appeared worried not satisfied with her plight. "I'd like you to leave."

"I will. I promise. But can you give me a minute? Please? Just a minute to listen to what I came to say? Maybe not," he offered in answer to his own questions. "You're *so* frightened of me. You don't *need* to be. But you can't possibly believe that, can you?"

"No," Galen murmured. "I can't."

"Okay," he said, backing away too, creating as much space between them as the marbled foyer would allow. "I'm sorry. This was a foolish impulse. It's just that tonight, when I heard Lucas's voice — the pain, the rage — I realized he'd been in prison all these years. I put him in that prison, Galen. But he went there willingly, caged himself, even though he never needed to be caged at all. I've learned so much over the years. So

308

much I've wanted to share with others. That's why I wrote my book. And then tonight when I heard his voice . . . well, I had this fantasy that with your help I could set him free. But I can see from your fear, from your terror, that my approach was misguided to say the least."

Brandon drew a breath and sighed. "You've given me my minute. I've forced you to. And now I'll leave. But I'm going to write to Lucas, as I've written to him so many times before. Maybe this time, though, with your help, my letter won't be returned unopened. Convince him to read it, Galen. Please. For his sake, for his *sanity*, for his freedom from a guilt he should never, *ever* have felt. And thank you for listening. Please accept my apologies for frightening you."

With that Brandon Christianson pressed the brass button embedded in marble beside the gleaming elevator doors. In moments the doors would part, and he would be gone, and she would be safe, and soon it would be midnight, and she would be on her way to the airport.

But wasn't she already safe? Safe *enough?* Manhattan's Lady Killer was dead. Brandon Christianson was not that monster. He was another monster, and he'd spent twenty-two years in prison, and Brandon was right, the man she loved was in prison still, and somewhere along the way Brandon had found God. *Speaking with God* didn't speak to her, but it spoke to millions, a source of comfort, of inspiration, of calm.

Brandon *had* to lie to her about his identity. She wouldn't have let him in had he not. And he'd promptly admitted the truth, and in his hurried confessional there had been other truths, anguished ones, about Lucas. His rage, his guilt, his pain.

Her gray-eyed panther was caged, imprisoned by his past. And now, as promised, the man who claimed he could set Lucas free was leaving, to write a letter which, she knew, Lucas would never read.

"Wait." Galen's voice was soft and strong. "You said you needed my help?"

"Yes. I hoped you would convince Lucas to see me, and maybe even be present when we meet."

"Why me?"

"Because of your relationship with Lucas."

"I . . . we don't really have a relationship."

"You don't? If Lucas told you about me, Galen, and about Jenny, I'd say you definitely *do*. As would Viveca. She's who told me you were staying here with Lucas. She also has the distinct impression there's something *significant* between the two of you."

"Viveca." There was apparently a connection between Brandon and Viveca that Lucas had chosen not to share — but which Galen might have guessed, given Viveca's certainty that she could induce the unnamed author of *Speaking With God* to come out from behind his glittering golden cross. "You and Viveca are?"

"Cousins. And tonight we were at her place, catching up on recent events, when the final chapter in Lady Killer horror began to unfold. Do you know who the killer is?"

"No."

"Well, I'll tell you if you like. The Lady Killer denouement is the reason I'm here, the impetus for my impulse to come to you for your help after hearing Lucas's voice. Maybe if I could tell you what happened, what I heard . . . would that be okay?"

Galen didn't hesitate. She had to help Lucas if she could. "Yes. It would."

Galen hesitated then, as her brain and her heart waged a silent debate about danger, safety, risk. The issue of risk was moot. Her heart had already made the commitment to hear Brandon out.

"Why don't we sit in the living room?" she suggested. One of her lavender phones sat atop the glass-top coffee table, an easy reach from where she would sit, and Brandon would sit on the opposite couch, farther away.

"Thank you," he said quietly. "That would be nice."

Brandon followed her into the living room, and obeyed her silent gestures — where he would sit, where she would — precisely. He draped his cashmere coat over the couch that was his and waited to sit until Galen had done so.

Galen sat, as did he. But Galen wore her coat still.

Brandon began to speak only after he realized she was not going to take the coat off.

"I said I'd tell you what happened at Viveca's tonight. And I will. But I think I should tell you first what I'd say to Lucas if I had the chance. If you decide there's no point in my saying those words to him, then there's really no point in my going into great and disturbing detail about the events of tonight. All right?"

"Yes. All right."

"Lucas is wrong about me, Galen. That's the bottom line. And I can see from your reaction that you don't believe it for a second and that you're suddenly very worried about letting me stay. But hear me out. Please. You're in no danger from me. None at all. The only danger is for Lucas, for his heart and his soul."

Brandon paused, waited, and only when Galen nodded slightly did he resume.

"I don't dispute Lucas's ability to sense evil. He has that gift. It's definitely real. And it's a blessing for all the victims and their families that he's helped. But Lucas's gift wasn't such a blessing for me. Or my family. Lucas told the parole board that he sensed evil, *my* evil, on the night precious Jenny died and for two nights before. I'm absolutely certain, Galen, that Lucas believes what he said is true. But he was only nine years old when Jenny died and he was devastated by her death. It's not uncommon, psychologists say, for a child so badly traumatized to subconsciously revise reality, to shift the sequence of events and even to alter memories entirely. It's normal, natural, and even necessary for emotional survival. What happened, I think, and the experts with whom I've discussed this theory agree, is that sometime *after* Jenny's death and *before* my first parole hearing, Lucas sensed his gift. But because of the impact of childhood trauma that I've just described, he believed the gift had been there earlier. But it wasn't, Galen. It *couldn't* have been. Because Jenny Kincaid died by accident, *accident*, not by design."

Liar! It was the word Lucas had signed that winter evening before running into the darkness to discover Jenny's body. But even as *liar* screamed within, another memory came to Galen, her *own* memory, the remembrance of a daydreaming girl who because of trauma — and the belief of betrayal — had misremembered for so long the happiness that mother and daughter once had shared.

"I killed Jenny," Brandon Christianson confessed in the sudden silence. "But it was an accident. It doesn't make much difference, *any* difference, to Jenny. And despite what Lucas may have told you, I've always accepted full responsibility for her death. I just wouldn't admit to a murder I did not commit. I killed her, but I didn't murder her, and the difference *to Lucas* is immense. He couldn't have sensed her impending murder, because there was no such thing. Which means he couldn't have prevented it, and cannot be in any way to blame, and he needs to stop being consumed, being destroyed, by his guilt. And that, Galen, is what I'd say to Lucas if I had the chance. Do

314

you think there's any point? Would he listen? Could he hear?"

Galen thought of Jenny. How could she not? And what Galen remembered at that moment was what Lucas had told her about Jenny's ability to read lips, how she would read a conversation a room away and then ask, her eyes dancing, Do you hear what I see?

Would Lucas hear Brandon's words? Perhaps. If he could see what Galen saw now, the solemn expression of contrition and of hope.

"I don't know," she answered. "But I'd like to hear the rest, what happened at Viveca's tonight."

Brandon took a moment to shift from the distant past to the far more recent one.

"I've been in Spain," he began, "since before Christmas. I returned about noon today. Even before leaving JFK, I learned that the power was out at my Greenwich home. So I came into the city and Viveca offered to put me up for the night. We were in her apartment, talking, catching up, when Adam called. He was worried about John, he said. Desperately afraid that John had gone off the deep end, that he had already done unspeakable things. Adam was going to convince John to accompany him to

Viveca's and they'd take it from there. Commitment was what Adam had in mind. Emergency admission to some private psychiatric facility where John could get discreet and confidential care. Viveca decided it would be best if I wasn't there when John and Adam arrived. Of course I agreed. I had other friends in Manhattan, one in particular I'd promised to see. Viveca had a key to the apartment adjacent to hers, which she gave me for backup in case my friend wasn't home."

"Which she wasn't," Galen said, recalling the icebound visitor the police had discovered in the apartment next to Viveca's on Park.

"I don't even know. After spending about a minute outside, I decided that the chill of the night coupled with the jet lag I was feeling made the neighbor's apartment sound pretty good. I didn't even tell Viveca, didn't really have a chance. A SWAT team descended, very quietly, about a minute after I let myself in. They had an arsenal of weapons, as well as some really impressive surveillance equipment, state-of-the-art gadgetry that enabled them and me — and Lucas in a van somewhere outside — to monitor everything that was happening next door. Adam arrived without John. But John

316

would be coming, Adam said. It was important to John's delusional mind that he arrive on his own. In the meantime Adam told Viveca what he already knew, what John had confessed, that he was Manhattan's Lady Killer."

Galen had guessed from what Brandon had said already that that would be the case. Still she whispered, "Oh, no. Not John."

"That was Viveca's reaction, too, and then some. She worships John, always has, and she's always believed that if Marianne hadn't come along, she and John would have been together. Who knows if that's true? Not that it matters. What matters is that Viv has always cared about John, and when Adam told her what John had done, that he was a murderer, she was terribly upset. It was a shocked hysteria, desperate but silent. I wanted to comfort her, to leave her neighbor's apartment and go to hers. But the SWAT guys wouldn't permit it. Besides, Adam was comforting her, even as he was trying to help her understand. I want you to understand, too, Galen. What I heard, what *Lucas* heard, exactly as we heard it. Which means, I'm afraid, it would be best to tell you in pretty much the same way and with the same words that Adam told Viveca. But I need to warn you, it's dis-

turbing, and if you'd rather I did some para-
phrasing . . ."

"No. I want to hear what you heard."
What Lucas heard.

Brandon drew a deep breath. "All right.
Well. In essence, the killing spree, the Lady
Killer rampage, was because of Marianne.
And Kay."

"Kay?"

"She was John's lover during the months
before Marianne's death. It might have been
an understandable affair, an escape from
the grimness and decay of his personal life,
had it been his first. But John had had lovers
for years. His sexual appetites were vora-
cious. And unusual. He liked bondage, the
binding of women, the power, the punishment, the control. It was John's dirty little
secret, one that could never be shared, either in words or in deeds, with his beautiful
patrician wife. Marianne was a goddess, and
John loved her. Which meant his sordid
sexual tastes had to remain hidden. And
they had for all the years of their marriage.
Then came Kay. She was the best lover, best
accomplice, John had ever found, as reck-
less, as depraved, as daring as he. She liked
the violence, the punishment, and she knew
exactly how to play the game, to goad John
into his most punishing. Kay especially en-

joyed taunting him with the prowess of her previous lovers, one lover in particular, the one she would never forget."

"Lucas."

"Yes." Brandon spoke with quiet apology. "I'm sorry, Galen."

"It's okay. Please continue."

"Kay's taunting of John with her memories of Lucas was part of the game. If John ever felt truly threatened by the incessant comparisons, he didn't share his feelings of inadequacy with Adam. Why would he? But for whatever reason — boredom was the one he gave, coupled with Marianne's deteriorating health — John ended his affair with Kay. Or tried to. But it was an ultimately fatal attraction. Kay would not let him go. Within days of Marianne's death, when all of Manhattan was in mourning for Marianne and grieving for her devoted husband John, Kay threatened to reveal all. She kept a journal, she told him. It was sexually explicit, she said, and named names — notably his. It might be, she imagined, of great interest to Rosalyn St. John, not to mention the straitlaced shareholders in John's vast media empire, and it might tip into sheer madness the frail and fragile Fran, who was barely surviving her sister's death as it was. Kay left that threatening message on John's private line at KCOR, and later that night he went to Kay's apartment in a rage and killed her. And you know what? This is disturbing, Galen. But you need to know. John *enjoyed* murdering Kay. Immensely. It was the ultimate bondage, the most supreme control. He especially enjoyed a grisly detail, the piercing of her just-dead eyes with a sewing needle. That was totally spontaneous, he told Adam. An impromptu inspiration. Kay was sewing when he arrived, replacing a missing button from a coat, and since such domesticity seemed so alien to the brilliant prosecutor, John couldn't resist commemorating it in some way. Galen? You're shivering."

"It's a chilling tale."

"Yes. It is. Maybe I should stop. Maybe that's enough."

"No. I want to hear everything, and in Adam's — John's — words."

"Okay," Brandon agreed slowly. "Well. John only needed to murder Kay. But he enjoyed the killing so much, why stop? But who should he kill next? Kay's journal, which he took from her apartment the night of her murder and which was as explicit as she had threatened it would be, provided the answer. John would kill Kay's enemies, a little posthumous revenge for poor depraved Kay. Her enemies, as it turned out, were Lucas's women. Kay had a long list, compulsively compiled, a collection of any woman ever associated with Lucas in any way. Kay made a mission of finding these women. She was *obsessed*. And it was easy. Since she and Lucas worked together often, she could logically, offhandedly, mention his name to whomever she met whenever she chose. Sometimes, apparently, those fishing expeditions paid off. In response to Lucas's name, some woman's name, some *other* woman's name, would be mentioned back. Kay assumed, *imagined,* that every woman on her list had been to bed with Lucas . . . as she herself had not been. That's right, Galen. Kay and Lucas *weren't* lovers. Her journal made that abundantly clear. She had wanted to be his lover, had *tried* to be, but Lucas had rejected her. He had told her, one New Year's Eve, that he was involved with someone else. Monica, Kay decided, when she learned through a casual remark made by a photographer named Paul that Monica and Lucas had met on a plane flight from Denver. And then there was Marcia, who at Lucas's urging had acquired a porcelain peacock for a real-estate tycoon, a tidbit recounted by said tycoon at a political fund-raiser Kay attended at his Long Island mansion. The list went on and on. John could have gone on and on. And John had a name of his own. Dr. Brynne Talbot. The renowned oncologist who had failed to save Marianne and who, during her months of care and friendship with both Marianne and Fran, had found Marianne reading an article about a case Lucas had solved and mentioned that she'd known him in college. John enjoyed killing Brynne. A lot."

"Just as he enjoyed tormenting Lucas."

"Yes," Brandon said. "He did. And Adam said as much and why: because of Marianne not Kay. John didn't care about Kay. He *wouldn't* have cared even if she'd had a sexual relationship with Lucas, which we know she did not. But Marianne . . . John *cared* about Marianne, deeply, *possessively.*"

"Are you saying, did Adam say, that Lucas and Marianne were lovers?"

"No. In fact, and this I know mainly from my own conversations with Viveca, Marianne and Lucas saw each other only rarely, and only by chance, at charity events and the like. But once, long ago, Marianne and Lucas had known each other very well, as I'm sure you know. Marianne and Fran were Jenny's closest friends, as was Lucas. Marianne and Fran and Lucas were the victims who survived. Do you know, Galen, what happens to such victims, especially when they believe — as they did, incorrectly — that Jenny had been murdered?"

"Yes," Galen replied, recalling what Lucas had told her when they'd discussed his relationship with Lawrence following Jenny's death. "At least I think I do. The survivors may not see each other, but the emotional bond between them remains strong, sometimes stronger" — *more fierce,* Lucas had said — "than before."

"That's right. And over the years Lucas became a hero to Marianne, beginning of course with his efforts to keep me in prison for the entire twenty-two-year sentence that had been imposed. John spent his marriage, he told Adam, listening to Marianne rave about Lucas, how *brilliant* he was, how noble, how honorable, how brave, as if he were some mythic slayer of dragons. Marianne raved in private and on the air, every time she reported one of Lieutenant Lucas Hunter's many successes. John wanted Marianne all to himself, in *every* way. But part of her belonged to Lucas, the larger-than-life hero with whom no one could compete or compare. John hated Lucas, *loathed* him, and when the opportunity presented itself to murder women

Lucas had known . . . yes, John enjoyed the torment such carnage caused Lucas." Brandon paused. Waited. Then said, "What do you think?"

"What do I think?" Galen wasn't thinking, only feeling, only shivering beneath her turquoise coat.

"Do you believe it? Does it ring true?"

"I'm not sure what you mean."

"Neither did the SWAT team. I told them, even as we listened, that I wasn't buying the story, that something was very wrong. What was wrong, they insisted, was that the entire escapade was going to be a bust. John McLain obviously wasn't going to show up, much less be caught *and stopped* in the act, which was what they'd been told was what was going to happen, *had* to. In the midst of that grumbling we heard for the first time from Lucas, by radio from the van. 'Get ready,' he said. 'Be ready to go in.' The communication with the command center remained open after that, so we also heard Lucas's instructions to the sharpshooters on the roof across the street. He told them to be ready, too, and wanted to be certain they had a clear line of sight. They did. Adam Vaughn's head was squarely in their crosshairs."

"Adam's?"

"It was *his* story, not John's. The pretense that John was the killer was Adam's only hope of catching Viveca off guard. Which it definitely did. She was so upset about John, so distraught, that she didn't see the glaring flaws in the story Adam was telling — even though I could see them simply based on things Viv had told me, including once, years ago, a confession for which she felt great guilt. She had the feeling, she said, that celebrated war correspondent Adam Vaughn had actually *enjoyed* his battlefield reporting. The more horrific the scene the better. That sounds sadistic, doesn't it? Which the Lady Killer definitely was. And which from everything Viveca had ever shared with me, John McLain was not. And it was Adam's Fran, not John's Marianne, who idolized Lucas. I knew that personally, but Viveca knew it too. It was Fran, we learned at my first parole hearing, who had written to Lucas to make certain he'd be there. And it was Fran who showed up at every parole hearing thereafter and who knew what Lucas did to deny my parole. And anyone who ever saw one of Marianne's newscasts knew that she *never* raved on the air about Lucas, certainly not in a way that was different from her admiration for anyone else. But Fran undoubtedly *did* rave about Lucas, quietly, privately, and perhaps incessantly to Adam."

"Fran," Galen echoed. She had never met Adam's wife, the bereaved sister who had been sleeping, a round-the-clock slumber of grief and pills, since the Lady Killer had begun his evil prowl. But Galen had seen that sister as a girl, in the photograph taken the day Jenny died. Even then, Fran had been so fragile, so frail, the kind of woman, wife, to whom a husband's aberrant sexual proclivities could not possibly be revealed — as Kay had threatened to do. "Adam confessed?"

"No. He died seven seconds after the sharpshooters confirmed to Lucas they had him in their sights and less than a heartbeat after Lucas gave the command to shoot."

"But . . ."

"Did Lucas screw up? Is he a cold-blooded killer, too? No. Because during the first six of those seven seconds, Adam made his move. He took a knife from his overcoat so slowly that Viveca didn't see it coming, and in a single motion imprisoned her with one arm as he pressed the blade into her neck. He might have played with her a while. Or might not have. Lucas wasn't about to find out."

Played with her. The three words — not

magical, merely menacing, merely mad —
shivered to Galen's soul. *Played with her.*
Those weren't Adam's words. Adam was
dead.

But they were a killer's words nonetheless.

Brandon's.

Galen reached for the phone and stood.

Too late.

Brandon had her wrist, and then the
phone, and in a motion that rivaled the one
with which Adam had imprisoned Viveca,
he captured both wrists behind her back
and bound them with a white stocking made
of silk. A bride's silk stocking.

"I got this from a dresser drawer in the
bedroom when the SWAT team rushed next
door to pick up the pieces, I imagine, of
Adam's skull."

"What do you want?" Galen asked. But
she knew, she knew, too well.

Brandon answered first with a smile, arrogant and wicked, and then with words, so
arrogant too, as he shoved her back onto the
couch. "Vengeance is mine, said the Lord."

"The *Lord's*, not yours."

"Just one of the many places where the
Good Book and I part ways. One of the
many things about which I felt I needed to
speak with God."

"You're crazy."

"As a fox. I'd been raging all that time in Marbella, fuming about the Lady Killer. It infuriated the hell out of me that he was tormenting Lucas as I'd been planning to do for so long. I just hadn't decided how and when. And then tonight happened, and this — you, Galen — was handed to me on a silver platter. It was an impromptu inspiration, like Adam's needle pricks to his victims' eyes. The idea began, I must admit, when Viveca suggested there might be something between you and Lucas. The idea of killing you, that is. But I might have toyed with the notion for a while, and maybe even discarded it, if Lucas discarded you. But then the Lady Killer scenario started to unfold, and I listened to Adam talking about murder. *Murder.* Do you know how *arousing* that is? I knew Adam was the killer right away, and I was jealous. Restless, and yes, *crazy* with need. It's been seven long months since I strangled that hooker in Cannes. Strangling has always been my thing, beginning with Jenny. But hearing Adam talk about using a knife, *carving* female flesh . . . well, I omitted that particular description earlier. I honestly didn't think I could say it without giving myself away. Do you see how perfect this vengeance is? The sublime sym-

328

metry of it all? Adam goes to Viveca, disarming her with lies, and I come here and do the same thing to you. With a little bondage thrown in for good measure. But there aren't any SWAT teams or sharpshooters nearby. I can pull the knife as slowly as I please from my overcoat pocket. It's a good knife. I do believe our dear departed Adam Vaughn would have approved. It's yet another item borrowed from Viv's accommodating neighbors once the SWAT team was gone."

"You'll never get away with this."

"Actually, Galen, I will. Lucas will realize it was me. I *want* him to. But I've got my passport with me, and funds to last me forever overseas, and there are any number of women who'd be happy to take me in. Literally. It would be nice if you were still a little warm, only a little dead, when Lucas discovers you. But that might be *cutting* it a bit too close. It will be hours before he returns — assuming he can tolerate Viveca's hysterics that long. Hours. You'll be ice. Oh, well. Shall we begin?"

He was going to begin. Galen saw the lust, the madness, in his eyes. There would be no more talk. But there would be foreplay, the slow removal of the knife from his cashmere coat, *as he was doing now.*

And what could she do? Scream, of course. But to no avail. The ice cave was too private, too insulated, to permit the escape or intrusion of sound.

Her hands were bound behind her back, bound so tightly by a bride's silk stocking that already her fingers were becoming numb. But her legs were free. She could run. *Run.* Where?

The elevator? Brandon would reach her long before the doors parted in response to whatever pressure she managed to apply to the illuminated button embedded in marble.

Her bedroom then, the sanctuary where so recently, at least for her, there had been love. Was there a lock on her bedroom door? She didn't know, had never looked, had never once thought to lock Lucas out.

Not like Mark. *Mark.* Who had taunted her with a knife, as Brandon was doing now, and even with her hands unbound, with Mark, she had made no attempt to defend herself with violence. To defend herself at all.

But there was so much to defend now. She would not let Brandon Christianson do this to Lucas. Again.

The *terrace.* Even with her numbing fingers and from behind her back, she could and would be able to unlatch the glass door. She knew that lock very well. And once outside she would run to the fountain, its icicles glistening with moonlit rainbows, and on those knife-sharp promises she would sever the bride's stocking that bound her wrists.

Then she would run to the edge, to the ledge — and off.

Lucas would believe, when her body was found on the ground below, that she had gone to the terrace, as she had done before in the middle of the night, and had slipped on the ice and fallen to her death.

He would feel guilt that he hadn't warned her to be more careful, and perhaps he would even feel loss. But that was so much better for his heart, for the rest of his life, than finding her as he had found Jenny . . . murdered by Brandon.

"Going somewhere?" Brandon asked, knife gleaming, as Galen stood. "Really, Galen. Where can you go? But as long as you're standing, let's get rid of that monstrosity of a coat, shall we? It's coming off, Galen. As is everything else."

He grabbed her by a fluffy turquoise lapel. It wasn't an imprisoning grasp. Brandon assumed she was already imprisoned, hobbled by her tightly bound wrists and frozen by her fear.

But Galen surprised him, pulling away, spinning away, and twisting with such force, more than she needed, that she stumbled slightly. Just enough. Too much. Brandon grabbed her with anger this time. With violence.

He shook her with violence as he spoke.

"You will pay for that little stunt."

He was strong, empowered by madness, and Galen had no arms. But her balance, so awkward with her hands bound behind her, was far less precarious when he held her, even as he shook her with such rage.

It was quite easy, really, as if she were a ballerina. Or a Rockette. Galen kicked, a ferocious blow that might be stunning for some men — as selected self-defense experts maintained — but which for others merely fueled the powerful rage.

As it fueled Brandon's. He pushed her away, a brutal thrust from which she could not possibly recover and which hurled her with punishing force precisely where he wanted her to be punished: against the white-stone fireplace where on a fairy-tale day bright orange flames had crackled and danced.

The stone was silent now. But there was fire. In her chest. As her ribs collided with a sharp corner of unyielding rock. Her flesh gave way, as did her fragile bones, and deep within a pierced artery began to weep. To sob.

There was a second impact, her head striking more stone as she fell. Then she was on the snowy carpet, on fire and gasping. But floating. Dreaming. Behind the darkness of lids too heavy to open.

She heard a voice and knew vaguely and without alarm that it belonged to the devil.

But her dreaming, floating mind extinguished the voice. Banished it entirely. And as the devil's hands unbound her wrists and undressed her until she was naked and exposed, her blurry consciousness believed them to be another man's hands. Such talented hands. And in the blackness she saw his eyes, glittering silver with his desire, and she believed, in this dream she believed, that they glittered, too, with his love.

And when the carving began? The deep, jagged cuts which seemed focused, obsessively so, on her small and naked breasts?

Galen's dream did not permit her to know what was happening. Or even to guess. But her floating brain needed an explanation for the sensation — which was not in itself particularly painful, especially in contrast to the pierce of shattered bones against her lungs.

And the dreaming explanation came. The talented, gifted, loving hands were pouring warm syrup on her breasts. It felt quite lovely. Warm and sweet.

And there would be even more lovely sensations when his tender, ravenous lips began to . . .

The dream paused, suspended, as the snow-white clock above where she lay began its midnight chime.

Its Cinderella chime.

She needed to leave! She had made a promise to call for her coach, the pumpkin in which she would begin her return journey to Kansas, after which she would descend to earth where she belonged, not in the wispy clouds of hope in this penthouse in the sky, before the snowy chimes finished their midnight song of joy.

She needed to place the call even as she was summoning the elevator.

But wait. The elevator was already coming. She heard the wispy joy between the chimes.

He was here. Home. To her. Before the witching hour. In time to save the fairy tale.

Lucas. Home. To her. At last.

And the dream for Galen truly began.

TWENTY-TWO

The dream for Galen.

And the nightmare for Lucas.

For what Lucas Hunter saw as he stepped out of the brass elevator was a ravaged snow angel.

She was naked, his modest Venus, and so *im*modest on the snowy carpet, her arms and legs spread wide by a devil. Her clothes lay in a turquoise heap nearby.

She was bleeding, as in his nightmare of gleaming knives and naked Barbies. The jagged slashes wept from her collarbone to her breasts, glistening crimson tears that spilled onto her ice-pale, blue-white skin.

Naked. Bleeding. White. Blue.

And *alive*. Barely. Her savaged chest gasped with despair.

Lucas rushed to her, knelt beside her.

"Galen," he whispered, as he had whispered when they had loved, and he touched her beloved face.

She was so cold.

Lucas whispered her name still, and the most tender of reassurances, as he searched so desperately for the gush of blood that was stealing her life. But the lethal pulsing could not be seen. It came from a severed artery deep in her chest.

And the savage knife wounds to her delicate breasts? They wept not gushed their crimson tears.

Gently, so gently, Lucas touched her angel arms, moving those pale white wings closer to her sides. And he brought her ice-cold legs together, too, giving her that modesty, that dignity, before he draped the entire angel in her beloved coat of turquoise fluff.

Then he reached for the lavender phone. Hers. Discarded on the couch.

Lucas saw the devil then, the shadow within the shadows, the silhouette of pure evil armed with vengeance and a bloodied knife.

And what did the devil see in the panther's gleaming eyes?

Murder. *Murder.* The absolutely certainty that Lucas could and would murder him with his bare hands. Neither the knife, nor his own twenty-seven-year quest for revenge, would afford the slightest protection against the fury that he saw.

Brandon should have killed him. Already.

He should have lunged at Lucas as he ministered to the bleeding corpse, the womanly shape that was barely womanly at all.

But Brandon had been so mesmerized, and so pleased, by Lucas's anguish that he had simply watched.

And, Brandon realized, a precipitous attack would have been for naught. Lucas had known he was there from the start, and he had been fully prepared to kill him if and when he approached.

Brandon cast a furtive glance at the elevator, his solitary hope for escape, then returned to the lethal gaze. And Brandon saw, amid the gleaming promise of murder, a look of arch disdain.

Lucas *could* kill Brandon, the contemptuous look asserted, whenever he chose. But unless provoked, Lucas would not bother with such slaughter now. Not when every wasted second, any wasted second, might cost Galen her life.

Lucas was dialing the lavender phone even now, watching Brandon and sending promises of death even as he pressed the numbers.

9-1-1.

And now Lieutenant Lucas Hunter was describing Galen's injuries and issuing succinct commands. He wanted a paramedic unit outside his building *now*. He would be there with the victim by the time the unit arrived.

The phone call was concise. Focused. Brandon heard every nuance and every word. There was *nothing*, he decided, not even a concealed command in some police-speak code, that would compel a squad of cops to the penthouse or dispatch the sharp-shooters who might be milling, still, on the rooftops just six blocks away.

I've won, Brandon realized. I've beaten the son of a bitch.

Unless provoked, Lucas Hunter couldn't be bothered with him now. Saving the scrawny newscaster was all. And if she died? If he failed? The failure would be pure tor-ture for Lucas, a torture greater even than Jenny, for Galen Chandler had been quite literally in Lucas Hunter's care.

Amazingly, Brandon found himself hop-ing that Lucas *wouldn't* fail, that by some miracle Galen would survive. A living Galen would be a living torment for Lucas, a woman so inconsequential to begin with now irreparably — grotesquely — scarred.

Brandon had done great damage to her meager breasts. No man would ever want her. Would *ever* want to touch.

No man. Especially a man like Lucas. But

might Lucas feel obligated, obliged? Might his guilt compel him to spend the rest of his life protecting her?

Maybe. For now, and with such care, Lucas was wrapping the turquoise coat around her blue-white limbs, a soft cocoon, and now he was lifting that fluffiness and whispering apologies for hurting her, for disturbing even with such tenderness her already shattered bones, and he was making promises to her, too, that everything would be fine.

Too bad, Brandon mused, that she was already a corpse.

A corpse in transit to the elevator and to the waiting medic van below. Lucas was so vulnerable now, and so dismissive of the threat Brandon posed, he didn't even look again toward the shadows where Brandon stood.

He merely turned his back and walked away.

Brandon almost lunged, *almost* succumbed to the sudden impulse to plunge the knife into Lucas Hunter's arrogant back. For even if Lucas sensed his approach, he wouldn't have time, would he, to lower Galen *gently* onto the foyer's ice-cold marble even as he made ready to turn and kill?

Maybe. Maybe not.

No. But the realization came too late. Brandon didn't realize, until the split second was over, that Lucas would sustain an attack from the front — that simply the sight of a battered suitcase and a Bloomingdale's shopping bag would stagger the lieutenant as if he'd been stabbed.

Had Brandon known the frontal assault was coming, he could have easily landed a mortal blow. But he hadn't known, and the moment had passed, and Brandon was philosophical. And pleased.

Victory was his. Beyond his wildest imaginings. No matter whether Galen Chandler lived or died. And by the time Lucas Hunter came looking for him, he would have vanished forever.

"Vengeance is mine," Brandon whispered to the bloodied carpet as the elevator doors closed. "Vengeance is mine."

The paramedics were experienced professionals. They had seen all manner of carnage and were trained, or had trained themselves, to withhold comment in the presence of the victim *always,* even if said victim was virtually dead.

Which she was. Galen Chandler. The KCOR anchorwoman who had soared from the depths of infamy to the height of fame

. . . and plummeted again to this.

This.

One of the paramedics swore softly, he couldn't help it, as he unfurled her turquoise cocoon. It was the chest injury that would kill her, the fractured ribs, the pierced artery, the lungs drowning in a deluge of blood that only a surgeon could stem.

That's what would kill her, was killing her. Literally. And swiftly.

And if by some miracle the van navigated the treacherously icy streets between here and Memorial Hospital and she made it to the operating room in time?

She would die every day for the rest of her life, emotional death, psychologic destruction, from the disfiguring scars on her savagely carved breasts.

The paramedic looked meaningfully from the carnage to Lucas, his expression posing the obvious question. Are we doing her any favors by trying to keep her alive?

The paramedic saw the answer and its fury before Lucas spoke. *"Help her."*

The paramedics did what they could, plumbing the depths beneath her skin in search of veins, any vein, which because of shock had clamped down to the tiniest of threads. As their needles pierced her flesh, and the driver drove as quickly as he could and as slowly as he must, Lucas knelt beside Galen's head.

"You're doing fine," he whispered as he touched her ice-blue cheek and caressed the curling flames that felt, too, like ice. "You're doing great."

"Keep talking to her, Lieutenant," a paramedic urged. "I'm suddenly feeling a much stronger pulse."

Lucas moved even closer, a kiss of warm lips against frigid temple. "I love you, Galen," he whispered for her ears, for her heart, only. *"I love you."*

"Whatever that was, Lieutenant, keep saying it. She's hearing you. And I've just found a vein."

Galen's veins opened, welcoming the necessary needle, as Lucas opened his veins, his heart, for her.

"Detective Chandler," he murmured, the faint tease necessary, essential, to prevent the flood, the torrent, of his fear. He kissed the eyelids that fluttered in reply, and then her mouth, kissing her still as he spoke. "Will you marry me, Galen? Will you be my bride?"

Sirens screamed, and the van skidded and slid.

But Lucas's mouth did not leave hers. And he felt, his lips did, his heart did, the softest curve of her smile.

TWENTY-THREE

Even as the trauma surgeons were working inside her shattered chest, the severed ligating arteries as they removed scalpel-sharp slivers of bone, plastic surgeons were closing the knife wounds on her breasts. The plastics maestros used tiny needles and placed every stitch, every suture, beneath the ravaged skin.

The closures were the best that could be done. By anyone. For now. The best chance for minimizing the scars. Later, much later and assuming she survived, revisions in her scars could be made.

While the surgeons repaired what could be repaired in the operating room, Casey from 6-North did some repair work of her own. On Galen's coat.

Casey had worked the evening shift, which ended at eleven. But Casey had lingered, many of them had, riveted to the television in the playroom where the hostages had been held. She was still there, still riveted — because the Lady Killer's identity

343

had yet to be revealed — when the call came from the ER at 12:22.

The caller was the triage nurse, and such a close friend, and so trustworthy, that Casey had told her not only that Galen was the benefactress of the Barbies but that Sunday afternoon's delivery had been made by Lieutenant Hunter himself.

Who was gorgeous.

And who was gorgeous still, the triage nurse thought as she waited for Casey to come on the line. Gorgeous, and desperate, in a quiet and terrifying way.

During Galen's brief stay in the emergency room, the lieutenant had done everything correctly and without any instruction whatsoever. He had permitted the ER staff full access to Galen even as he'd stood nearby.

And even after, as Galen was being whisked to the operating room, Lucas hadn't gone crazy at all — hadn't insisted on accompanying her gurney, *her,* into the sterile OR suite. And even after *that,* when Galen was in surgery and the trio of police officers had found him in emergency, in the trauma room where Galen had been, the homicide lieutenant had seemed all right, *fine.* With quiet calm he had told the other officers the identity of Galen's assailant, and where he was, and with comparable control Lucas had issued explicit commands.

But now. Now. Lieutenant Lucas Hunter was in Trauma Room 1, the nurse told Casey. Still, and so still. A black-clad statue drenched with blood.

As silent, as stark, as death.

They'd tried speaking to him. But if he heard, he didn't respond. Maybe he'd listen to Casey?

Casey seriously doubted it. She doubted there was anything at all that she could do. Especially when she saw him. Gorgeous, terrifying, and looking like death, as if he'd seen death, was seeing it still.

Casey's gaze left Lucas's face, had to, and fell on something the triage nurse had neglected to mention. Galen's turquoise coat. Lucas held the billowing fluff as tenderly as if he were holding Galen.

Which was fine, Casey thought. Lovely — except for the fact that its bright blue lining was vivid with Galen's blood.

"Lucas? It's Casey. From 6-North. Remember me?"

There was color on his taut and ashen face. More blood. Galen's. But his eyes were colorless, empty. And polite.

His voice spoke from the grave. "I remember."

"Good. So, Lucas, here's the deal. I'd really like to get those . . . stains off the lining of Galen's coat. The sooner, the better. A little hydrogen peroxide applied right now can make it as good as new. True, Galen could easily sew a new lining. But, well, I get the impression the coat itself means a lot to her. So maybe the lining does, too?"

Casey tugged gently at the coat, which was gently released. "Great. Thanks. This is *quite* a lining, isn't it? Pockets everywhere." Her hands grazed over the pockets, discerning by shape the items secured within. "Galen must use these inner pockets instead of carrying a purse. Very smart. She could probably sell a *few* of these coats to *every* woman in Manhattan, and that's just for starters."

Casey was chattering, and the hydrogen peroxide was working its magic, vaporizing the blood into a froth of bubbles that would easily wipe away.

And as for the other blood? On his coat and on his face? In another setting Casey might have made a swipe at the bloodstains herself, were he merely a cop in the ER on a case.

But he was a man, not a cop. A man lost in tormenting thoughts and unsurpassed fear. But a polite man, she had discovered. A gentleman, this gentle, anguished man.

She drenched a clean towel with a flood of peroxide and held it before him.

"Your face, Lieutenant. And your coat. Please." *Please.*

He complied, for which she felt a rush of euphoria as bubbling as the peroxide froth, and after she retrieved and tossed in a hamper the bloodied towel he had used, she displayed the damp but stain-free lining of Galen's coat.

"See how well this works? I think I'll take it upstairs, to the room in the Surgical ICU that will be Galen's, and hang it up to let it dry. I'll show you the OR waiting room on the way. Follow me, Lucas. Please."

Please worked again. They exited the ER just as the first brigade of media came rushing in. Casey showed Lucas to the waiting room, where the media could not follow, and after taking Galen's coat to the SICU, she returned to wait with him for news.

It was a silent wait, of torment for him, and such fear.

What was he *thinking?* she wondered. It was impossible to tell. He needed *not* to be thinking, not thinking at all. But Casey doubted very much that Lucas Hunter would permit himself the luxury of such escape.

Wherever Lucas was, the place of no escape, it was a vast dark cave of punishment, of pain. And, perhaps, perhaps, of prayer.

But it was he, even before she, who sensed the presence in the doorway. Lucas stood to face the truth, which came in the form of Dr. Diana Sterling, the trauma chief, whom he had met on official police business more than once before.

"She's out of surgery, Lucas, and we're already getting her settled in the SICU. Barring complications, the greatest threat to her survival is past."

"Diana. Thank you." It was a whisper of joy.

To which Diana smiled. "Galen may not be feeling very thankful, not for the next twenty-four hours at least. We're going to be controlling everything, we have to, her breathing, her heart rate —"

"Her pain."

"*Especially* her pain. The goal is to re-expand her lungs as much as possible and as soon as possible, to perfuse and oxygenate every cell that was compressed by the blood. Which means we mechanically ventilate, relax her musculature, and keep enough narcotic on board that she won't reflexively resist the deepness of the breaths. The drugs will have the additional benefit of sedation.

It would be best for her if she spent the next twenty-four hours sound asleep."

"May I see her, Diana?"

Diana sighed, and just to emphasize her reaction, in case he'd missed it, she spoke the word. "Sigh."

"No, Diana? I can't?"

"You saved her life, Lucas. Your voice did. In the van." He made her heart beat, the paramedic had told her, and gave her a blood pressure that came from nowhere. *From him.* "But I worry that if she hears you now . . . she awakened fairly ferociously from anesthesia. Too ferociously for her own good. We were delighted to see the consciousness, because of the head injury she'd sustained, but it took a while to get her calm." Diana Sterling sighed anew. "You can see her, Lucas. From a distance. But not a word. Not a touch. She's asleep now and in a perfect balance to begin to heal."

"Okay. I want" — *always, always* — "what's best for her."

Diana smiled. "If she awakens, and it's best for her to have company, I will find you, Lucas. I promise."

"Thank you," he whispered. Again.

Thank you. Lucas whispered it so many times that day, gratitude for the steady

349

stream of updates delivered by Galen's doctors and nurses to the waiting room across from the Surgical ICU.

Galen was still sleeping, they reported, which was *terrific,* exactly what she needed, and her vital signs were ever more strong.

Casey stopped by before her shift, she was working days, and again after. The ice was melting, she told him. Virtually gone.

Galen was sleeping, and the ice was melting, and at four-thirty on that Wednesday afternoon . . .

"Lucas?"

"Lawrence."

"I just heard. How is she?"

Fine, Lucas Hunter's strong lean hands began to sign. *She's going to be fine.*

I'm so glad, Lawrence Kincaid signed in reply. Then, looking at his own fingers, which might have been so rusty — should have been but were not — Lawrence signed even more. *It's been years since I've done this.*

Me, Lucas signed, *too.*

It was not forgotten, not by these two men, not this wondrous language of Jenny's, this dancing silence which for six shimmering years had been a language of great joy.

When Lucas spoke again, he spoke the Queen's English. But the dancing joy shimmered still.

"I've asked Galen to marry me."

Lawrence smiled. "And?"

"I think she said yes." Lucas smiled, too. "I'm sure she did."

They spoke of the present, not the past. Of Galen. And when a nurse appeared with the latest update — that Galen was still sleeping and doing *great* — both men replied in unison, "Thank you."

And when they were again alone, Lawrence Kincaid said, "I should have adopted you."

"Adopted me, Lawrence?" Adopted *me?*

"I wanted to, Lucas. I was planning to. I'd discussed it with my attorney, but hadn't yet approached Helena. It might have been necessary, easier, for Helena and me to have married, at least for a while. Which would have been fine. But then . . ."

"Jenny died."

"And you left. And that shouldn't have happened, Lucas. If I'd adopted you, if I'd already done it, you would have stayed. There would have been no question about it. You would not have returned *by default* to England, because I was so consumed with my grief. And my rage. I cared so much about Brandon's punishment that I was blind to everything else. Especially the important things. By the time I opened my

351

eyes, I'd lost you both."

Both. Jenny. Lucas. *Both* of his children.

"I don't know what to say." But Lucas didn't need to say anything. His dark gray eyes, so astonished and so grateful, said it all.

Lawrence had some suggestions nonetheless. "You could say I was a worthless excuse for a father."

"No, Lawrence. I would never say that."

"Or for a man."

"No. Not that either."

"You might at least point out that it's a little late, almost three decades late, to be telling you this now."

"No," Lucas said softly. "It's not too late."

In the ensuing silence, emotion signed itself in the shimmering air, an invisible dance of remembrance and of joy.

Eventually the renowned playwright spoke again.

His new play, *Bellemeade*, was in rehearsal now, and it was a story of family, of *the* family he and Jenny and Lucas once had been. It had taken all this time, all these decades, to get the story precisely right. But at last he had. And assuming the cast and crew hadn't already walked out in protest, because he'd vanished for the dinner break and had yet to reappear, *Bellemeade* was going to be what he had hoped, all he had hoped.

Especially if Lucas and Galen were in the audience on opening night.

"We will be," Lucas promised, and paused, and smiled. "And I hope, Lawrence, that you'll come to our wedding, too."

TWENTY-FOUR

Diana Sterling sent Lucas home at 8 P.M.

Galen was doing very well. Extremely well. She would be extubated in the morning. Lucas could see her, talk to her, then.

"In the meantime," Diana said gently, "may I prescribe a good night's sleep for you?"

"Sure, Diana. You may."

It was a prescription, however, that Lieutenant Lucas Hunter did not heed.

He did not sleep.

He sewed.

All night.

And at dawn he dressed the tiny plastic doll and combed her flame-hued hair, a cascade of fire that fell to her waist, and he wrapped her in a lavender tissue-paper cocoon.

Lucas was at Memorial Hospital, waiting outside the SICU, when the anesthesiologist removed the endotracheal tube from Galen's throat.

Fifteen minutes later he was permitted to see her.

She looked so small, propped amid the pillows that provided softness for her damaged chest, and so white.

And so alive, suddenly, radiantly alive, when he walked into her room.

"Lucas."

"Hi," he said softly, wanting to touch, to hold, but caressing her only with his gentleness. For now. His gentleness. "Does it hurt?"

"Only when I breathe." She smiled. "Or don't breathe."

"I'm so sorry."

"It's *fine*, Lucas. *I'm* fine. I've just had a twenty-four-hour nap, and Dr. Sterling promises that after just a few short days of taking deep breaths I'll get to go . . ."

"Home."

"Yes." *Home.* That was the word she would have spoken. But . . . her shrug ignited an inferno of flames within her battered chest, a searing reminder, a punishment perhaps. For where *was* home, that illusive wondrous place? Was it in Kansas with Julia? Or with her mother in the house she once had fled? Or was home the place where rainbows danced in icicles from a

355

wedding-cake fountain, a place of fairy tales and loving and dreams *and lies?*

"Galen?"

"Yes?"

"I brought you something." Lucas handed her the lavender cocoon. "I got her last night at FAO Schwarz. I had no idea there was a Barbie that looked so much like you."

"There isn't," she murmured, a protest which she might have embellished had her gaze not drifted from the doll's long curling flames and bright blue eyes to her clothes, the striped robe and cotton gown that were identical, *identical,* to what she herself wore. Her slender fingers touched the fabric. "You *made* these."

"I tried."

"More than tried," she whispered. The workmanship wasn't expert, merely meticulous, a crafting of great care, tiny, methodical stitches placed precisely where they were supposed to be. "Look how perfectly you did the sleeves."

"There was a possibility for a while, for quite a while, that the robe was going to be sleeveless."

"I can't believe . . . Thank you."

"Oh, Galen, don't thank me. Not for anything."

Galen looked from meticulous seams, sewn by strong and gentle hands, to the fury of granite. "For everything, Lucas. *Everything*. If you hadn't returned when you did . . ."

"What do you remember?"

Everything. The entire wondrous, floating dream. Admittedly, it had started somewhat imperfectly, her own wispy clouds of hope obscuring the near-lethal truth.

"I think I remember it all."

"Tell me. If it's not too disturbing to recall."

"It's not. Given the ending. I'm fine, Lucas. *Fine*. So. Let's see. Brandon dropped by the penthouse at precisely eleven-twenty-nine. I let him in. Like an idiot. Without confirming that he was really the police sergeant he claimed to be. But I knew from the breaking news on television that the killer was dead." *And there was, you see, this billowy cloud of hope.* "Once he reached the penthouse, it took very little time to realize who he was."

"Because he attacked you."

"No. He *charmed* me. He gave me this very sincere, very credible, mumbo jumbo about wanting to meet with you so you could heal. He maintained his innocence of course, and he even came up with a fairly

357

plausible explanation of how the chronology of your memories might have been disordered by the trauma of Jenny's death. Anyway, I *fell* for it and dropped my guard. Just like Viveca dropped her guard with Adam." *Adam.* "Was it really Adam, Lucas? Was Adam really the Lady Killer?"

"Yes. He really was." It was a fact which had not been officially confirmed until late yesterday afternoon. While Galen slept. "Someone must have told you that this morning."

"No. Brandon told me. That night."

"Brandon?"

"He was there, Lucas. With the SWAT team in the apartment next to Viveca's. Didn't you know?"

"No."

"So you must have sensed him. That's why you returned to the penthouse so soon."

"Yes," Lucas said softly. "I sensed him. But," his voice was softer still, "that's not why I returned."

"It's not?"

"No. It's not. I'll tell you all about that" — *all about you* — "as soon as you've finished telling me about Brandon. If that's okay. If you have the energy."

"I do. There was that twenty-four-hour

nap." And she would stay awake forever, her heart would have it no other way, to hear what he had to say . . . the words that matched the tenderness of his eyes. "Let's see. Where was I? Oh yes, being completely fooled by Brandon. Well, not completely. I figured it out just moments before he confessed that hearing Adam talk about murder had made him crazy. *Crazier*. Made him want to kill. With a knife. When he made his move, I made mine. Tried to. He'd tied my wrists behind my back, so my balance wasn't very good. Neither was the self-defense kick I tried. He shoved me into the fireplace. That's how my chest was injured, and as I fell I also hit my head. I didn't lose consciousness, but everything was floating after that. Floating, and not terrifying at all. Even when he undressed me. I wasn't able to fight him, so I just surrendered. And floated."

Galen paused, her eyes closing briefly, searching the memories of that floating mist and finding the dreamlike remembrance of Brandon — no, *Lucas* — pouring warm syrup on her breasts.

"What are you remembering?"

"Nothing." She opened her eyes. *Nothing that makes any sense*. She smiled. "Then the clock started to chime midnight, and I heard the elevator. You. And the rest is history." Her smile became a frown.

"What, Galen?"

"I didn't think I'd ever completely lost consciousness. But I must have. I remember you talking to me, and I heard you call 911. But I don't remember anything between you and Brandon. He was *there,* in the penthouse. He heard the elevator, too."

"He was there. But we didn't speak. And he kept his distance. He left the penthouse after us." Lucas paused, struck anew by the clarity with which he had known Brandon's movements after he and Galen left the penthouse . . . and how calmly he had informed the three officers of those movements when they came to speak with him in the emergency room. "He took my car and was bound for JFK."

"But was arrested en route."

"No. He resisted arrest and led the pursuing officers on a high-speed chase."

"On the ice."

"Yes," Lucas confirmed quietly. It had been a dangerous pursuit for the officers. But they hadn't backed off, just as Lucas wouldn't have, for the icy streets were empty. No innocent bystanders were at risk. The jeopardy was for the officers only, and they had accepted that peril for Lucas, and for Galen, because of what Brandon had done. And the ice on that night had been friend to good and foe to evil. "Brandon lost control, spun out, crashed. He died instantly. The officers were fine."

"*Good.* About the officers, and especially about Brandon." Galen shrugged, but felt no punishing bursts of flame. "Not a very charitable sentiment, I guess."

Lucas smiled. "Just about as much charity as he deserves." Lucas Hunter grew solemn then, not from death but from life, from love, from dreams, from hope. "Do you remember anything else?"

"Like what?"

"Well," he said softly, "like anything I might have said to you on the way to the hospital? Any questions I might have asked?"

His eyes were glittering, ravenous, ferocious, wanting something, *wanting her,* so much. "Like what?"

"Well." Lucas touched the pale satin of her cheek, and then the trembling warmth of the lips that had curved so softly beneath his. "Like I told you I loved you. Which I do, Galen. I do. So much."

"Lucas."

"And like I asked you to marry me, to which — and this is the part for you to remember very clearly — your answer was yes."

"It was?"

"Wasn't it?"

Yes. Yes. Yes.

But she frowned, as Lucas had feared she would. He stopped her words with a gentle kiss.

"My turn. Listen to me, Galen. Hear me. Please."

"Okay."

"Okay. I'm in love with you. I didn't believe it was possible for me to fall in love. I thought I'd closed myself off to that long ago. But I have fallen in love, Galen. With you."

"I never believed I could fall in love, either. But I have, Lucas. I *have*. With you. Because of you."

"But you were leaving," he said quietly. "Your suitcase and shopping bag were in the foyer, and everything else was in the pockets of your coat."

"Well, I . . ."

"Thought I'd made love to you to provoke the killer." Lucas saw the truth in her eyes, and Galen saw the rage *at himself* in his. "I should have told you more. I should have told you what I sensed Sunday night: that it was Adam, and that he was very close to killing again, that he wouldn't be able to resist for very long. I had to confirm what I'd sensed and get everything in place as quickly as I could. Which I did, even sooner than I'd hoped, because I missed you. Desperately. I didn't believe he would call that night. I believed I was ahead of him by at least a day. But it still hadn't been my plan to make love to you that night. I knew it was almost over, that *he* was almost over. But . . ."

"I seduced you."

"You'd seduced me long before that night. But I would never have made love to you — not our first time — had I known I couldn't hold you and love you and tell you all the things I wanted to say to you all night."

"But the killer called," she whispered. "How did he know that we'd made love?"

"He didn't know, Galen. He was just ready to kill. No matter what you said to him when he called, and no matter what we had done or not done, he was going to kill that night and make you feel as if it were all your fault. He called. And I left."

"You had to."

"Yes. I did. And I had to focus on what Adam was saying to Viveca, to sense if possible the instant just before he went for his knife."

"Which you did."

"Yes. But it was a struggle, because I kept thinking about you, worrying about the girl who'd been called a scarecrow by her classmates and who'd been taunted — sexually and *about* her sexuality — by Mark, by Adam, and even by Rosalyn St. John. I knew you knew about *love*, Galen, from Julia and Winnie and Gran. And from your mother, too, I think, before Mark came into your lives. I believed you loved me, and I even believed that you knew I loved you. But because of the cruelty of Mark and others, I worried you wouldn't understand that I wanted you sexually as well. And if you believed my lovemaking was a lie, you would doubt everything, including my love. Which, I think, is what happened after I left."

"I . . ." Galen looked from his searching eyes to the Barbie she held, and frowned.

"I thought about that, too," Lucas said quietly, reading her thought. "I wondered whether your vision of what a woman should look like, what her figure should be, had been influenced by the impossible plastic shape after all. But I decided that what you'd said was true. The Barbies, for you, are friends. And symbols, I think, of love. Had your mother's Barbie been a rag doll, or a GI Joe, that's the doll you would have cherished. And clothed. And you've always clothed the Barbies very modestly, as you clothe yourself."

"You were thinking about all this while you were listening to Adam?"

Silver glinted in his serious gray eyes. "I was. And I was vowing that as soon as Adam was captured, or dead, I'd turn everything over to Peter Collings, the other officer in the van, and come home to you. Peter deserved recognition for all the work he'd done on the case, and I trusted him to make the call to John."

"To John?"

"So that he could tell Fran."

Fran, Galen thought. Adam's frail and fragile wife, who'd been Jenny's closest friend, and with whom Lucas shared a fierce if distant emotional bond. Once Lucas had realized the killer was Adam, *of course* he had thought of Fran, worrying about her and wanting to protect — to be certain Fran heard the devastating truth about her monster husband in the gentlest way. But from John? The brother-in-law who was barely surviving Marianne's death himself?

"John," Galen murmured.

"We spoke on Monday," Lucas said. "I called him. It was an expansive conversation, comprising many topics, including KCOR's coverage of the case. I'm sure John never guessed the real reason for my call, which was to confirm some details about Adam. But I made a discovery during that call, one I hadn't expected to make — that John's concern for Fran, his protectiveness and his worry, surpasses even his own immense grief. I had planned to be the one to tell Fran about Adam. I thought that you and I might tell her together. But I realized it was John who should break the horrifying news. It was something he could do, needed to do, and would *want* to do for Fran. And Marianne."

"So you told John about Adam?"

"No. I simply told him that I felt the case was about to break and that because of the station's involvement I needed to be able to reach him at all times. Adam had told me, intentionally I suppose, that John had made a habit of disappearing for hours and sometimes days since Marianne's death. John agreed that he would be available, that he wouldn't take the drives away from Manhattan that he'd been taking and that he'd carry his cell phone with him on his midnight, all-night, walks."

"So you knew that John would be available to go to Fran whenever you or Peter

Collings called him."

"Yes. And to be certain that it was John, not Rosalyn St. John, who told Fran the news, a team of cops had been posted outside Fran's home since Adam's final phone call to you, and an intercept had been placed on Fran's phone."

"You thought of everything."

"Not everything," Lucas replied quietly. *Not Brandon.* Lucas vanquished the harsh thought, her loving blue eyes vanquished it for him, and he smiled. "I did, however, make advance arrangements about Fran. Which is fortunate because, as I was telling you, my thoughts that night, while I was supposed to be listening to Adam, were mostly about you. I had a few more thoughts — about you — if you'd like to hear them."

"More?"

"Just a few. I wondered what if you'd been sexually precocious as a girl, and with the impossible Barbie shape. What if your classmates had teased you about that? And what if Mark had made taunting comments in the other extreme?"

"And?"

"And," he said softly, "I decided you would have had the same disconnect about how beautiful you are. How beautiful. And

367

how sexy." Lucas smiled at her beautiful, sexy frown. "I see you're disconnecting still. We're going to have to work on that, Galen. In bed. I thought we had a pretty good start the other night, that you might have sensed, in some way, my passion and my lust?"

"You think I'm . . . sexy?"

"Galen." His gaze was intimate, eloquent, intense. "I know you are."

"And you said something about lust?"

"Yes, lust. *Wanting.* Primal. Elemental. You have some elemental misconceptions, Galen, thanks to the cruelty of humans, not the innocence of dolls. I'd be very happy to spend the rest of my life showing you just how flawed those conceptions are. Is that prospect appealing to you in any way?"

"Yes," she whispered. "In every way."

"Good." His smile vanished. But the intimacy and the desire did not. "I was on my way home to you, Galen, already on my way home when I felt Brandon's evil. And I saw, even before I reached the penthouse, what he was doing to you."

"Oh, Lucas, you *saw?*"

"Yes." *I saw my snow angel bleeding and being carved.* Lucas had run on the ice without a falter, without a slip. The ice which would kill a killer had not dared, would not dare, undermine its own. "I'm in

368

love with you, Galen. In love, and in lust. But you need to know, always know, that even if I could never touch you again, I would want to spend the rest of my life with you. Loving you."

At last, at last, Lucas saw springtime in her blue, blue eyes . . . and Galen knew, at last, what truth looked like in his. It shimmered, it glittered, it glowed, molten silver with neither shadows nor pain.

"But we *can* touch," she whispered.

"Oh yes," Lucas answered. "We can."

TWENTY-FIVE

She slept, she dreamed, she healed.

And she spoke to the man she loved in conversations that floated as she did from joyful consciousness to essential sleep.

"When will we marry?" she wondered.

Soon, he promised. Whenever she liked and however she wanted. In the hospital, today, would be fine. Or, if she wanted something more formal, more traditional, they could do that, too. She could make her own wedding gown, and the dress for her maid of honor, Julia. And maybe, Lucas suggested softly, something for the mother of the bride?

Traditional. Like the diamond he gave her on the third afternoon. It was brilliant-cut and flawless and cradled in the traditional Tiffany setting, the pure golden band with its white-gold prongs. It was breathtaking, this crystalline piece of perfect glacier. Rainbows in icicles. Fire in ice.

Like him.

Her husband to be.

"What will I do?" she mused aloud one morning and without a trace of alarm.

"Do?"

"When we're married," she clarified, dreamily. "When I'm your wife."

"Whatever you like. You could, if you wanted, become a world renowned fashion designer. Easily."

His suggestion was gentle, loving, proud. But with it the dreaminess faded ever so slightly, as Lucas had thought it might. His gifted seamstress dreamed only of making clothes for those she loved — special clothes for Winnie, her mother's wedding gown, imaginative ensembles for the cherished dolls of sick little girls. Galen might make dresses for her own wedding, too, for that intimate celebration of love, just as she had made for herself a billowy coat of turquoise fluff because the color had been Winnie's favorite and matched exactly the mittens Galen treasured so.

"Is that what you'd like me to do, Lucas?" To *be?*

"No."

"What then?"

"Do you want the selfish, sexist answer?"

"Yes," she murmured as dreams filled her spring blue eyes anew. Sexist from this man felt so sexual, and so unselfish, at least to her. "Please."

And his answer was unselfish, of course. For Lucas knew it was what she wanted, too. "I'd like you to be at home."

"The penthouse."

"Unless you'd like to move. Maybe we should, Galen, given what happened there."

"What happened in the penthouse is our love. It's our home, Lucas. It's where I want to live . . . and do whatever sexist things you have in mind for me to do. And they are?"

"Homemaking. In our home. Sewing. Gardening. Loving our babies."

"Our babies, Lucas?"

"If you want."

"Oh," she whispered. "I want. Our babies. And you."

He kissed her eyes, her nose, the soft edges of her mouth. "You may have me, Galen. More than you want."

"Impossible."

"I hope so. Because I'm not sure what I'm going to do. I've been wondering if, with Brandon's death, my ability to sense evil will be gone. If maybe what I've been feeling all these years was Jenny's spirit, restless and roving, and now at peace at last."

"Jenny's," Galen echoed. "Or yours."

"Or mine. Probably mine." Whatever the

reason, there was a lightness in his soul, a brightness where once everything had been so black. But maybe that was Galen. Maybe that was love.

Lucas would have spent every second of every visiting hour of every day with her, at her bedside, watching as she slept and whispering his love to his love when she awakened from her dreams.

But Galen banished him. There was paperwork to do. The final, official reports on Brandon Christianson and Adam Vaughn. After which and forever those cases would be closed, and after which, at least for a while, maybe decades, Lieutenant Hunter was going to take some time off.

If Lucas attended to the paperwork of Brandon and Adam during the day, Galen reasoned, then maybe he would sleep at night. Which he needed to do. Had he slept at all since the ice storm within the penthouse had begun?

Besides, she told him, she and her Barbie were rarely alone and never bored. She spoke to Julia by phone every day, and as she drifted in and out of wakefulness, a parade of visitors drifted in and out of her room, to visit and confess.

Viveca arrived, a new Viveca, chastened, apologetic, and hoping that someday, some-

how, Galen and Lucas would be able to forgive her. She had *believed* her cousin, truly believed Brandon's lies, and she had made some awful mistakes on his behalf, including that despicable episode with Lucas in college — a confession which Galen declined to hear.

"It's past history, Viveca. Whatever it was. And Brandon is past history, too. For all of us. He was a *psychopath*, Viveca. There was no way you could know."

And Paul arrived. Paul, who felt guilt about a range of things, beginning with his unkindness to her.

"You were understandably upset," Galen countered. "About Marianne and Monica and Kay. Besides, let's face it, everything you said about me was true."

"But unforgivably mean."

"*Forgivably.* And forgiven."

Paul felt guilty as well about his betrayal of Wally. It was he who'd brought the photo of Wally's ersatz family to Lucas's attention, as if Paul had actually believed Wally could possibly be to blame.

"You *had* to let Lucas know," Galen said. "No matter what you believed. Because what *if?* Have you told Wally what you did?"

"Yes."

"And?"

374

"He says he's relieved not to have to pretend anymore."

"Why *was* he pretending?"

"Because it was easier. It began, he said, quite by accident. He'd bought a new wallet and before he'd removed the photo that came with it, someone noticed it, admired it, admired *him* for the first time in his life. He has some issues to deal with. And he's going to. He's also going to visit you. Sometime. Once he recovers from what sounds like the flu."

Paul's greatest guilt was that *he*, however unwittingly, however casually, had mentioned to Kay Monica's flight from Denver to New York with Lucas ... from which Kay, in a flight of pure fantasy, had deduced that Lucas and Monica were lovers and had added Monica's name to the long list used as a *hit* list by Adam Vaughn.

"It's *not* your fault," Galen insisted. "Kay was disturbed, and Adam was a psychopath, and you could not possibly have known."

Paul arrived a second time, the next day, with a gift, proof of the photographer, the artist, he was. It was portrait of Galen, a single frame from the video taken that Sunday at dawn, after the hostages had been freed, and Lucas had left to see the savaged body of Brynne, and Galen had insisted on addressing the camera and all of Manhattan in her mittens and coat.

The artist, Paul, had been quite right. Between the turquoise of her coat and the flames of her hair, her winter white face had virtually disappeared. In a color photo, that is. But when that same frame was developed in black and white, what showed, what glowed, was the face of a woman already deeply, already irrevocably, in love.

The doctors drifted in and out as well. Dr. Diana Sterling and others. They listened to her heart, her lungs, and peered under what seemed an extravagance of bandages, after which every white-coated visitor proclaimed her to be healing well.

Remarkably well. Which meant, they decided, that Galen Chandler was either the most stoic woman on the planet or they had vastly overestimated the degree to which her shattered ribs and ravaged lung would wage their fiery war.

There *was* a blazing conflagration. But Galen felt the fire as warmth, and as a reminder of that other warmth, that illusion of warm syrup being poured onto her breasts, that odd yet enduring dream.

Or was it a dream? Had Brandon poured some hot liquid onto her after all? Were there burns, perhaps, healing well and with a total absence of pain?

Yes, Galen realized. For as she got stronger, and even though she asked no questions other than when would she be going home, Dr. Diana Sterling spoke to her about her wounds.

It was a solemn discussion, and reassuring and calm, during which Diana was clearly referring to the wounds on her breasts . . . wounds that Galen had never seen. She might have looked during the dressing changes that happened several times a day. During those times, however, she lay on her back and closed her eyes and counted the seconds until her nakedness would be concealed again.

She also could have looked privately. But she hadn't, even though she nodded as if she had, as Diana offered solemn yet reassuring words about wound healing, scar maturation, and the ever-improving techniques of scar revision one could choose.

Galen told herself she would look at her wounds, her burns. But she didn't. Hadn't.

Until the day came. At last. The *eve* of the day when she could go home at last to the man she loved.

Lucas had left her that night with the caressing promise, as his lips touched hers, *tomorrow.*

She would be released at noon. Before that, however, her nurses would help her shower and shampoo, permitting only the faintest mist to fall on the places on her chest that were remarkably yet not entirely healed. Then she would dress in the turtleneck and jeans Lucas had brought for her, and her turquoise coat, and . . .

It was nine o'clock. P.M. On every other night Galen would have been asleep. But on this eve of going home, she was wakeful, happy, excited — and curious.

She wanted to see the remarkable healing. Needed to. For tomorrow night she and Lucas would share the hyacinth bed. Hers. They would save his, which would become theirs, until their wedding night.

It was too soon to make love. But Lucas could hold her, they could hold each other, and it would be best, she reasoned, if she knew in advance the places beneath the bandages that should not yet be touched.

The mirror was in the private bath of her private room. It was a half-length mirror above the sink and silvery like his eyes, the only mirror that really mattered.

Or so she had believed.

Galen looked first at the only place where there was pain, where the fire smoldered still when she breathed. Her skin, she discovered, was yellow and blue and black, the natural shades of a healing bruise. There was a small round scar where the chest tube had been, and a more substantial one through which the surgeons had gained emergent access to the sobbing artery deep within. As emergently as they had needed to enter her chest, however, the surgical incision was discreet, a semilunar line that hugged the curve of her ribs.

A bruise. And two inconsequential scars. All of which would fade in time to nothing.

And the other wounds? The ones about which Diana Sterling had spoken to her with such solemn calm, and which Lucas had seen on the night he had rescued her, and which had come with warmth but no pain?

No pain.

And then excruciating pain, as Galen saw what lay hidden, lay lurking, beneath the pristine snow.

Wounds. Not burns.

A chaos of madness, of vengeance, of rage. They were random, these deep jagged slashes where she'd been carved. Yet they held such evil purpose, to maim, to mangle, to destroy.

And then there was a scream, the silent, keening wail that was the sound of a woman in love whose heart had simply shattered.

TWENTY-SIX

"Hi."

"Hi," Lucas echoed softly. It was 10 A.M. The snow-white clock and lavender phone had chimed for a moment in unison, a duet of joy which he heard at its onset because he had just turned the vacuum off, satisfied with the result. The new piece of carpet, the replacement for the pristine patch where the snow angel had bled, blended flawlessly with the old. The florist had promised the flowers, a bouquet of springtime, by ten-thirty, and he and Galen had agreed, when he had left her last night, that he would arrive exactly at noon. They wouldn't even speak before, they'd decided. They would forsake their first morning phone call as a sweet and final torment. But now Galen was calling. "Shall I come get you now?"

"No. I'm not at the hospital."

Lucas Hunter didn't know, might not know for a while, whether his ability to sense evil had died with Brandon. But as his entire being filled with ice, far colder and more ominous than all that had come before, Lucas knew with certainty that he still could sense death.

Could *feel* death.

The death of a dream.

"Where are you, Galen?"

"On a meandering journey to Kansas."

"Galen . . ."

"May ninth."

"What?"

"That will be our wedding day, if that's all right with you. It's on a Sunday this year, which also happens to be Mother's Day. And it feels right to me that the date I left Kansas will be the same as when you and I begin our life together. And I'll *need* until May, Lucas. I really will. I *do* want to make my wedding gown, and Julia's dress, too, and I'm going to see my mother, I have to, and maybe I'll invite her to the wedding and as you suggested even make her dress. I've been thinking about the guest list. Lawrence, of course. And maybe John and Fran and —"

"Galen?"

"I'd like to get married on the terrace, by the fountain, if that's okay. Which is another reason we have to wait until May. The flowers. I spoke with a very nice man who owns a nursery in Bronxville and ordered a zillion little flower pots of tulips, hyacinths, and daffodils in lavender and pink and white. All of which are available in those colors, *including* the daffodils."

I know, Lucas thought. And you can have those flowers today. I've ordered those bridal flowers. Today. We can get married. *Today.*

"When are you going to plant the flowers?"

"When I return. In a month. It's best, the nurseryman said, to wait to transplant them until *after* the final frost."

But, my faraway love, what if this is the final frost? "Galen. Talk to me. Please."

Lucas heard her deep intake of breath and he wondered, amid all the other worries, if the breath had been so deep it caused her piercing pain.

"I need time, Lucas. Not to decide about loving you, or marrying you. I love you forever and with all my heart. But I need to heal a little more, in all ways. Which means returning to Kansas to see my mother."

"Is there a reason I can't go with you? Not to see her, unless you want me to, but to be with you all the times between?"

Yes. There is a reason. Yes. "I just need to do this on my own."

382

"What aren't you telling me?"

Everything. "Nothing. Lucas, please, don't worry. And *please* don't be mad. I'm planning to call you every night. If you want me to."

"I do. Every night. Every day. And if you want me with you, I'll be there."

"I know."

"Where are you now?"

"On my meandering route."

"Not by air."

"No. The doctors said no air travel for a while."

"So by train?"

"Yes. A slow train. Slow *trains.* A few hours a day with overnight stops to rest. I told Julia it would be at least a week before I arrive."

"Let me be with you, Galen, to take care of you from here to Kansas."

"I'm *fine.* Really. My leisurely pace is as much to think — to reflect, to remember, to prepare — as it is to rest."

"There's more."

"No. Lucas, please. Trust me. Believe in me."

"I do, Galen. But I miss you."

"I miss you, too. But think of the reunion we'll have."

She promised that she would call him every evening.

And she did, beginning that night.

And she did the next night, too.

They talked for hours. About healing. About reconciliation. About family. She wondered about the half brothers he had never known, the legitimate sons of the earl.

All I need is you, Lucas told her. *You.*

Galen didn't call the next night.

And his world froze. Became dark. Black. But purposeful. And intrusive.

Lucas searched for her in all the ways law enforcement could. Beginning with the phone calls she had made from her hospital bed. To Julia. To him. And, on the morning she left, to the nursery in Bronxville to order, the nurseryman confirmed, her pastel plants. That was all.

He spoke with Diana, who reported that Galen had been dressed already when she made her first morning rounds. And so eager to leave, so ready to go home to Lucas that Diana had expedited her discharge then and there.

And Lucas spoke with the woman in the billing office to whom Galen had given a check to cover her entire bill. Which terrified him. *Why?* Because, the woman explained — as Galen had explained to her — Galen was so accustomed to checking out of motels, from her Gavel-to-Gavel days, that it was habit to settle her account as she left. She seemed fine, the woman said. Cheerful. And taller, she added, than she had imagined from TV, and more delicate, and more pale. And so *pretty*, she said.

Lucas went next to Ophelia, where Galen's credit card had been used by Galen an hour after paying her hospital bill. The Ophelia manager remembered Galen well. Her radiance. Her joy. Galen wanted the bridal negligee, the satin one with embroidered roses. It wasn't available in her size, so the manager placed a special order, which would arrive long before May ninth. And, at the manager's suggestion, she also special ordered sheets for their wedding bed, his bed, in white satin with roses, too.

Roses on snow.

She would be a beautiful bride, the manager opined. With her flame-colored hair and her white-satin skin.

Lucas's final stop, because that was where the trail ended, was Galen's bank, where she had transferred funds from savings to checking, to cover the hospital bill, and then withdrawn some cash, a substantial amount. But she had not closed her account.

She'd made a phone call, however. In a private office that the courageous anchorwoman had been welcome to use. A local call, precisely at ten. To him.

Then nothing. Nothing more. No calling-card phone calls, no credit-card purchases, no checks. Had she left Manhattan by train, or car or bus or plane, her ticket had been paid for in cash.

"I'm sorry, Lucas," Julia told him when he called. "I haven't heard from her since she called to say she was coming to Kansas and would be here in about a week. But I didn't expect to hear from her. She said she was going to meander, and think."

"Did she say anything else?"

"Yes. She did. She said she loves you, Lucas, with all her heart. It's such a good heart, such a giving heart."

"I know," Lucas whispered. "I know."

Another day. Another night. And nothing. Just loss. Just fear.

Lucas was staring at the phone number for Bess Chandler, debating whether to make that call, knowing that he would, that he had to, when his penthouse phone rang. His. Not hers.

And with a double-ring.

"It's Diana, Lucas," she said from twenty-two floors below. "I have news about Galen. May I . . ."

But the latch on the heavy steel door had already been released.

TWENTY-SEVEN

"Where is she?"

"In Boston. In a hospital. One of the best in the world."

"And?"

"And she had additional surgery two days ago and has not yet awakened."

"I have to get to her."

"I know you do. The one-fifteen shuttle from La Guardia has lots of seats, and I've already given the airlines your name, and the taxi I took from the hospital is waiting downstairs for you. All of which means you have time, Lucas, to let me tell you what I know and to answer what questions I can. I'm not saying that will make the time between now and when you reach her easier, but at least you'll be more informed. And more focused."

"You're right, Diana. Thank you. Tell me. Please."

"Okay. Let me begin by telling you what's going on right now. Galen is absolutely stable. Her vital signs are normal and she's breathing on her own. She appears to be sleeping, but it's deeper than that." Diana's hand stopped the obvious question even as she provided its answer. "Every imaginable neurologic parameter has been studied, and she's being managed by the best of the best, and there's nothing — *nothing*, Lucas — to indicate any brain damage whatsoever. *Any* damage in fact of *any* kind. Galen just hasn't awakened from anesthesia. Yet. But there's every expectation that she will. She may be wide awake by the time you reach Boston."

Boston. What was she doing there? Meandering by way of Boston to Kansas? If so . . . "There was an accident."

"No, Lucas. There was nothing accidental at all. Galen planned to be in that Massachusetts hospital at this time. It was a plan that was hatched, unbeknownst to me, the night before she was discharged from Memorial, when she looked for the first time at the wounds made by Brandon's knife and when she *realized* for the first time what he had done."

"But . . ."

"I know. We all assumed that Galen knew about the wounds and that she remembered every detail of Brandon's assault."

"She did remember, Diana. She *does*. She's very clear that she never lost consciousness." And I *saw* her, groggy but awake, as Brandon was carving her delicate flesh. "She knew."

"Yes, and no. She felt what Brandon was doing to her as a liquid warmth without pain, and she had concluded that as real as the memory seemed, it had to be false. She revised her conclusion the day I spoke with her about the wounds, but even then she didn't realize he'd used a knife. She imagined burns, and since there was no pain, assumed they weren't terribly significant. Or maybe," Diana suggested quietly, "deep down she did know but didn't want to look. In any event, when she saw what Brandon had done, she had the page operator contact whomever was on call for plastic surgery. Bottom line, the resident who answered the page had done some of his training in Boston and knew that a promising but experimental technique had recently been approved for clinical trials at a medical center, *the* medical center, there."

"Experimental," Lucas whispered.

"Experiments are the basis of research, Lucas. You know that. And research is how most medical and surgical advances are made. And by the time the clinical-trial phase is approved, enormous preliminary investigation has already been done."

"What research, Diana?" *What experiments has my lovely Galen agreed to?*

"Well, as you and I discussed, as Galen and I discussed, the traditional approach to scar management is to permit the wounds to heal, to mature. Sometimes even with massive injury the mature scars can be quite subtle. So the traditional approach is to wait and see. Months. Sometimes longer."

"And the experimental approach?" he asked very quietly.

"Early intervention, ideally within ten days, while the most active — aggressive — phase of tissue response to injury is taking place. The often overzealous areas of healing tissue are surgically resected, after which the research compound is applied. It's an elegant mixture, designed to temper the response to injury so that, when it works, the result may be no scarring at all."

"When it works. And when it *doesn't* work?"

"The scars may be worse than those of the original wounds, had they been permitted to heal on their own."

"And?"

"And, for various reasons, the scars can be quite refractory to the traditional revision techniques."

"*And,* Diana?"

"And, because of damage to adjacent nerves, there can be significant pain. Chronic pain."

Lucas swore softly, fiercely, inarticulate words which were eloquent in tone alone.

"Galen knew the risks, Lucas, and was willing to accept them."

"Because of what some on-call resident happened to say?"

"No. Although I can assure you the resident in question is in significant trouble. Even though the plastic surgeons were involved in Galen's care, I was her physician of record. And this particular resident had never even seen her before. No decisions, and probably not even any *discussions,* should have taken place without involving me. But that night, after talking with Galen, our rogue resident placed some calls to Boston and set the whole thing up. I knew nothing until today, when the resident *happened* to ask if I'd gotten feedback yet from Galen's doctors in Boston. He'd assumed Galen had told me. She had promised, he claims, that she would. *Not* that anything Galen may or may not have said excuses his misconduct in any way. But that's for me to deal with."

"Galen probably did make that promise." His voice was harsh, bitter, cold. "She didn't want you to know, Diana, because most of all she didn't want me to."

"She wanted to *surprise* you, Lucas. Which is not only *obvious,* but it's also the reason she gave the psychiatrist pre-op."

"The psychiatrist?"

"It's part of the protocol, an essential part really. Such consultation is advisable even when traditional cosmetic surgery is involved. And in a research setting, especially given the small but real downside risk . . ."

"The researchers are reluctant to enroll anyone who's there for the wrong reason."

"That's right. Or anyone who has unrealistic expectations. And, of course, anyone who couldn't handle an adverse outcome should that occur."

"So this psychiatrist decided that Galen's reason, that her selfish, sexist fiancé couldn't *bear* to touch her scars, was a valid one?"

"*No.* That was *not* Galen's reason, nor would the psychiatrist have validated it if it were. Galen *knows* you love her, Lucas. With scars or without. That came through to the psychiatrist loud and clear. And *she* loves *you.* She didn't want Brandon to be part of your lives, that's all, *of your love.* She wanted no reminders of Brandon Christianson for either of you."

Diana was wrong, Lucas thought; Lucas *knew*. Galen didn't want the reminder, the torment, *for him*. "And if the experiment failed, Diana? If the scars were worse than before and couldn't ever be repaired? And she was destined to spend the rest of her life in pain? Did the psychiatrist happen to ask her what would happen then?"

"*Of course*. That's the most important question of all. You would be married, she said, as planned, because your love was far stronger than Brandon's evil."

"And the psychiatrist believed that?"

"Absolutely."

Lucas closed his eyes. *Which means, my precious love, that you have perfected the ability to lie. Because of me. For me.* Galen would not return to him, to their love, if the experiment failed. She would not permit him to spend the rest of his life looking at what had happened to her because of him.

"Lucas?"

"Yes?"

His eyes opened, and Diana saw darkness. Blackness. "Galen is *going* to wake up, and although I know it couldn't matter less to you — not now, maybe never — her response to the protocol compound is already

393

the best they've ever seen. Galen was *very* confident going into the procedure. She *knew* it was going to work. And it looks as if she was right."

The operation was a success, but the patient died.

Diana read correctly the anguished thought and offered a gentle distraction, the hope of one. "You're supposed to be asking me, Lieutenant Hunter, how I can ethically reveal what I've revealed, especially the details of a confidential psychiatric interview. The reason is Bess Chandler."

"Galen's mother."

"Yes. Galen listed her as her legal next of kin."

"Her mother," Lucas said softly. "Not me."

"You're not her legal next of kin. Not yet. And remember, Lucas, Galen wanted this to be a surprise."

No she didn't! the thought pierced and screamed. Not if it failed. She would have vanished then. Forever.

"Bess Chandler didn't arrive in Boston until this morning. She'd been at a teachers conference in Kansas City and didn't get the messages Galen's physicians had left for her until her return late last night. But this morning, literally on her arrival on the ward, she asked where *you* were. She believed you needed to be notified no matter what Galen had said."

"She and Galen must have spoken. Galen must have told her about me."

"No. She didn't. Apparently they haven't spoken for years. But I got the impression that she'd followed Galen's career, *was* following it long before the Lady Killer's calls to Galen became national news. In any event, the happiest of the happy endings to that news story — Galen's engagement to you — was broadcast nationally as well. Galen's doctors were deciding who was going to notify you when I happened to call them. Bess Chandler gave the doctors permission to tell me everything, and for me to tell you." And now she had, and Diana felt Lucas's restlessness, his disperate need, to be on his way to be with his love. Still she asked, "Do you have any questions?"

"No." *Yes.* Why, Galen? *Why?* But Lucas Hunter knew the lovely, anguished answer. Galen loved him so much, *too* much, an excess, like his drinking once had been, that enabled daydreams . . . but could also destroy. "Thank you for coming, Diana."

"It's the least I could do. We blew it. Ethically."

"You wouldn't have arranged for Galen to go to Boston."

"No," Diana confessed. "Not that she wasn't an ideal candidate medically, and emotionally, because of your love. But precisely because of your love, its depth and its strength, I knew your relationship would survive the scars. So why take the risk?"

The cab was waiting as promised, and there was ample time to return Diana to Memorial Hospital and still make the 1:15 flight. But Diana wanted to walk. A nice, brisk, mind-clearing hike was precisely what she needed to decide how best to deal with the renegade resident.

Diana walked to the hospital, and Lucas began the short journey to La Guardia — a journey that was detoured by Lucas shortly after it began . . . to a theater where a play about family was being rehearsed . . . and where Lucas quietly commanded the cabbie stop and wait.

The theater was dark save for a single floodlight on the distant stage. But Lucas Hunter could see in darkness. It was his gift, his curse, his skill. And on this February day, Lawrence Kincaid could see in darkness, too.

And what Lawrence saw as Lucas approached was an expression he had seen before, on that night in his study at Bellemeade, when Lucas had so frantically signed, *Jenny needs us. Hurry. Please.*

Neither man spoke.

Nor did they have to.

And neither signed.

And when Lucas turned, to return back outside, Lawrence followed, as he had followed Lucas years ago on that life-shattering night.

TWENTY-EIGHT

"He loves her very much."

The quiet statement spoken to Lawrence came from Bess. Bess Chandler. During their journey from Manhattan to Boston, Lucas had shared with Lawrence what he knew about the estrangement of mother and daughter, when it had begun and why. It was a harsh story, a bitter one, fueled with the fear Lucas was feeling and the harshness he felt toward himself.

Lawrence had formed during that journey a clear image of the woman named Bess. Not a physical image, but the more important one, the human being within. She would be vain, self-absorbed, and neurotic in a flighty, whimsical way. And aware of the harm that had been done to her only child? Lawrence seriously doubted it. But if she *were* aware, he decided, she would wave it away without an ounce of remorse, or blame, or shame.

But as soon as he and Lucas had entered

Galen's hospital room, Lawrence had been compelled to revise fairly drastically his preconceived notion of Bess. She had been sitting beside Galen's bed, touching Galen's hand, wanting to be there, wanting that desperately.

The instant Lucas appeared, however, Bess had yielded her precious place — her precious daughter — to him. Gratefully, with heart-stopping relief, and without a word. She had stood in the doorway, lingered there, until as if certain she had no right to intrude, even with her nonintrusive gaze, she had withdrawn.

To the waiting room.

Which was where Lawrence found her.

Bess Chandler was gazing out the window, lost in thought and quite oblivious of him.

But Lawrence was so very aware of her. How *unexpected* she was. Beginning with her physical shell. Bess was in her early fifties, he imagined, a few years younger than he. And Bess Chandler looked the way fifty looked, could look, these days. Slender, fit, with an aura of energy and purpose, enough of each to live another fifty years at least.

Her hair was short, no-nonsense, a wash-and-go blend of sable and silver with highlights, natural ones, of flame. Tiny lines fanned from the corners of her light blue eyes. From laughter? Perhaps. Although they crinkled now as she frowned at the winter twilight.

But they *would* crinkle when she laughed. If she laughed. Lawrence had a sudden image of such laughter, and more: who Bess Chandler truly was . . . what she was.

He saw her tromping through the woods, leading a small band of Girl Scouts to a campfire, stopping to point out each and every wonder along the way. And later, after she'd shown them how to pitch their tents and they were roasting marshmallows over the dancing flames, he saw her mesmerizing her youthful followers with stories — good ones, not ghost ones.

Good ones.

Fairy tales.

Her girls would follow her anywhere, this woman named Bess, this sable-haired hen with her entourage of lively, peeping chicks. She loved the liveliness, and the peeping, and would have happily welcomed another flock, and another. The more, the merrier. Come one, come all. We'll have such fun, and you'll be so safe, *I promise.*

There it was. Lawrence saw it so clearly. The essence of Bess Chandler.

She was a mother. *A mother.*

Who had failed the one time it mattered, with the only chick that was ever truly hers.

And now as Bess spoke to him of Lucas's love for her child, Lawrence saw the immense sadness she felt. The irretrievable loss. And he remembered more words from his journey with Lucas to Boston, gentle words, a gentle truth, no matter how harshly it was spoken.

Galen wanted to see her mother, Lucas had said. She *needed* to. Something very powerful was beckoning to her.

Lawrence knew precisely what that powerful something was.

"Yes," he replied quietly. "Lucas loves Galen. Very much. As do you."

"Oh," Bess whispered. "I *do*. But Galen doesn't know it."

"I think she does. She was planning after this to go to Kansas. To see you."

The mother's blue eyes glistened with hope. "She was? Are you *sure?*"

"She was. And I am sure. Despite the way it ended, despite what happened with Mark, Galen remembered better times, happier times, with you."

Bess was stunned by his words, by what he knew. But her gaze, and her hope, did not falter. She was from Kansas. Like Dorothy, she knew when she'd met an authentic wizard.

"You know about Mark?"

"Galen told Lucas. Who told me."

Her hope, but not her gaze, wavered, and her voice became wary. "Did Mark ever . . . touch her? Before that night? Do you know?"

"No. He didn't touch her. He looked at her. Stared at her. And made comments that were humiliating and harmful. But that was all."

"*All.*" Bess's relief that Galen hadn't been physically molested faded swiftly to bitterness toward herself. "But that was enough. *More* than enough. And I let it happen. In my home. In *our* home. Galen's and mine. Not Mark's."

"Did you know?"

"No. *No.* Not until that night, when Mark was giving me his version of what had happened, when he was being so contrite *and so charming* as he tried to convince me, persuade me, of the truth. *His* truth."

"But you weren't convinced."

"No. But it took me a little while, *too long,* to even hear what he was saying. I was so stunned by what I'd seen. But when I heard him *at last,* I saw him at last for what, for *who,* he truly was." Her blue eyes clouded. "How, *how,* could I have been so blind?"

Blind. It was Lawrence's word for himself in the months, too many months, following Jenny's death. The months in which he had let Lucas go.

"It happens."

But the mother hen would have no sympathy. Just as Lawrence had permitted himself no sympathy from Lucas. "Only if you *let* it happen. Which I *did.*"

"Because something about Mark made you — let you make yourself — blind. Was it love?"

"Love," Bess echoed. "No. Although I'm sure I believed it was at the time. But it was really all about me, something selfish, or needy, or *greedy* about me." She shook her silver and sable head. "Our life was so good, just us girls, Galen and me. We had such fun. And yet I felt as though I was missing something. Something," she repeated quietly. "A man."

"You might have met the right man, Bess. The three of you might have become a family. There might have been more fun, more laughter, more love."

"But that isn't what happened, is it?" Bess answered her own question with a thoughtful frown. "Even though, in the beginning, it seemed good, *was* good, I think. And then . . ."

"Then?"

"Galen withdrew from me. We'd been so close, always so close, and then we were drifting apart, gradually yet relentlessly, and I didn't know why. Galen said everything was fine, *fine,* and even though I was worried, and not completely convinced, I didn't begin to guess the truth. I finally decided that we'd become like so many mothers and their teenage girls, that there had come the time, this teenage time, when we couldn't be close, when Galen needed to distance herself from me to assert her own identity distinct from mine . . . as the woman she would be. My worry was replaced by sadness. I missed my little girl. But I truly believed, I *let* myself believe, that that was what was happening to us."

"It doesn't sound, Bess, as if you had any reason to think it was anything else."

"Because," she said softly, "my lovely, generous daughter didn't *want* me to know. She was protecting *me,* even though I wasn't protecting *her.*"

"She loved you."

"Yes. And I loved her, more than anything or any*one* in the world. But somehow she didn't know that. I'd *failed* to let her know.

And by that night in May she'd come to believe that I would choose Mark, need Mark, love Mark, more than her. I don't know when her love turned to anger. I didn't see it. I *missed* seeing it. In fact . . ."

"In fact?"

"Well. After a while, and even though she and I were still so far apart, she seemed better. *Happier.* And whenever I asked her where she was going to be after school and in the evenings, she said with friends. And I think that was true. I think she *did* have friends."

"She did," Lawrence said, recalling what Lucas had told him about Winnie and Julia and Gran. "Good friends."

A smile touched her face, happiness for the daughter who despite the abandonment she felt at home was not alone. The smile vanished as Bess spoke again.

"But I didn't know who those friends were, and that night, after I told Mark to get out and stay out, and when I discovered that Galen, too, had left, I drove around town looking for her. I looked everywhere, not knowing *where* to look, and when she wasn't at school the next day, I kept looking. And looking. But no one had seen her. *She was gone.*"

"But not forgotten."

"Oh, Lawrence, I thought about her all

the time, every moment of every day. And I remembered, every moment of every day, the way she looked at me that night, as she fled the kitchen and I just stood there in shock. I didn't realize then what I was seeing, only that it was something I'd never seen before. But it was hatred, *and such pain,* for what I had done — for what I had permitted Mark to do. My beloved daughter hated me, with reason, for betraying her."

There was a time, Lawrence knew, when the daughter who had fled was found, when Galen became the sensational reporter for Gavel-to-Gavel TV. And Lawrence knew without asking what Bess's reaction had been. Relief, and pride, and temptation, such temptation, to reunite with the daughter she had lost.

But Bess had resisted the powerful temptation, its alluring promise, its soaring hope, for the same reason he had spent years, years, watching Lucas from afar, and with such pride. The wish for reunion was a selfish one, or so Lawrence had believed. A gift for parent not for child ... especially when it was the parent who would be asking forgiveness, for the unforgivable, from the child who had escaped, had survived, and who was succeeding so brilliantly on his or her own.

But Lawrence had been wrong.

"Galen was on her way to Kansas, Bess, to see you. And to invite you to her wedding. She loves you, and misses you, and remembers your love. She remembers your love most of all."

Bess Chandler's purse, made of cloth and by hand, lay on one of the waiting room's several vinyl chairs. She touched it gently, lingeringly, as she had touched Galen's hand.

"Galen made this for me when she was seven." Bess lifted the treasured gift and from its single compartment withdrew a blond-haired doll. A Barbie. Wearing a long flannel nightgown. "She was mine, and then Galen's. She's been on Galen's bed all these years. When the doctors called, I don't know, I just ran into Galen's room and grabbed her. And then . . . did you notice, lying beside her on the bed, there's another Barbie? She brought it with her, the doctors said, from New York. So I guess she doesn't need this one after all."

"Yes," Lawrence countered softly. "She does."

Bess looked from the Barbie to the wizard. "You're a nice man, Lawrence Kincaid."

"I'm a man, Bess Chandler, who's made

my share of mistakes. But maybe I've learned a little from them, too. Galen needs both of her Barbies. I'm sure of it. And she needs to hear, even while she's sleeping, of your love."

Love. My love. I love you.

Lucas whispered every combination of magic, all the magic words.

But still she slept. Day after day. Night after night.

Five more days. Five more nights.

She was Sleeping Beauty, and he was her prince, and there was no doubt that Lucas Hunter would fight his way — naked and armed only with his love — through a forest of the sharpest thorns.

The fairy-tale Sleeping Beauty had slept for a hundred years. And what of this Sleeping Beauty? In this fairy tale?

Galen might sleep for the rest of her life. And his. How could the doctors predict when she would awaken when they had no idea why she slept? No idea. At all. Galen was far beyond even the most attenuated consequence of anesthesia. And every neurologic test, sophisticated and otherwise, remained normal. Everything did.

And it made no sense that she'd had a heretofore unreported reaction to the protocol compound, something autoimmune, because there was nothing foreign, nothing man-made, in the elixir of tissue extracts she'd received. Besides, if her skin was any indicator, she was accepting the compound as if her own, and with a welcome that was quite extraordinary.

She might sleep forever, this Sleeping Beauty.

But she would have no scars.

"I'd like to take her home," the prince told her doctors on the seventh day. "I can do everything for her at home that you're doing here."

Yes, the doctors agreed. He could. He could hire nurses to care for her around the clock, and physical therapists to keep toned and mobile her snowy limbs, and there were specialists in Manhattan who could administer and monitor the parenteral nutrition she received, and —

And Lucas Hunter meant precisely what he said. That *he* could do everything for her. Everything.

He had been watching, everything, and there was nothing he couldn't do. Nor was there anything he didn't want to do. He would appreciate, before he took her home, a little formal instruction, step by step, to make certain he had it all exactly right.

Especially the intravenous feedings, the nutrition — far beyond glucose and saline — she was receiving through the large-bore catheter in her subclavian vein. Lucas needed, especially, to be shown precisely how to cleanse the catheter, and sterilize thoroughly its rubber diaphragm, before inserting the needle through which the nutrients would flow.

The needle. The gray-eyed panther had not been so good with needles on his first try, on that afternoon of scones and tea, or even on his second, although better, when he spent the night sewing a tiny bathrobe and gown.

But the talented hands of the lover would become very good with needles, with *this* needle, the one that would keep his Galen, his love, alive.

And so they returned to Manhattan, by ambulance and by car. A two-vehicle parade. Lucas and Galen rode in the ambulance, which seemed — without its flashing lights and screaming sirens — too much, far too much, like a hearse. And Lawrence and Bess traveled in the car behind.

The ambulance attendants made the journey as far as the street beneath the penthouse, but no farther. Lucas carried Galen the rest of the way . . . over the threshold of his building, beyond the heavy steel door, and into the elevator and up, then across the marble foyer and the carpet of snow to the lavender bedroom that they would share, they had decided, until their wedding day.

Lucas placed his beautiful sleeping daffodil beneath the plush comforter of the canopied bed.

"What can we do?" Lawrence asked from the doorway of the pastel bedroom.

Lucas looked surprised, as if he'd forgotten that Bess and Lawrence had accompanied him, as if he'd believed that already he and Galen were alone.

In their home.

"Nothing, Lawrence. Thank you. We're fine."

"I'm going to remain in Manhattan," Bess said. "I'll get a room nearby, and I'll be here every day, Lucas, at whatever time you say."

"No. I'm sorry, Bess. But no."

It was not, Bess knew, a rejection of her. Lucas had accepted her. For now. For Galen. He even believed, she thought, in her love.

And Bess believed something, too: that alone with Lucas was the best place Galen could be. But she worried, with a mother's love for him, about the man who would keep her daughter so loved and so safe.

"How about if I do your grocery shopping for you?"

Grocery shopping? Lucas's expression was blank. He would be giving Galen everything she needed through her veins.

"Food for you, Lucas."

"I'm fine. Thank you."

"Tell me, please. Isn't there anything I can do? For Galen? For you?"

Bess believed he would say no. And she even imagined that she might have pushed beyond endurance the politeness to which Lucas clung despite his fear.

Go away! he would shout, a release of frustration and despair. Go *away.*

And then, because there was no release, the politeness would return. Please, Bess. *Please.* I need so desperately to be alone with her.

But Lucas did not shout.

And he said, very softly, "Yes, Bess. There is something."

"Tell me." *Please.*

"You can make her wedding dress."

TWENTY-NINE

"Oh. *Lucas.* You're there."

"Who is . . . Julia."

"Yes. It's Julia. And, well, it's been almost two weeks since you called, wondering if I'd heard from Galen, and haven't — I *still* haven't — and I've left messages, because you haven't been home, and even though I thought that the two of you had probably eloped and were off on some grand and lovely honeymoon, I just wanted to be sure that everything was fine."

He should have called her. Galen would have *wanted* him to. But he hadn't, nor had he checked messages. There were none that could possibly matter. His voice was gentle with apology for Galen's friend.

"Everything isn't fine, Julia. And I'm sorry. I should have called you. Galen's . . ."

Sleeping, still. And it had been almost a week since he had brought her home.

Lucas told Julia what had happened, and when he stopped speaking, and within a heartbeat, Julia told him in reply, "I want to be there, Lucas. To help Galen. And you. I'm not a nurse, but I have experience. My sister . . ." her voice faltered.

"Winnie."

"Yes," she whispered. "Winnie." Her voice became stronger. "I took care of her, and so did Galen, and it was good to have both of us helping, even though, even when, I could have managed on my own. Would you let me help you, Lucas? Would you let me help you help her?"

"No. Thank you, Julia. Not yet."

Not yet. *Yet.* It was a concession, a confession, Lucas had believed he would never make. But he could envision a time, a year from now, five years, when he might need help — for Galen's sake — a time when he might have descended so far into his silent madness that he could no longer care for her as she needed to be cared for.

For now, and he hoped forever, he alone would care for her, would protect the modest woman he loved. He was her husband, in all the ways that mattered, in the solemn promises they had already made.

Lucas kept at bay all thoughts of the time when Galen would awaken. Or *if* such time would ever come . . . as if only then would their life, their marriage, begin. *This* was their life. *This* was their love. At least it was his.

But Lucas wanted so very much more for her.

So he planted, for her, the flowers she had ordered from Bronxville.

Galen, the accompanying note from the nurseryman read. *I've handpicked the best plants I could find, in white and cream and lavender and pink. If you plant them now — and you can, because I believe we've seen our last frost — the flowers will be in glorious bloom for your wedding in May.*

The pastel blooms, on that day in May, would be, would have been, splashed by drops from the wedding-cake fountain overhead. The nascent flowers were watered as well, on the rainy day when Lucas planted them, sprinkled by the dampness of rain and by the hot, soggy anguish of his tears.

Lucas rarely left her side. His journey to the terrace to plant Galen's flowers was the longest, ever, that he was away. And it terrified him. As did sleeping.

But he forced himself to sleep, in her room but not her bed, for the rare fitful moments that he could. For her. To delay as long as possible his descent into madness, the vast and aching darkness from which he knew he would never return.

Lucas had promised both Lawrence and Bess that he would let them know if there was a change, any change at all. But as February became March, and Lawrence Kincaid had heard only silence from the penthouse in the sky, he broke that silence with a phone call.

Lucas shared his news. Galen was sleeping still, there was no change. And Lawrence shared his. Bess had returned to Kansas, where she was sewing Galen's wedding gown and waiting for word of her daughter. Lawrence confessed a little more, that he and Bess spoke by telephone every day.

Lawrence provided Lucas with an array of phone numbers, followed by a stern yet loving command, the sort of instruction a worried father would give his son.

"I want you to call me, Lucas, at least once a week. I won't intrude, either in person or by phone. But you have to keep me informed. Please."

Lucas agreed. He would call Lawrence without fail every Sunday afternoon at one. It was a fair request, Lucas knew, and — he knew this, too — a necessary safeguard for Galen. Lawrence might detect even before Lucas did how much trouble he was in. *Even* before? It was likely, more than likely, that Lucas might not detect his deterioration, the impending darkness, at all.

His mind felt so acute, so clear. But it was an illusion, he feared, the sort of eerie clarity one felt when starved of food and of sleep — a light, bright, shimmering clarity that was as sparkling and pure as the years in Chatsworth before Jenny's death.

Lucas promised to call Lawrence every Sunday without fail, and even though Lawrence said that he would keep Bess informed, Lucas decided to call her, too, and Julia, not as sentinels for his sanity but because Galen would want him to.

Lawrence would monitor his madness, as would the only person permitted into the privacy of their home.

Dr. Diana Sterling came once a week to examine Galen and draw her blood. The bloodwork, like the exams, was a necessary aspect of Galen's care, to make certain the nutrients Lucas was giving her were in balance and correct.

Diana also provided expert and unsolicited consultation about Lucas.

"You don't look good," she told him directly and without preamble as she stepped into the marble foyer on April twenty-first, the seventieth day of Galen's sleep.

"I'm fine."

"You're very thin and you haven't slept."

417

"I'm fine, Diana." An odd light glimmered in his exhausted gray eyes, part shadow, part glow. "But there's something I need you to check."

"Something on you?" she asked quietly. A lump, a lesion, a mass? Why not, she thought with sudden anger. It made perfect sense that this man who had saved lives and slain killers, only to be rewarded by the enormous sadness of Galen's inexplicable sleep, would now be dying himself. Of cancer. *Why not?* If fate continued to have its sinister way with him, the gentleman lieutenant would probably die just moments after Galen awakened. "Lucas?"

"No. Not me. Galen."

It was a lump of sorts, a gentle rounding, as if a tiny bulb had been planted deep beneath the snow, for safekeeping until it bloomed. But the soft swelling in Galen's lower abdomen was hardly a lesion — except for the shadowed anguish amid the glowing brilliance its presence carved in Lucas Hunter's heart. A husband's heart.

And a father's.

"Is she . . . ?"

"Pregnant," Diana finished. "Yes. I think so. I'm comfortable doing the neurologic exams on her, Lucas. It's something I'm fully trained to do. But her pregnancy needs to be managed by a specialist in OB. I'd recommend Carolyn Barclay. In fact, I'd be happy to give her a call right now."

Diana's voice drifted off, and she frowned. She had been presuming that Lucas would choose to keep the pregnancy, would choose to nurture his baby as he was nurturing his future bride. But there might never be a wedding, and he would have a child to raise even as Galen slept, and maybe it was too much, too great a burden, a heaviness too immense to bear.

But there was no heaviness in the voice that answered her.

"Yes, Diana. If you could call her. Please."

They had agreed, bride and groom, that May ninth would be their wedding day. Mother's Day.

But they had not set a time.

So Lucas chose a time for them — the precise moment the wedding day itself began, as soon as the snowy mantelpiece clock finished its midnight chime.

Its Cinderella chime.

Lucas brought to chattering life the long-silent fountain. And beneath the silvery light of stars and through a sudden blur that neither his fatigued mind nor his starving heart could control, he watched the diamond-bright spray drift from the white-stone wedding cake to the pastel blooms in the garden below.

Then he went to his bride and bathed her, as he did every day, and washed, as he did, her flame-colored hair. The shining flames were longer, flourishing even as she slept, nourished through her veins by him.

Lucas whispered to her, as he did every day and every night. But on this night his words of love were new.

"It's our wedding day, my love. It's just begun. I thought we'd sleep first, and when it's daylight, when it's warm, we'll go to the terrace. The sheets you ordered from Ophelia, the embroidered roses on satin snow, are on the bed in the other room, in our bedroom, and this, do you feel this softness against your skin? It's the negligee you ordered. It's beautiful, Galen. You are so beautiful. I love you. *I love you.*"

Lucas carried her to the bed, their bed, and he showered, too, for his bride, and for the first time since their baby was conceived, he lay beside her, and held her, and eventually, and for the first time since that night, since *before* that night, Lucas slept. Truly.

And he dreamed.

Truly.

And she dreamed.

And she awakened.

In his arms.

It was a gentle awakening and a misted one, a shimmering of moonlight through gauzy curtains, and of her own gauzy thoughts.

Galen wasn't alarmed, for she was safe in his arms. She felt only that glorious sanctuary . . . until she saw his moonlit face.

Then there was great alarm. His beloved face was a ravaged skull in the golden moonbeams, a skull with skin, just enough stark whiteness, to cover the harsh angles of his aristocratic bones. There was color on his ice white flesh, if black were truly a color at all. Black-on-black, where his sooty lashes lay atop the pools of ink beneath his eyes, and framed in black, his hair gleaming in the moonlight, dark and damp *and long.*

She wanted to awaken him, to kiss him back to health, to plead with him not to die. But there was something else on his ravaged face, a look of peace, the pristine peacefulness of snow, and the snow-white purity of dreams.

He was sleeping, dreaming, and the pools beneath his eyes told her how much he needed the rest, and perhaps as well the dreams. And her alarm for him had shattered the mists that cocooned her awakening mind. She had no answers. Yet. But she would find them while he slept.

His sleep was so deep, his dreams so enchanted, that her watchful, wary panther did not awaken as she left him, as she slid, such an easy slide of satin on satin, from his arms.

Satin on satin. Her *wedding-night* satin.

Galen rose from their wedding bed in their moon-misted bedroom. The mist whirled as she rose and her legs wobbled on the snowy carpet. But guided by something so powerful it stilled the whirling and steadied her legs, she walked to the lavender room at the end of the hall.

Where she found everything. Every anguished and joyful answer. The intravenous pole beside her canopied bed. The dolls, *both* of them, atop the downy comforter. The chaotic nest of blankets on the floor nearby. The discharge summary from the hospital in Boston. The meticulous notes that had been kept every day since, nursing notes in his masculine and ever-more-chaotic script.

The most recent entry, by her panther turned shepherd, was dated May eighth at 11:59. *Still sleeping.*

There were other notes as well, charted

less often but meticulously too, by Doctors Diana Sterling and Carolyn Barclay. Galen's hands drifted as she read the entries by Dr. Barclay, drifted to the place of such joy. She made more discoveries en route to the gentle swelling — the skin where Brandon had savaged her, unblemished now and new, and the small square of sterile gauze that protected the indwelling catheter through which she was fed.

Through which Lucas fed her. And their baby. Their *daughter.*

Even as he starved himself.

Galen ran, no she flew, back to the bedroom where he slept. It was a soundless flight, and it slowed as she neared the bed. She didn't want to awaken him, not if he slept so deeply still and dreamed such nourishing dreams.

He slept, but in her absence the peace was gone, and Galen saw, between the sooty black lashes and the inky black pools, the moonlit glistening of tears.

She went to him, and curled anew in his arms, and with a most gentle kiss, Sleeping Beauty awakened her prince.

"Galen," he whispered with disbelief, and with fear. It had happened. The madness.

"Yes, my Lucas. It's me. I'm awake. And I'm real. And I know everything, and I'm *so sorry* for what I've put you through."

"Galen?" It was a query now, of wonder, of love.

She cradled his skeletal face in her healthy hands, and kissed his mouth, his eyes, his tears.

"I'm back," she whispered. And then, because her own tears threatened to drown her words and to blur too much the face she wanted to see, she managed a soft and soggy tease. "I'm back, Lucas Hunter, with a vengeance."

"Oh, Galen," he murmured, believing, beginning to believe. "I love you, I love you, I love you."

They kissed, and whispered, and when it was impossible to speak, they held each other in silence, in stillness, as if they were rainbows shimmering in ice.

And then they kissed again, when it was impossible not to, and whispered because that was essential, too. And sometime during their moonlit awakening, panther and snow angel became one.

It was a gentle joining, a gossamer union of wonder, but it was held together, they were, by the fearsome power of hope . . . and by the glorious splendor of being home.

At last.